STALKING *the* VAMPIRE

ALSO AVAILABLE BY MIKE RESNICK

IVORY: A LEGEND OF PAST AND FUTURE

NEW DREAMS FOR OLD

STALKING THE UNICORN

STARSHIP: MUTINY
BOOK ONE

STARSHIP: PIRATE
BOOK TWO

STARSHIP: MERCENARY
BOOK THREE

STARSHIP: REBEL
BOOK FOUR

STALKING the VAMPIRE

A FABLE of TONIGHT

A John Justin Mallory Mystery

MIKE RESNICK

an imprint of Prometheus Books
Amherst, NY

Published 2008 by Pyr®, an imprint of Prometheus Books

Inquiries should be addressed to
Pyr
59 John Glenn Drive
Amherst, New York 14228–2119
VOICE: 716–691–0133, ext. 210
FAX: 716–691–0137
WWW.PYRSF.COM

12 11 10 09 08   5 4 3 2 1

Library of Congress Cataloging-in-Publication Data

Resnick, Michael D.
    Stalking the vampire : a fable of tonight : a John Justin Mallory mystery / Mike Resnick.
        p. cm.
    ISBN 978–1–59102–649–5 (pbk. : acid-free paper)
    1. Private investigators—Fiction. 2. Vampires—Fiction. 3. Manhattan (New York, N.Y.)—Fiction. I. Title.

PS3568.E698S728 2008
813'.54—dc22

                                                                            2008026155

Printed in the United States on acid-free paper

To Carol, as always,

and to Mallory's (and my) ladyfriends:

Lesley Ainge
Catherine Asaro
Joan Bledig
Laura Frankos
Cokie Cavin
Linda Donahue
Linda Dunn
Laura Frankos
B. J. Galler-Smith
Paula Goodlett
Adrienne Gormley
Janis Ian
Michaele Jordan
Fiona Kelleghan
Kay Kenyon
Nancy Kress
Yvonne MacDonald
Julia Mandala
Maureen McHugh
Heidi Ruby Miller
Debbie Oakes
Kristine Kathryn Rusch
Josepha Sherman
Jane Yolen
and The Female Person from Colorado

CHAPTER 1
6:30 PM–6:55 PM, All Hallows' Eve

It didn't look much like a detective's office.

One side contained a desk covered with doilies, a teapot that could only be described as precious, pencils and pens neatly aligned by a telephone, and a framed tintype of a chubby woman, rifle in hand, posing with her foot on the neck of a dead gorgon.

The other side of the office looked like it hadn't been cleaned in months, if not years, which was exactly the case. There were a pair of pneumatic Playmates taped to the wall, on which Mallory's partner had meticulously drawn bras and panties with a Magic Marker. There was a large wastebasket, surrounded by eleven crushed paper cups that Mallory had tossed in its general direction, missing each time. One drawer of the desk held the office bottle, another a stack of unread pulp magazines, a third a change of underwear and socks.

The kitchen—the place had formerly been an apartment—held an ancient refrigerator that, at the moment, contained three six-packs of beer, a supply of sliced lemons for his partner's tea, and seven half-gallons of milk for the office cat.

John Justin Mallory leaned back in his chair, feeling every one of his forty-five years. He'd tossed his trenchcoat over a chair, but he still wore his battered fedora. His feet rested comfortably on his desk, a fresh paper cup held a shot of Old Peculiar, and he held the *Racing Form* up so that Periwinkle, his magic mirror, could read it over his shoulder.

"So what do you think?" asked the detective.

"You know very well what I think."

"He's got to be ready today," said Mallory. "I feel it in my bones. I mean, how the hell many races can he lose in a row?"

"According to the *Form*, it's sixty-four and counting," said Periwinkle.

"But look at the odds," persisted Mallory. "Ninety-nine trillion to one, in a five-horse field. Whoever heard of odds like that?"

"Probably the tote board doesn't go any higher," replied the mirror.

"O ye of little faith. How can a horse with a name like Flyaway not win every now and then?"

"Do you really want me to tell you?" said Periwinkle, stifling a yawn.

A feminine creature, who seemed human at first glance but decidedly less so upon further examination, stretched her feline body languidly atop the refrigerator. "They should make him run in handicap races, so he'll have a better chance," she said.

"He's in a handicap today," said Mallory. "The other four horses are spotting him from ten to sixteen pounds."

"I meant a *real* handicap," replied the cat-girl, purring gently. "Like a quarter-mile head start against a field of blind three-legged horses."

"Try not to be so encouraging, Felina," said Mallory. "It'll go to my head."

"Good," said Felina. "Maybe it'll push all thoughts of betting on Flyaway down to your left elbow."

"Not very likely," intoned Periwinkle.

Felina hurled herself through the air and landed on Mallory's desk. "Then since your elbow's not busy, you can skritch my back."

Mallory reached out a hand and absently scratched between her shoulder blades while still reading the *Form*.

"That's wrong!" protested Felina.

"What's wrong?"

"You're scratching," she complained. "I want you to *skritch*."

"What's the difference?"

"It's like the difference between night and almost-night," she said helpfully.

"Fine," said Mallory, rubbing the small of her back. "Let me know when I'm doing it right."

She stretched and purred noisily, and before she could answer him—not that he needed one—the office door opened and Mallory's partner entered. She walked to her own desk, set down a brown shopping bag filled with purchases, smoothed some wrinkles out of her dress, brushed a wisp of gray hair back from her pudgy face, and exhaled deeply.

"You wouldn't believe how crowded it is out there," said Winnifred

Carruthers. "I'm exhausted! It took me almost an hour just to get a jar of incense, and the line for black candles was endless. Everyone's doing their last-minute shopping."

"I thought they were supposed to do it on Christmas Eve," said Mallory.

"That's in the Manhattan you left behind, John Justin," she replied. "In *this* Manhattan, everyone celebrates All Hallows' Eve."

"Call it anything you like, but where I come from, it's Halloween."

"The younger generation calls it that," acknowledged Winnifred. "But to the traditionalists, it will always be All Hallows' Eve. You should be more noticing, John Justin. The whole city's getting ready for the celebration."

"I should think this Manhattan had suffered through quite enough ghosts and goblins and things that go bump in the night without setting aside a day to celebrate them," remarked Mallory dryly.

"You're looking at it all wrong, John Justin," said Winnifred. "It's a festive occasion." She smiled happily. "My nephew Rupert has come to visit for a week. He just arrived yesterday. I hope he likes some of the gifts I bought him."

"I'm sure he will," said Mallory. "If I know you, you bought him a big enough selection to choose from." He went back to studying the *Form*.

"Oh my goodness!" exclaimed Winnifred. "You're reading the *Racing Form!*"

"So?"

"So that poor creature is running again tonight, isn't he?"

"Running *again* implies that he ever ran before," said Felina.

"There's an awful lot of sympathy in this office for a horse who's never yet worked up a sweat," said Mallory irritably, "and not much for the guy who keeps betting on him."

"Perhaps it's because the horse doesn't know any better," suggested Periwinkle.

"There's a dog down the street who keeps running away from his owner," said Felina. "Maybe we could feed him Flyaway and slow him down."

"One of these days he's going to win, and the payoff is going to make history," said Mallory.

"If you bet him to show, and he starts in the fourth race of the day and finishes third in the ninth race, do you still win?" asked Felina.

"Enough already," said Mallory. He put the *Form* back down on his desk. "All right, it's a holiday of sorts. I'll skip the track and take you out to dinner."

"It's All Hallows' Eve," said Felina, rubbing against him. "Let's be generous and take the fat broad too."

"I was talking to the . . . to my partner," said Mallory. "You're staying here and guarding the office."

"There's nothing here worth taking," protested Felina.

"Well, I like that!" snapped Periwinkle.

"What use is a magic mirror that never shows cat movies?" sniffed Felina.

"There *are* no cat movies," replied the mirror.

"All you ever show is women taking their clothes off," said Felina. "What fun is that?"

"*What?*" demanded Winnifred, glaring at her partner.

"That's not so," said Mallory defensively. "Sometimes I watch wrestling."

"Naked ladies wrestling in the mud," said Felina, wrinkling her nose in disgust.

"It's an art form," said Mallory, "not a sporting contest."

"It's obscene," said Winnifred severely.

"It's boring," said Felina.

"I could show you naked ladies sky-diving, if that's more to your taste," offered Periwinkle.

"Can't you show anything but naked ladies?" said Winnifred.

"My job is pleasing my audience," said Periwinkle. "If you asked me what *I* would like to show . . ."

The mirror became a screen, and characters moved through an exotic-looking bar.

"So it's *Casablanca*," said Mallory. "Big deal. There's Dooley Wilson at the piano, and here comes Peter Lorre with the letters of transit." Then: "No, I'm wrong."

"You're right," said Periwinkle.

"But that's not Bogart, and the girl certainly isn't Bergman." He peered at the screen. "The guy looks like Ronald Reagan."

"And Ann Sheridan is the girl," said the mirror.

"So it's not *Casablanca*," said Mallory.

"It *is*. This is the film they would have made if they'd signed their first choices. We can make it a double feature with Clark Gable and Humphrey Bogart, John Huston's first choices, in *The Man Who Would Be King*."

"Forget it," said Mallory firmly. "If it isn't Bogey and Bergman, it's not *Casablanca*."

"All right," said Periwinkle with a melodramatic sigh. "I did my best. Some people are rooted in their ignorance. Some people just refuse to be culturally uplifted."

Reagan and Sheridan were instantly replaced by Bubbles La Tour, who was gyrating her hips so fast that it almost made Mallory dizzy to watch her.

"That's quite enough of that," said Winnifred harshly.

"Whatever you say," replied Periwinkle. Bubbles La Tour was immediately replaced by the fifth inning of a 1938 American Association baseball game between the Miami Monorchids and the Gainesville Geldings.

"You know," said Mallory wistfully, "I can remember the good old days, when all I had to contend with were thieves and muggers. And I had to leave my office to find them. There weren't any uppity mirrors or spoiled ninety-pound office cats in *my* Manhattan."

"For better or worse, *this* is your Manhattan now, John Justin," noted Winnifred.

"But only as long as he feeds and skritches me," said Felina.

"You are a walking appetite," complained Mallory.

"I'm too comfortable to walk," replied the cat-girl. "I'm a lying-down appetite."

"Speaking of appetites," said Winnifred, "you mentioned something about dinner, John Justin?"

"Yeah, what the hell, why not?" said Mallory. "If it's really a holiday, it seems a shame to send out for pizza."

"Sounds good to me," she replied. "Where shall we go?"

"Anywhere you want. I just want to stop by Joey Chicago's bar on the way, and maybe lay down a sawbuck or two on Flyaway with Harry the Book. Then, if you like, we can pick up your nephew and all have dinner together."

"Rupert was still sleeping an hour ago," she said. "I think it would be better not to disturb him."

"Sleeping?" repeated Mallory. "The kid must be a real night owl."

"He's a healthy young man, and he's new to the big city," agreed Winnifred. "He was out exploring it all last night."

Mallory shrugged. "If he made it back, I guess he can take care of himself."

"Once he gets his hours straightened away, I'm going to take him to the art museum and the symphony," said Winnifred.

"Yeah, a nice healthy young man will love that," said Mallory, trying to keep the sarcasm out of his voice." He paused. "So where am I taking you for dinner?"

"You know, I haven't had unicorn steak in years."

"Do they serve it in New York?"

"I know just the place," said Winnifred. "The Mystic Skewer. It's on the corner of Sloth and Gluttony."

"Then let's go," said Mallory, walking over and holding his arm out to her. She reached for it, then suddenly swayed as if she was about to faint.

"Are you all right?" he asked solicitously as he helped to steady her.

"Just a slight dizzy spell," replied Winnifred, leaning against him. "Probably I overexerted myself shopping."

"I don't know," said Mallory. "I've never seen you tired before."

"We're all getting older, John Justin. It's hard for me to believe it, but I'm in my sixties."

"In fact," continued Mallory in worried tones, "I've never seen you this pale before. Maybe we should stop by a doctor, just to be on the safe side."

"I'll be fine," Winnifred assured him. She moved free of his supporting arms. "I just needed a moment to rest. I'm ready to go now."

"You're sure?"

She nodded her head. "I'm sure."

"Do that again!" said Mallory sharply.

"Do *what* again?"

"Nod your head like that," he said, staring intently at her.

"Is something the matter, John Justin?"

"Just do it!"

She shrugged and nodded her head.

"*Shit!*" muttered Mallory. "Come over to the light."

"What is it?" asked Winnifred, worried now.

"If I tell you, you're going to think it's some kind of Halloween joke," said Mallory. "Felina, get over here, look at where I'm pointing, and tell me what you see."

"Two little holes," said the cat-girl.

"And where are they?"

"On her neck."

"Are you quite serious?" asked Winnifred.

"Why the hell would I lie to you?" said Mallory. "How long have you been having these dizzy spells?"

"Just today," she said. "Once while I was shopping I had to stop and sit down for a moment until it passed, and then right here. But as you can see, they don't last for very long."

"No others?" he demanded.

"No."

"Think hard."

She frowned. "Well, just one."

"What time last night was it?"

Her eyes widened in surprise. "How did you know?"

"Because your nephew didn't arrive until yesterday afternoon."

"Surely you can't be suggesting that Rupert—?"

"What else has changed in your life since yesterday afternoon?" said Mallory. He looked out the window. "Dinner can wait. Even Flyaway can wait. We've got to get over to your apartment *fast*."

"Why the hurry?" asked Winnifred. "He'll still be there, and we can put an end to this foolishness. He told me that he wasn't going out to celebrate until seven or eight o'clock."

"I'm not worried about his going out."

"Then what?"

"I want to make sure we confront him before it's dark."

Winnifred's apartment was three blocks from the office, in one of the sturdiest buildings Mallory had ever seen. There was a uniformed doorman—his tail kept peeking out beneath his long coat—who opened the door for them, and a moment later they were in the elevator. She had a brief dizzy spell as it approached the seventh floor, but by the time it stopped she was fine again.

"Why are you staring at me like that, John Justin?" she asked as they got off.

"I'm trying to decide whether you should stay home and rest or go down to the hospital for a transfusion."

"I'm doing neither," she said. "This is All Hallows' Eve. It's a night to celebrate."

"Start by not falling down," said Mallory. "You can work up to celebrating later."

"You're looking at this all wrong, John Justin," said Winnifred. "If I *have* been bitten by a vampire, this is the best night of the year to find the guilty party. Every creature of the night comes out on All Hallows' Eve."

"You've been bitten," Mallory assured her. "And we don't have to go hunting for Transylvanian counts with bad accents. The thing that bit you is sleeping down the hall in your apartment."

"Rupert isn't a *thing!*" she said harshly. "He's my nephew, and I'm sure there's a logical explanation for all this."

"I don't know," he replied dubiously. "If I've learned anything at all during my two years here it's that *this* Manhattan doesn't abound in logical explanations."

"Nonsense," she said firmly, seeming more like herself. "We'll speak to Rupert and get to the bottom of this."

They stopped before a door.

"This is it?" asked Mallory.

"Yes."

"Give me your key."

"I can unlock my own door, John Justin."

"Hand it over. You're not going in there first. I don't know what's on the other side of this door."

"Well, *I* know," she said. "This is my home, for goodness' sake!"

"To quote a blonde bombshell I lusted for when I was a kid, I don't think goodness has a hell of a lot to do with it."

He took the key from her, inserted it in the lock, turned it, and slowly opened the door.

"It's dark as a tomb in here," he complained.

"I'm saving on electricity until we get our next case," explained Winnifred. She reached over to the wall and flipped a switch, and suddenly the room was bathed in light.

"Goddamn!" exclaimed Mallory. "Now, *that's* impressive!"

"I'm very proud of it."

"You should be," said Mallory, still staring at the wall to his left. On it were the mounted heads of a gorgon, a chimera, a banshee, a unicorn, a dragon, and half a dozen other beasts he couldn't identify. Below them was a gun rack filled with high-powered rifles of varying makes and calibers. "You ought to will these to the museum."

"I already have." She paused. "The only thing missing is the Yeti. I spent two years hunting for him in the Himalayas. I came across his tracks a few times, but never actually saw him. The weapons are all retired, of course—keepsakes of a more exciting life. An excitement I thought was gone forever, before I met you."

"Hi, Winnifred," said a voice. "Welcome back."

Mallory jumped back and studied the wall, trying to determine which head had spoken.

"Who said that?" he demanded.

"I did," replied the voice, and suddenly a glowing bird that constantly changed colors flew past all the doily-covered chairs and couches to perch on Winnifred's shoulder.

"This is Dulcet, my songbird," said Winnifred.

"Don't ever let Felina see her."

Winnifred smiled. "Why do you think I keep her here instead of at the office?"

"I don't believe I've ever seen anything like her," said Mallory, fascinated by the bird's changing colors.

"She's imported from Italy," explained Winnifred. "Sing something for my partner, Dulcet."

The bird burst into a lilting aria from *Madame Butterfly.*

"Isn't it beautiful?" said Winnifred.

"Very nice," answered Mallory. "A little highbrow for my taste."

Dulcet immediately began singing "That's Amore."

"That's enough for now, thank you," said Winnifred, and the bird fell silent.

"What's this?" asked Mallory, looking at a small glass case that contained a silken veil and a crushed rose.

"It's from a very long time ago," she said uncomfortably, and immediately turned her attention elsewhere. "Oh! I forgot to set food out!"

"How the hell many beggars get past your doorman and make it to the seventh floor?" asked Mallory, following her past shelves filled to overflowing with romance novels, DVDs of love stories, and CDs of every sentimental love song Mallory had ever heard plus a few hundred he had thankfully missed.

"Not for beggars," she said, scurrying to the kitchen and pulling some items out of the refrigerator. "Well," she amended, "not for the kind you mean, anyway." She walked to a window, opened it long enough to place the foodstuffs on a broad ledge, and closed it again. "It's for the harpies. They get so hungry this time of year. And there's a darling miniature pegasus that just began showing up two weeks ago."

Mallory frowned. "That's kind of contradictory, isn't it?"

"I don't follow you, John Justin."

He gestured first to the heads and then to the little pegasus that was just dropping down to the window ledge. "Do you kill them or nurture them?"

"Every creature on the wall was intent on ripping me to shreds," she answered. "Even so, I gave each of them a sporting chance. But these poor little babies"—she gestured to a trio of approaching harpies—"just want a little food and a safe place to eat it."

She suddenly reached out a hand and steadied herself against the wall.

"Damn!" said Mallory. "I've never been here before, and it was so interesting I almost forgot why we came. Where's your nephew?"

"He's sleeping."

Mallory looked out the window. "Twilight," he announced. "He should be waking up."

And as if on cue, a slender young man, a few inches shorter than Mallory, with unkempt wavy brown hair, suddenly opened a bedroom door and walked out into the living room, clad in pajamas, a bathrobe, and slippers.

"I heard voices," he said, blinking his eyes as if trying to focus them.

"Rupert, this is my partner, John Justin Mallory," said Winnifred. "John Justin, this is my nephew, Rupert Newton."

"Just don't call me Fig," said Rupert. "I hate it when they call me that."

"Is there anything else I should call you?" asked Mallory, stepping closer to him.

"Like what?" asked the young man, puzzled.

"Oh, I don't know," said the detective with a shrug. "Vlad, maybe. Or Nosferatu."

Rupert jumped back as if he'd been stung. "How did you know?"

"I'm a trained detective," said Mallory dryly. "Besides, your aunt is pale as a ghost and keeps trying to fall down."

"I'm sorry, Aunt Winnifred," said Rupert. "I didn't mean to."

"Then you *are* a vampire?" she said, surprised.

"Not yet, I suspect," said Mallory, studying the young man. "But he *knows* a vampire, don't you, Rupert?" He pointed to Rupert's neck. "You see? Just like yours, though he's obviously had it a lot longer."

"A week," confirmed Rupert miserably.

"How'd it happen?" asked Mallory. "Did you go out with a girl who had a reputation for giving dynamite hickeys?"

"You're making fun of me!" protested Rupert.

"Kid, there's nothing funny about being one of the undead," said Mallory. "I'd say I want to help you, but I don't know how. My first job is to protect your aunt."

"I don't want to hurt her!"

"I believe you," said Mallory. "But there are still a few rays of sunlight in the sky. How will you feel about it two hours from now?"

"I'd never harm Aunt Winnifred!"

"How do you think I knew what to look for?" demanded Mallory. "Winnifred, turn your head." She did so, and he pointed to the two holes on the side of her neck. "Do you even remember doing that?"

Rupert stared at his aunt, wide-eyed. "No," he said. Then, "I thought it was a dream."

"Okay," said Mallory, "so once the urge or the hunger or whatever you want to call it hits, you don't know what you're doing, and after you've done it you don't remember it." He turned to Winnifred. "Like I said, he can't stay anywhere near you."

Winnifred seemed about to object, then changed her mind and remained silent.

"You don't want to harm your aunt," said Mallory. "I don't want her harmed. Will you let me relocate you to a hotel until I can find someone who can help you?"

Rupert nodded his agreement. "How will you keep me there? In my dream, I got stronger at night."

"We'll see to it that you don't have any reason to leave," said Mallory.

"How?"

"The Goblins are playing the Gremlins at the Garden tonight, and it's on TV," said Mallory. "If I leave you sitting in front of the television set with a bottle of plasma and a straw, can you think of any reason why you won't stay there?"

Rupert started salivating slightly at the mention of plasma. "No," he said, wiping his mouth off with the sleeve of his robe, and Mallory could see that his canines were a little longer than average. "No, I can't."

"Where will you get the plasma, John Justin?" asked Winnifred.

"The local blood bank."

Rupert started drooling again, and his left eyelid began twitching.

"I won't be a party to theft," said Winnifred firmly.

"I'm not stealing anything," said Mallory. "I plan to buy it with the twenty I was going to put on Flyaway."

"They'll never sell it to a private citizen."

"Yes, they will."

"What makes you think so."

"Because I'll have Rupert with me," answered Mallory, gesturing to the salivating, twitching young man. "And I'll explain that they can either sell it to me now or they can hope Rupert doesn't remember where they are an hour or two from now when it's totally dark out." The detective smiled. "He may not be as potent as your .550 Nitro Express, but there are certain advantages to having an embryonic vampire in your arsenal."

CHAPTER 3

7:22 PM–7:52 PM

"I really don't get any stronger at night," said Rupert as he and Mallory walked down Second Avenue.

Mallory paused as a yellow elephant, with a driver and two passengers in its howdah, came down the middle of the street. "I'll never get used to what passes for cabs here," he muttered.

"Here?" repeated Rupert curiously. "Where are you from, Mr. Mallory?"

"I have the strangest urge to say that I'm not in Kansas anymore," replied Mallory. He shrugged. "Oh, well. Could be worse. Could be Checker cabs."

"Getting back to the blood bank, Mr. Mallory . . ."

"Yeah?"

"Like I said, I really don't get stronger at night."

"Okay, you know it, and now I know it. Let's keep it our secret, and if *they* don't know it, maybe we'll get what we need."

"I feel just terrible about this."

"Not to worry," said Mallory. "I don't remember my pulp literature and B movies all that well, but I'm pretty sure it takes more than one bite to turn you or your aunt into a vampire." He stared at the young man. "Who the hell nailed you?"

The boy shuddered. "Draconis."

"Draconis?"

"Aristotle Draconis."

"He's a vampire?"

"He must be. I woke up just in time to see him leaving my stateroom."

"Your stateroom?" repeated Mallory. "You didn't fly here from Europe?"

Rupert shook his head. "I'm afraid of heights, so I took the *Moribund Manatee*."

"Something doesn't make sense here," said Mallory. "But I thought vampires couldn't travel across water."

"I thought so too," said Rupert. "I guess we were both wrong," he added ruefully.

"What does this Draconis look like?" asked Mallory.

"Tall," said Rupert. "Very tall, almost seven feet. And thin, like a skeleton. And he dressed all in black."

"Clean shaven?"

The young man nodded. "Yes. With dark burning eyes."

"You want to expand on that?" said Mallory. "In *my* Manhattan I'd know what it means, but here it could literally mean that his eyes were on fire or shooting off sparks."

"They looked like they could," said Rupert with a shudder. "And there's something else."

"Yeah?"

"I saw him walking around the deck on the first day, and he was so pale I thought he might collapse at any minute. I mean, I know you think Aunt Winnifred was pale, but it was nothing compared to *him*. He was almost chalk-white."

"All right," said Mallory. "Tall, emaciated, and chalk-white. I'll remember it."

"No," said Rupert.

Mallory frowned. "But you just said—"

"He was pale the *first* time I saw him," said Rupert. "But when he left my stateroom, his coloring was normal. Darker than normal, even."

"I think we'll operate on the assumption that it wasn't from a tanning parlor," said Mallory. "Do you know anything else about him?"

"I overheard him saying that he was looking forward to exploring America. I got the impression he'd never been here before."

"Good."

"Good?" repeated the boy.

"If he doesn't have a destination in mind, there's every likelihood that he's still in Manhattan. The city's worth a couple of days on anyone's itinerary. That means I might be able to find him."

"Believe me, you don't want to find him," said the young man earnestly.

"Why not?"

"He's terrifying," said Rupert. "What are the odds that he'll come after Aunt Winnifred out of all the people in New York? You'll live a lot longer if you never meet him."

"And what if he comes after *you* again?" asked Mallory.

Rupert's eyes went wide with terror. "Why would he?"

"Maybe he likes the way you taste. Maybe he needs to bite you a few more times to turn you into a fellow vampire, or an eternal servant. Maybe he's a gay vampire and he thinks you're pretty. You could fill half a dozen books with what I don't know about vampires. In fact, I think a hell of a lot of romance writers in my Manhattan already have."

"You *really* think he might come after me?"

"I'd call it a possibility."

The young man's hand shot out, grabbing Mallory's sleeve. "Then I take back everything I said. You've *got* to catch him!"

"The first thing I've got to do is get you off display," said Mallory as they approached the blood bank. "Then I'll check on Winnifred again to make sure she's okay, and then we'll worry about Aristotle Draconis."

"But—"

"That's the way it's going to be," said Mallory, increasing his pace. Rupert watched him for a moment, then realized that he was standing there alone and broke into a run to catch up with the detective.

They reached the blood bank in another minute, and Mallory walked up to the front desk.

"Excuse me," he said, trying to get a nurse's attention.

"That all depends on what you've done," replied the nurse.

"I beg your pardon," said Mallory, confused, "but I'm not quite sure what you're talking about."

"Excusing you," answered the nurse. "We can forgive high alcohol contents and poor cholesterol readings, but we cannot accept blood that is infected with measles, mumps, tonsillitis, lumbago, rheumatism, arthritis, tennis elbow, gingivitis, flat feet, acid stomach—"

"Stop," said Mallory before she could rattle off thirty more disqualifiers. "We're not here to donate blood."

"We don't buy it on holidays," she said severely.

"You misunderstand. We're here to *buy* some blood, or at least some plasma, for the young man."

"What type?"

"It doesn't make any difference."

"We have to know before we can inject it," insisted the nurse.

"He's not going to inject it," said Mallory. "He's going to *drink* it."

The nurse stared at the pale young man. "Ah, yes," she said. "I can see now: the pale skin, the dilated pupils, the hint of enlarged canines, and of course there's no hair on the back of his hands."

"Should there be?"

"Only if he'd been bitten by a werewolf," said the nurse, "in which case you'd be better advised to go to a butcher shop than a blood bank."

"Now that that's settled, how much for, oh, I don't know, half a gallon of blood?"

"That's out of the question," said the nurse. "We can't spare that much."

"We're willing to pay . . . *now*," said Mallory meaningfully. "I can't speak for later, when he's desperate."

She stared at Rupert, who was starting to drool again. "He looks pretty desperate right now."

"I don't know if I can control him," said Mallory.

She pulled a cross and a string of garlic out from a hidden drawer under the counter. "Not to worry," she assured the detective. "*We* can control him."

Rupert held his hands up before his face. "Take it away!" he yelled.

She put the garlic and cross back into the drawer. "You were saying?" she asked with a pleasant smile.

"Nothing," said Mallory. "Come on, kid—we'll have to find it somewhere else."

"Just a minute," said the nurse.

"Yes?"

"It really wouldn't do to have your young friend attacking strangers on the street. He might pick on the wrong one and get seriously hurt." She lowered her voice confidentially. "It's not generally known, but most of the grocery stores sell blood this one night of the year, since there are so many creatures out celebrating. It's not legal, but the police tend to look the other way."

"Thank you," said Mallory.

"You didn't hear it from me."

"My lips are sealed. Come on, Rupert."

He left the blood bank, accompanied by the young man, who took a deep breath of the evening air and let out a heavy sigh. "Ah! That's better!" He turned to Mallory. "I've been allergic to garlic all my life."

"Then it wasn't because you're turning into a vampire?"

"I never could stand the stuff. Makes my eyes water."

"All right," said the detective. "I think I'm going to put you up at my apartment. Why waste the money on a hotel? If Draconis is looking for you, he's no more likely to look in my apartment than in a hotel room. There's no way he can know you're connected to Winnifred, and even if he were to find out, he still wouldn't know that she's my partner." He paused. "There's a market right around the corner from my place. We'll get the blood there. And once you're ensconced in my apartment, I'll get together with Winnifred and dope out our next step."

"I'm very grateful, Mr. Mallory," said Rupert. "I've always hated vampires. Now it looks like I might become one."

"That's something else we've got to do—see how to reverse the damned thing and turn you back into a normal young man. Your aunt is a lot better at research than I am. I think I'll have her do that while I'm trying to locate Draconis."

"*Pssst!*"

Mallory stopped and saw a green-skinned goblin gesturing to him from between two apartment buildings. "Hey, Mister—pretty goblin girls!"

"The name's Mister Mallory," said the detective in bored tones. "Mister Pretty Goblin Girls lives on the next block."

"A humorist," muttered the goblin. He turned to Rupert. "Pretty goblin girls, dirt cheap."

"Not interested," said Rupert.

"Well, then, exceptionally ugly goblin girls, wildly expensive, if that's to your taste."

"No, thanks."

"Goblin boys, perhaps?" said the goblin.

"Go away," said Mallory.

"Goblin octogenarians?"

Mallory and Rupert increased their pace.

"Blind deaf mute goblin quadruple amputees?"

"You really have one?" asked Mallory.

"Sure," said the goblin. He pulled a hatchet and a sledgehammer out of his overcoat. "Give me five minutes."

"Forget it," said Mallory. "I was just curious."

"Curiosity killed the cat," said the goblin. Suddenly he snapped his fingers. "How about a dead cat?"

Mallory kept walking.

"Okay for you!" yelled the goblin after him. "But don't be surprised if the price has tripled by midnight!"

"I'll only be surprised if someone pays it," said Mallory as they walked out of earshot. "How're you holding up, kid? It's only another block."

"I'll be all right," answered Rupert.

"There's the sign," said Mallory after they'd gone another thirty yards.

"Noodnik's Market," read Rupert.

"Don't let him throw you," said Mallory. "He's a nice enough guy. He just likes a challenge."

"I don't understand."

"You will."

They continued walking, past Ye Olde Antiquarian Book Shoppe, which sold only volumes dealing with antiquarian books; Ming Toy Yingleman's authentic Greek grocery shop; the elegant Industrial Espionage Cartel, with reinforced titanium bars over its darkened windows; and the Herbal T Store, featuring a huge selection of T-shirts created by the famed Hollywood designer Morris K. Herbal.

Finally they came to the grocery store and entered it. Seymour Noodnik immediately approached them.

"Hi, Mallory," he said. "It's All Hallows' Eve. Hell of a night to be out on a case."

"I'm not."

"You're not searching for a serial killer, or better still, a trio of lewd lady exhibitionists?" said Noodnik, trying to hide his disappointment.

"Nope. I'm just here to buy something."

"Crocodile wings," suggested Noodnik. "I got a special on 'em."

"Crocodiles don't have wings," said Mallory.

"Not anymore," agreed Noodnik, wiping off a butcher knife. "I can make a price on a dozen."

"Not interested."

"Okay, then—canary teeth."

"Forget it."

"You're a hard man to please, Mallory. How about a pair of fighting fish?"

"Let me guess," said Mallory. "They come equipped with guns and knives."

"No, their names are Ethel and Wilbur, and they hate each other. She nags, and he cheats on her with an angelfish whenever she goes to her club meetings."

"Will you shut up for a minute and let me tell you what I want?" said Mallory.

"You're usurping my function," said Noodnik. "My job is to sell you."

"So let me explain what I want you to sell me."

Noodnik frowned. "That's not part of the job description. How about a leather helmet with goggles for a flying snake?"

"Damn it, Seymour, are you going to shut up and listen to me or am I going to go down the street to Gregory the Greengrocer's?"

"All right, all right," said Noodnik. Then, confidentially: "He used to be Gregory the Tangrocer before he ate that bad rigatoni."

"I need half a gallon of blood," said Mallory.

"What kind?"

Mallory looked puzzled. "The usual—red."

"Elf's blood? Dragonfly's blood? Gorgon's blood?"

"What kind does a vampire drink?"

"It depends," answered Noodnik.

"On what?"

"On what kind of vampire you're talking about. Is it a Republican? A Democrat? A Royalist? How many arms has it got? At a rough count?"

"Why don't you just look at him yourself?" said Mallory.

"You mean he's *here*?" demanded Noodnik. "Near my customers?"

"He's harmless."

"I'll bet that's what all the hadrosaurs used to say about *T. rex.*"

"He's a kid. He was just bitten last week."

"How many times?"

"How the hell do I know?" said Mallory irritably. "Rupert, come over here."

There was no response.

"Rupert!" yelled Mallory. He looked around. "Where the hell did he go?"

A small, balding man with canines that were almost an inch long, giving him the look of a chubby bulldog, approached them.

"I hate to intrude, but I believe the young man you're looking for ran out the door a minute ago."

"Was someone chasing him?" asked Mallory.

"Or was *he* chasing someone?" interjected Noodnik.

"I believe he was running in terror," said the small man.

"Oh, come on," said Noodnik. "My prices aren't that high. Maybe I jacked them up a couple of hundred percent for All Hallows' Eve, but still . . ."

"Did you see which way he went?" asked Mallory.

"I'm afraid not."

"Damn!" muttered Mallory. "Where do you look for a runaway vampire in the middle of Manhattan?"

"Perhaps I can be of help," said the small man.

"I thought you didn't know which way he went," said Mallory.

"That's quite true, sir. I lost sight of him before he'd gone five yards."

"Well, then?"

"He *is* a runaway vampire, is he not?"

"Yeah."

"And I heard Mr. Noodnik ask if you were here on a case, so clearly you're a detective."

"What are you getting at?"

"Just that you and I should team up—if you will buy me the blood you were going to buy the young man."

"You don't know where he is," said Mallory. "Why the hell should I buy you anything, and why should we team up?"

"We need each other. You know all about runaways but nothing about vampires." The man smiled a very toothy smile. "I, on the other hand, know nothing about runaways, but I know almost everything there is to know about vampires."

Mallory looked at the little man, then out into the empty street.

"Seymour, give my friend here a bottle of blood." He extended a hand. "My name's Mallory."

"John Justin Mallory?" said the little man excitedly. "The one who found that unicorn and solved all those other cases? This is an honor!" He took Mallory's hand and shook it vigorously. "Bats McGuire's the name, blood-sucking's the game."

"You sure this is a good idea, Mallory?" asked Noodnik.

"I'll be all right," said Mallory. He turned to Bats McGuire. "Let's not waste any time. Are you ready to go?"

"Right." The little vampire turned to Noodnik. "Keep the blood on ice for me. I'll be back for it once we accomplish our mission." He led Mallory to the door.

"Got a special on caskets" were Noodnik's parting words.

CHAPTER 4
7:52 PM–8:26 PM

"Who bit him?" asked McGuire as they walked along the street.

"Some guy called Draconis," said Mallory. "Ever hear of him?"

The little vampire shook his head. "No. And I know most of the vampires in town. He must be in from Chicago or maybe Kansas City."

"Try Europe."

"Why? I'm happy right here."

"I mean, Draconis just arrived from Europe."

"Well, that makes things easier," said McGuire.

"It does?" responded Mallory. "How?"

"Those European vampires are a traditional lot. He'll probably have brought his coffin with him, filled with his native soil." McGuire grimaced at the thought. "Me, I'd much rather sleep on satin sheets at the Plaza or the Waldorf. Anyway, the case is solved."

"What are you talking about?"

"You're a detective. Just track down Draconis's coffin and wait for him. He probably believes all that bullshit about not going out in the sunlight."

"I take it you don't?"

"I burn easily—but I don't turn to dust," answered McGuire. He stopped as they came to a bar. "Well, now that the case is over, let's pop in here for a victory drink. Your treat."

"The case isn't over," said Mallory. "Knowing his coffin is somewhere in a city of seven million people and finding it are two different things."

"Not as different as busty naked ladies and Swedish temples, or 78 RPM records and left-handed golf clubs," said McGuire. "But let it pass. Let's think of our next move over a drink."

"I'm starting to think that knowing everything there is to know about vampires is not going to help you pull your weight," said Mallory dryly.

"You should be a little more appreciative," said McGuire defensively. "I've already told you something you didn't know about Draconis, and I've only been on the case for ninety seconds." He paused. "Now let's get that drink."

"Achmed Hamib's Desert Oasis," said Mallory, reading the flickering neon sign *Achmed Hamib's Desert Oasis* above the door. "I have a feeling they don't serve blood here."

"Just as well," said McGuire. "I hate the stuff."

"I thought you were a vampire."

"I am."

"Well, then?"

"When you were a kid didn't your mother make you eat your greens?"

"What's that got to do with anything?"

"You didn't like 'em, but they were good for you. Me, I don't like blood, but every now and then I have to drink a little. I find I can fool my body for days on end by drinking Bloody Marys."

"All right," said Mallory. "But just one."

They entered the bar, passed through an arched doorway past a truly impressive display of swords, some of which weren't made in Japan, and found a small table in the corner. A turbaned waiter approached them.

"A beer and a Bloody Mary," said Mallory.

"Very good, Sahib," replied the waiter. "And for your friend?"

"I'm having the beer; he's having the Bloody Mary."

"And a pinch of the specialty," added McGuire.

"Five dollars extra," said the waiter.

"*Inshallah*," said McGuire.

"*Inshallah*, my ass!" snapped the waiter. "You pay up front or you don't get a damned thing! We know you around here, Bats McGuire!"

McGuire turned to Mallory. "I hate to mention it, but you *are* treating."

Mallory pulled a five out and held it up. The waiter snatched it, stuffed it in a pocket, and walked off.

"What specialty costs as much as the damned drink?" asked Mallory.

"*Ouch!*" shouted the waiter from the back room. "*Goddamn, that smarts!*"

"What the hell was *that*?" demanded the detective, startled.

"The specialty," said McGuire. "He pricks his forefinger and mixes a couple of drops of blood in with the drink. That'll hold me until tomorrow."

"Why his forefinger?" asked Mallory. "Seems to me a thumb would be easier, or at least a little less painful."

"*By the pricking of my thumbs, something wicked this way comes,*" intoned McGuire. "I'll stick to forefingers, thank you."

The waiter, a bandage on his finger, emerged from the back room, carrying their drinks.

"I hope you choke on it!" he muttered as he handed McGuire his Bloody Mary.

"Keep it up if you want a nickel tip," shot back the vampire.

Suddenly the waiter's entire attitude changed. "A thousand pardons, Sahib," he said, bowing low to Mallory. "I hope I have done nothing to offend. May Allah give thee many strong sons and beautiful daughters."

"I'll settle for a fast track at Jamaica tomorrow," said Mallory.

"It's coming up muddy," said the waiter. "May Allah lend wings to the feet of Lowborn Prince."

Mallory held up a bill. "There's twenty in it if you and Allah can tell me where to find Aristotle Draconis."

"Doesn't he play third base for the Louisiana Lechers?" said the waiter.

"He's a seven-foot-tall vampire and he's in Manhattan right now."

The waiter frowned. "What's he doing in Manhattan? The Lechers are playing the Toledo Troglodytes in an hour."

Mallory put the bill away. "Thanks anyway."

The waiter lowered his voice. "Before you leave, *Effendi*, perhaps I could interest you in some exotic belly-dancing?"

"We're in a hurry."

"It will only take me a few minutes to change into my costume."

"*Your* costume?" said Mallory.

"Do you see anyone else here?"

"Some other time."

The waiter shrugged. "Your loss."

"Doubtless," said Mallory as the waiter walked away. The detective turned to McGuire. "Finish that drink. I've got to check on my partner."

"I thought *I* was your partner," complained the little vampire.

"You're my companion for the moment. *She's* my partner. And the young man we're looking for nabbed her on the neck last night. I want to make sure she's not out doing the same thing to someone else."

"She won't be," said McGuire. "It takes more than one bite to inspire the thirst in a victim."

"The kid was only bitten once."

McGuire shook his head. "He only *remembers* being bitten once, but if he drank some of his aunt's blood, then you can draw one of two conclusions. Probably Draconis was feasting on him all during the trip from Europe, and the young man slept through it. They usually do, you know. I mean, it's quite painful to be bitten in the neck. Fortunately, we have a mild anesthetic in our saliva."

"Fine," said Mallory. "That's one conclusion. What's the other?"

"That the young man is kinky beyond belief and needs to see a good shrink."

"Let's stick with the first," said Mallory. "I saw the bite marks on his neck."

"Okay," said McGuire, finishing his drink. "It's probably the more reasonable assumption."

"All right, let's go."

They walked out into the night, avoided the crowd watching dragon races on the next block, took a pair of side streets, and soon arrived at Winnifred's apartment. The doorthing—Mallory had some difficulty thinking of him as a door*man*—recognized the detective and passed the two of them in, and a moment later they emerged from the elevator onto the seventh floor.

Mallory knocked on her door, and Winnifred, looking a little less pale, opened it.

"Who's your friend?" she asked, staring at Bats McGuire.

"An expert on vampires," replied Mallory.

"Yes, he certainly looks like one," she said. "Come on in. May I offer you some tea?"

"No, thanks," said McGuire. "We just had something to drink." He stared at her trophy wall. "That's quite a collection you have here, ma'am."

"Call me Winnifred, or Colonel Carruthers."

"I especially like the banshee."

"You know something about banshees, Mr. . . . . ah?"

"McGuire, ma'am, Bats McGuire. And yes, some of my best friends are banshees."

She stared coldly at him. "Banshees are a vicious and surly race."

"Yes, ma'am, they certainly are," he agreed promptly. "You don't dare turn your back on them for a second. But when you're a forty-seven-year-old unemployed vampire, you take your friends where you find them."

Winnifred turned to Mallory. "I assume Rupert is safe in some hotel room?"

"He flew the coop," said Mallory.

"He turned into a bat?" said Winnifred, surprised. "I didn't think he was that far gone."

"Poor choice of words," replied Mallory. "We stopped at Noodnik's—you know the place; we nailed Skippy the Card Shark there a few months ago—and he saw something that scared him and ran off. It could have been Aristotle Draconis, the vampire from the boat; it could have been something else. We won't know until we find him. Mr. McGuire here has offered to help."

"It's a big city, John Justin," said Winnifred. "We'd best split up."

"You're not going anywhere," said Mallory. "I want you to stay home and get your strength back."

"Are we equal partners, John Justin?"

"You know we are."

"Then stop giving me orders," she said. "We're splitting up." She walked toward her bedroom. "You wait here for a moment. I'll be right back."

She entered the bedroom and closed the door behind her.

"Probably gone to put rouge on her cheeks so she won't appear so pale," suggested McGuire.

Mallory shook his head. "Not her," he said. "She's got something else in mind, but I'll be damned if I know what." He shrugged. "Oh well, we'll find out soon enough."

"She's quite a hunter," said McGuire, studying her trophies.

"The best," said Mallory.

"And a romantic, too," added the vampire, glancing at the shelves of love stories.

"Not quite as successful," commented Mallory. "But she deserved to be."

McGuire spent another few minutes looking at the accumulation of a lifetime spent proving herself against the fiercest beasts of the jungle while hiding from beasts of the cities—the ones that wore suits, carried briefcases, and drank martinis. Then the bedroom door opened again, and Winnifred stepped out.

She was dressed in khaki shirt and shorts, hunting boots, and a pith helmet. She strode over to her gun rack, where she pulled out her favorite, a .550 Nitro Express.

"I'm ready now," she said.

"You can't go out alone," protested Mallory. "Look at you. You can barely lift the damned gun."

"It's a rifle, John Justin," she corrected him. "You carry guns in hip pockets. You blow away vampires with a Nitro Express." She turned to McGuire. "No insult intended."

"Winnifred, this is ridiculous, maybe even suicidal. You're in no condition to come face to face with something that's probably impervious to bullets."

"I've also got my hunting knife and my wits," she said. "They've served me pretty well in the past."

"You haven't been in the jungle for almost ten years," said Mallory, "and you've lost a lost of blood. I don't want you facing Aristotle Draconis alone."

"I won't be."

He frowned. "I thought you said we were splitting up."

"We are."

"Then—?"

"There's a phone in my bedroom," she said. "While I was changing, I called my former safari team—my gunbearer, skinner, and tracker trolls. They'll be here in five minutes, and then the old crew will be off to hunt for this Draconis."

"I'm not going to talk you out of it, am I?" said Mallory.

"No."

Mallory sighed. "Then I wish you a safe and uneventful hunt. The only things I can tell you about Draconis are that his first name is Aristotle, he's seven feet tall, skinny as a rail, and dresses in black."

"Then that will have to do," she replied. "We should decide where to meet in a few hours to compare notes and further coordinate our hunt, John Justin."

"Yeah, no sense going over the same ground twice. I'll start south of Central Park, you take from the park north, and we'll meet"—he checked his wristwatch—"at half past midnight."

"Where?"

"May I make a suggestion?" said McGuire.

"Shoot," said Mallory.

McGuire threw himself to the ground, then got up rather shamefacedly when he realized that Mallory was not giving an instruction to Winnifred.

"There's a charming little bistro called the Belfry at the corner of Eldritch and Eerie, very near the south end of Central Park. I know the owner, and he can give us a private room where we won't be overheard while exchanging information."

Mallory looked at Winnifred. "What do you think?"

"I suppose it's as good a place to meet as any," she replied.

"Okay," said Mallory, walking to the door. "There's no sense our hanging around until your crew shows up. We might as well get busy."

"I'll see you at twelve thirty," said Winnifred. "Or perhaps sooner, if it's a successful hunt."

McGuire accompanied Mallory to the elevator, and a moment later they walked out into the night.

"All right," said Mallory. "You're the vampire expert. Where would a young, very frightened almost-vampire go?"

"I've been a vampire since I was seven years old," said McGuire, "but if it was just occurring now, I'd seek out other vampires to find out what was happening to me, what kind of life I was facing."

"Makes sense," agreed Mallory. "Where is he likely to find the greatest concentration of vampires?"

"I should think the answer would be obvious," replied McGuire.

"The zoo?" suggested Mallory.

"Of course not," said the little vampire.

"Maybe some graveyard?"

McGuire shook his head. "No. There's only one place he'll go—the Vampire State Building."

"The Vampire State Building," repeated Mallory, staring at him. "You're kidding, right?"

"Am I smiling?" replied McGuire.

CHAPTER 5

8:26 PM–9:18 PM

It was the Empire State Building in the Manhattan Mallory had left behind, but as he was constantly discovering at the most inopportune times, he wasn't in *his* Manhattan anymore.

If he'd had any doubts, they were dispelled when he and McGuire came to the front entrance. Like most office buildings, it had a uniformed doorman. Unlike most, this one hung upside down from the top of the doorway.

"Hi, Boris," said McGuire. "I wonder if you can help us out?"

"Sure," said the doorman, stifling a guffaw. "Which way did you come in?"

"Boris fancies himself a humorist," explained McGuire.

"No problem," replied Mallory. "I've got a fat seventy-three-year-old aunt who fancies herself a sexpot."

"Boris, this is my friend, John Justin Mallory," began McGuire. "He—"

"Mallory?" repeated the doorman, pushing off and somehow landing lightly on his feet. "You're the guy who found that unicorn?"

"Yeah," said the detective. "Pleased to meet you."

"Has he . . . uh . . . joined the club?" asked Boris.

"No," answered McGuire. "At least not yet. We're here on a case."

"You're working for him?"

"Like I said, he's my friend. I'm just helping him out."

"Okay," said Boris. "Got a nice broad neck, though."

"If anyone nabs him in the neck, it'll be me," said McGuire. "Now, are you gonna listen to him or not?"

"Don't go getting offended," said Boris. "It was an honest question. What can I do for you, Mr. Mallory?"

"I'm looking for a young man who's run away," replied Mallory. "About five feet eight, maybe a hundred and sixty pounds, brown hair, brown eyes, couple of puncture marks on his neck. His name's Rupert Newton."

"You sure he's *run* away?" asked the doorman. "I mean, if he's one of us, he could have *flown* the coop, so to speak."

"I don't think he's a fully fledged member of your fraternity yet," said Mallory. "My guess is he'd want to seek out some vampires and find out what's been done to him, what he can do about it, what he can look forward to."

"Well, then, he's come to the right place."

"Have you seen him?"

"No," answered Boris. "But then, my vision isn't what it used to be. Before the change, I mean." He paused. "I suppose he *could* be here."

"He'd have shown up in the last ten or fifteen minutes."

"It's possible, then," said Boris. "I was off having a bite"—McGuire giggled at his choice of words—"until about two minutes before you showed up."

"It's a big building," said Mallory. "Where would he be most likely to go?"

"Well, it *is* our holy night, so most of the offices are closed," answered Boris. "If he's here at all, he'll be on the ninetieth floor."

"Why the ninetieth?"

"It's the only one that's open."

"Thanks," said Mallory, stepping through the doorway and into the building. "If you see him coming out, do me a favor and grab him until I can catch up with you."

"Grab him?" Boris's left eyelid began twitching and the muscles in his jaw tightened. "With pleasure."

"One other thing," said Mallory, turning back to the doorman. "Does Aristotle Draconis work in this building?"

Boris shrugged. "Check the registry. We've got thirty thousand people working here." He paused. "Well, *some* of them are people," he added.

"Come on, Bats," said Mallory, heading off to the elevator.

McGuire scurried after the detective, and a moment later the doors slid shut behind them. The small enclosure was immediately flooded with music.

"'Strangers in the Night,'" commented McGuire as he identified the tune. "Ah, the memories that brings back!"

Mallory frowned. "I don't remember anything in the lyrics about biting."

"What a kidder!" said McGuire. "Next, you'll be telling me it's supposed to be a love song."

"I wouldn't dream of it."

The song ended as they passed the sixtieth floor, to be replaced by another.

"Ah!" said McGuire with a happy smile. "'Fangs for the Memory.'"

"So what are we likely to find on the ninetieth floor?" asked Mallory.

The little vampire shrugged. "Trial lawyers, literary agents, all the usual bloodsuckers. I mean, it *is* the Vampire State Building."

"Somehow I don't think Rupert would be looking for a lawyer *or* an agent."

"No sense guessing what we'll find," announced McGuire as the elevator came to a stop and the doors slid open. "We're here."

The first thing Mallory saw was a huge poster announcing that a band named Vlad and the Impalers would be performing on All Hallows' Eve at the annual Zombies' Ball.

"Vlad and the Impalers?" said Mallory. "Are they serious?"

"They're the hot new group," McGuire informed him. "Though it'll be tough to top last year's band."

"Let me guess: Lassie and the Wolfwomen?"

"Silly name," said McGuire. "No, it was Igor and the Graverobbers."

"It figures," muttered Mallory.

"Personally, I always liked Guy Lombardo," admitted McGuire, "but one has to keep up with the times."

"Well, let's look around and see who or what's up here," said Mallory, walking past the poster. He found himself in a broad corridor lined with offices and tasteful store windows. He walked past a couple of doors, then stopped and read the neatly printed sign in a small window. "'Bat Ecology for the Newly Changed.'"

"That certainly sounds likely," agreed McGuire. "No, wait."

He pointed to a little note taped to the door: *Closed for the holiday.*

Next was an AAA office. "American Auto Association?" suggested Mallory. "What the hell would they be doing in the Vampire State Building?"

"American *Aeronautics* Association," McGuire corrected him.

Mallory peered through the window. He saw stacks of maps, a number of books listing the best caves in America, and a desk with a sign: *File Your Flight Plans Here.*

An incredibly slim woman, dressed all in black, with black hair and bright red lips, sat at the desk. When she saw Mallory staring at her, she winked and smiled at him.

"What do you think?" said McGuire.

"Not my type," replied Mallory. "I prefer 'em alive."

"I meant, do you think she can help us?"

Mallory shook his head. "The kid didn't have wings twenty minutes ago. I don't imagine he's sprouted any since then."

"No, you're right," agreed McGuire. "If he'd . . . *changed* . . . we'd have found his clothes. Take it from me, it's damned hard to fly when you've got a wingspan of forty inches and you're wearing a suit, a tie, and a pair of jockey shorts. Or even boxer shorts, for that matter."

They passed a trio of offices, and then Mallory came to a halt before the Advisory Council for the Newly Converted. "This looks like the kind of place he'd come," announced the detective. "It's certainly where *I'd* come if it had happened to me." He turned to McGuire. "You stay out here, and if you see a kid who fits Rupert's description, give a holler."

"I'm not very good at hollering," said McGuire. "I never know what to yell. 'Yoicks!' seems somehow out of place, and of course 'Excelsior!' is just too old-fashioned. I could scream 'Stop thief!' of course—but if he's not a thief, we could have a defamation suit on our hands."

"Okay, don't yell," said Mallory disgustedly. "Whistle."

"I can't."

"You can't whistle at all?"

"Only 'Bloody Mary Is the Girl for Me.'"

"Then yodel."

"I've never yodeled before."

"Goddammit, McGuire!" said Mallory impatiently. "Just pound on the window and I'll take it from there."

"What if I break the window?"

"What if I break your nose?" growled Mallory.

"Okay, okay, I'll think of something," said McGuire.

Mallory just glared at the little vampire for a moment, then turned and entered the office. A portly man, all smiles and dimples, stood up from behind a desk and walked over to him, hand extended.

"Greetings, my good man, greetings!" he thundered. "How may I help you? We represent the finest academic institutions in all Manhattan. If you're having difficulty finding your way around, I can arrange sonar lessons from the great Vladimir Plotkin himself."

"No, thanks," said Mallory. "I—"

"Perhaps a correspondence course on Arteries and How to Find Them," suggested the man. "Or we have a special this week: two tickets to the opera plus three private Squeaking on Key lessons."

"Can I get a word in, please?" said Mallory.

"I apologize," said the man. "My only excuse is my enthusiasm to help the newly converted."

"I don't qualify," explained Mallory. "I'm just looking for someone."

"Oh, we don't arrange liaisons here, my dear sir. You'll want the dance studio on the fourth floor. Their advertised specialty is How to Vamp for Your Man. Always a nice selection down there."

"I'm looking for a young man who *is* among the newly converted," said Mallory. "I was hoping he'd come here."

"Are you the . . . ah . . . *converter?*"

"Just a friend. If he came here, it would have been in the last half hour."

The man shook his head. "No, it's been at least two hours since our last visitor. You might try Ebbets Field; I understand the Louisville Sluggers are in town. Our crowd just goes bats over them." He practically choked holding back a self-satisfied chuckle.

"How about Aristotle Draconis?" asked Mallory, ignoring his pun. "Tall, skinny, definitely not a newcomer to the practice."

"No, I'd remember a name like that."

"Okay," said Mallory with a grimace. "Thanks anyway." He turned to leave.

"Is your young friend from America?" asked the man.

"Yes."

"Too bad. The Acme Coffin Company, down on forty-eight, is having a special on soil from the Old Country. Sooner or later your young friend is going to have to sleep—though probably not until morning. If he was from Transylvania, he'd have to find an outlet that sells his native soil, unless he brought it along with him. And now," he concluded, "if there's nothing further, I'm going to be closing the office down until tomorrow."

"I would have thought you did most of your business at night," remarked Mallory.

"Oh, absolutely we do—but this is All Hallows' Eve, my good sir. It's our night to howl." He suddenly looked embarrassed. "Well, to squeak, anyway."

Mallory walked to the door. "Thanks for your time."

"I'm sorry I couldn't help you," said the man. "But you might consider making the usual rounds before the partying really gets hot and heavy."

"The usual rounds?"

"The young man is aware of the pending transformation, is he not? I mean, that's why you thought he might come here."

"Right."

"Well, then, he's going to have to prepare for some major changes in his lifestyle. For example, he'll need super-strength sunscreen. No more than half a dozen pharmacies carry it. He'll need highly polarized shades . . . sunglasses to the uninitiated. Sooner or later he has to eat, so he'll undoubtedly want to buy a portable AIDS testing kit before he consumes any of his victim's blood. If his canines are anything like your friend's there"—he pointed to McGuire—"he may want to visit a cosmetic dentist before they pierce a hole through his lip."

"There's a lot more to being a vampire than I thought," remarked Mallory.

"Oh, indeed there is, sir," agreed the man. "If you would like to come back tomorrow, we can continue our discussion, but I really must close up shop now."

Mallory walked out of the office, followed by the portly man, who locked the door and headed off to the elevator.

"Learn anything?" asked McGuire.

"A bit about vampires," replied the detective. "Nothing about Rupert or Draconis."

"There are still a few lights on," said McGuire.

"We'll look, but I don't think we're going to find anything."

They began walking down the corridor, with Mallory reading the signs aloud as they went: "Anemics Anonymous . . . Transformations, Inc. . . . the Lonely Veins Club . . . You know, if I hadn't seen the bites on Winnifred and the kid, I'd have a hard time believing some of this."

McGuire suddenly stopped as they came to a haberdashery. "Look at those velvet capes!" he exclaimed. "I would kill for a cape like that!"

"I think that may be a prerequisite to wearing it," replied Mallory.

"And that salesgirl!" enthused the little vampire. "Look at the teeth on her! She can bite my neck any time she wants!"

"Stop drooling on my shoe."

"My God, what a pair of wings she must have!"

The salesgirl looked up and saw McGuire staring at her. For a moment she looked surprised. Then she gave him a big toothy smile.

"That's it!" announced McGuire. "I'm in love!"

"Fine," said Mallory, starting off. "Stay here. I've got work to do."

"You don't mind?"

"No insult intended, but you haven't been all that useful so far."

"You cut me to the quick, Mallory."

"Wishful thinking."

McGuire turned back to the store, just in time to see a handsome young man, dressed in a tuxedo, walk up to the salesgirl. She threw her arms around him and exposed her neck to his teeth.

"Boy, talk about fickle!" muttered McGuire. "And I would have married her!"

Mallory looked surprised. "You would?"

"Well, we'd have had the honeymoon first and maybe visited half a dozen sex clubs to make sure we were compatible . . ."

"I've never seen anyone fall in love and get jilted so fast," remarked Mallory. "You coming or staying behind?"

"I'm coming."

"There's only one more store with its lights on," said Mallory, looking down the corridor. "We'll take a quick look and then decide what to do next."

"It's a poster shop," observed McGuire as they approached it. "See, there's Bela Lugosi. And there's a young Frank Langella. He's the one who made young girls *want* to be bitten. Without him, there'd be no billion-dollar romance novel industry."

"*Is* there one?"

"Young women gobble them up the way young men consume girlie magazines."

"Doesn't anyone write romance novels *without* vampires?" asked Mallory.

"Have you been to a bookstore lately?" replied McGuire.

"Not really."

"We're the New Thing," said McGuire proudly. Suddenly he frowned. "On the other hand, getting laid anywhere but on the printed page isn't any easier than it ever was. I blame it on anti-vampire prejudice in high places."

"Perhaps," said Mallory. "Or it could just be that you're an ugly little wart with bad manners and worse breath."

"Is that any way to speak to a friend of long standing?"

"We've only known each other for maybe an hour," replied Mallory.

"Well, that's as long as most of my friendships usually last," said McGuire. He wrinkled his brow thoughtfully. "Probably it's jealousy. Or maybe envy. Or, as I was saying, it could simply be a misguided dislike of vampires."

"Let me know when you're through feeling sorry for yourself," said Mallory.

"Right," said McGuire. He was silent for a moment. "Five . . . four . . . three . . . two . . . one. Okay, I'm through. For the moment, anyway. Let's go."

"Just a minute," said Mallory, staring intently through the window.

"What is it?"

"This wasn't a wasted trip after all," said the detective, pointing to a poster showing a skeletally thin black-clad man and promising that the noted European poet Aristotle Draconis would make one of his rare public appearances at Madison Round Garden at eleven o'clock on All Hallows' Eve.

"Where to now?" asked McGuire as the little vampire and Mallory emerged from the elevator on the ground floor and walked to the exit.

"We've got almost two hours to kill before this Draconis shows up," answered Mallory. "There's no sense wasting it. You're a vampire. Where would you go to hide?"

"That's a very broad question," said McGuire as they emerged into the cool night air. "Would I be hiding from the police—and if so, the vice squad or the fraud squad? Or from another vampire? Or maybe I'd be hiding from Harry the Book, who's been trying to collect what I lost at Jamaica yesterday. And of course I always hide from overly aggressive redheads called Thelma, because you never know which one might turn out to be the one I made some silly promises to when dazzled by the midday sunlight. Or I could be hiding from the AAA Ace Credit Company. Or . . ."

"Shut up," said Mallory wearily.

"Yes, sir."

"You sound like you spend you entire life in hiding."

"It's not easy being an unemployed middle-aged vampire," said McGuire defensively. "I know, from the outside it looks like it's all blood and bites, but the general public has absolutely no idea." He stifled a manly little sob and wiped his nose on his shirtsleeve.

"Is there any way to convert back into a normal human being?" asked Mallory.

"One of *them*?" demanded McGuire with an expression of absolute contempt.

"Sorry I asked."

"I apologize," said McGuire. "It's hardly your fault that you're not at the top of the food chain."

"Getting back to business," said Mallory, "where are we likely to find a kid who's been bitten once or twice, hasn't joined the glorious ranks of the vampire brigade yet, and—now, I know this is difficult for you to come to grips with—doesn't *want* to be a vampire?"

"Doesn't *want* to?" repeated McGuire. "One of the insane asylums, of course. Bellevue, probably."

"I don't believe I'm getting through to you at all," said Mallory. "At least you were *trying* to be helpful before."

"Helpful is my middle name," said McGuire. A pause. "Actually, Oglethorpe is my middle name, but I've never been very fond of it. Perhaps if I'd actually *known* any Oglethorpes . . . Still, I suppose it could be worse. Could be Frothingham."

"Shut up."

"Yes, sir."

"Where would someone go if he didn't want to run into a vampire?"

"Ah!" said McGuire, his face brightening. "You mean, where would a prey animal hide?"

"Right. And make it within a mile of Seymour Noodnik's grocery store."

"What were you doing there in the first place?" asked McGuire.

"Picking up some stuff to eat."

"Like ripe young girls with bulging jugular veins?"

"Calm down. I was going to put the kid up at my apartment, and since I'm almost never there, I figured I should lay in some supplies." Mallory grimaced. "I haven't bought any milk in about three months. How long does it stay good?"

"Not *that* long."

"Just as well," said Mallory with a shrug. "I don't think my refrigerator's working anyway."

"So where *do* you spend your time?" asked the vampire.

"Mostly at the office. It's just a block from where I live—well, on those occasions that I live there."

"Well, that makes it easy enough," said McGuire. "As far as the kid knows, you're his one protector. He'll gravitate to your apartment or the office."

"His aunt is a protector, too, and he knows her far better," Mallory pointed out. "Why would he choose me?"

"Because Colonel Carruthers could be stalking through the middle of

Central Park with her trolls," answered McGuire. "At least he knows where to look for you."

"Oh, shit!" muttered Mallory, suddenly heading off. "I know where he'll be! Come on!"

"Your apartment or your office?" asked McGuire, his little legs moving rapidly to keep up with the detective.

"He's never been to either. He doesn't know where they are. He'll be at Winnifred's apartment."

"That doesn't make sense," offered the vampire. "He left Noodnik's quite some time before you and I visited your partner, and he hadn't shown up."

"That's because I'm not a stranger to Manhattan, and I'm not looking into every shadow to see what might be lurking there ready to pounce on me," answered Mallory.

"I don't know . . ."

"I've been waiting half an hour for you to come up with a better suggestion. Have you got one?"

"No, but . . ."

"Shut up."

"Yes, sir," said McGuire.

They'd gone about two blocks when a goblin stepped out of the shadows, blocking their way.

"Encyclopedias?" it asked in its sibilant voice. "Nice cut-rate encyclopedias, only been read by half-blind little old ladies?"

"Weren't you just selling dismembered corpses or something like that an hour ago?" said Mallory disgustedly.

The goblin wrinkled its nose dismissively. "A drug on the market. And speaking of drugs on the market, how about—" it lowered its voice conspiratorially—"a bottle of (get this!) children's aspirin."

"Go away."

"You're right, sir," said the goblin. "You haven't been a child in days now. Any fool can see that."

"Yeah, I think that pretty much defines both the situation and the speaker," said Mallory. "Get out of my way."

"Subscriptions!" cried the goblin. *"Look! Colliers! Argosy All-Story! Mating Habits of the Tree-Dwelling Wildebeest!"*

"Bats," said Mallory, "count to five and if he's still blocking my way, bite him in the neck."

"How about a correspondence course on seven ways to prepare goblin for Thanksgiving?" offered the goblin, backing away.

Mallory began walking again. "Let's go."

"Banned eight-millimeter movies!" shouted the goblin after them. "Candy Barr! Joan Crawford! Linda Lovelace! Arnold Stang!"

Mallory stopped and turned. "Arnold Stang?" he repeated.

"I was just kidding," said the goblin. "But it got your attention, didn't it?"

"Bats, kill him," said Mallory, starting off again.

"Deep Ear! The Bratislavan Stallion! Behind the Mauve Door!"

"Uh . . . I don't know if I've ever mentioned it," said McGuire, softly enough so the goblin couldn't hear, "but I'm terrified of goblins."

"Just you, or all vampires?" asked Mallory.

"Just me. How do you think I got to be forty-seven?"

"Figures."

"The Devil and Arnold Stang!" yelled the goblin just before they passed out of earshot. "Half price! And I'll toss in a two-month supply of vitamin H!"

"Is there a vitamin H?" asked McGuire. "I've been feeling run down lately, and . . ." He paused and looked up at Mallory. "I know: Shut up."

They walked another block in silence, and then Mallory peered ahead and slowed down.

"I don't like the looks of this," he said.

"It's just a few cops and an ambulance," said McGuire.

"That's not an ambulance," said Mallory, and as they got closer McGuire could see a spavined, ancient horse harnessed to a wagon. "That's the death cart."

McGuire shrugged. "People die. No reason to take any notice of it, especially on All Hallows' Eve."

"Don't you recognize where you are?" snapped Mallory. "That's Winnifred's building."

"It is?"

Mallory pulled out his license, held it up, and elbowed his way through the small crowd of humans, goblins, gremlins, elves, and unidentifiables. A moment later he was looking down at the lifeless body of Rupert Newton.

"You know him?" asked a cop.

Mallory nodded. "Yeah. What happened?"

The cop shrugged. "We got a call that there was this stiff on the street, and this is what we found."

"Vampire?" asked Mallory.

"He's got a couple of holes in his neck, but they're not fresh. We'll schlep him off to the morgue and let *them* worry about it. You wanna come down and make an official ID?"

"Can I just do it here?"

"If you could, I wouldn't ask you to come down there. Don't give me a hard time; this is All Hallows' Eve. If the worst that happens is that we trip over a few dozen bodies between now and morning, we'll be ahead of the game." He paused. "You know where the morgue is?"

Mallory nodded.

"We got four more to collect. Figure we'll be there in an hour."

"Got you," said Mallory, stepping back as the cops moved forward to lift Rupert and put him in the cart.

"I'm sorry," said McGuire, as the death cart headed off down the street and the crowd began dispersing.

"Something's wrong," said Mallory.

"I know. You client is dead."

Mallory shook his head. "He's not my client. He's Winnifred's nephew. And that's not what's wrong."

"What's wronger than being dead?" asked McGuire.

"The kid was running for his life," said Mallory. "He was scared to death of Aristotle Draconis, who is the guy who nabbed him in the neck and started him on the road to vampirism, right?"

"Yeah?" said McGuire, trying to see where the detective was leading him.

"Well, if the cop was right, he wasn't killed by a vampire," said Mallory. "No fresh bite marks."

"Sometimes shock and fear will do it," offered McGuire.

"Is that your personal observation?" said Mallory sardonically.

The little vampire shifted his feet uncomfortably. "I believe I read it somewhere."

"There's another problem, too."

"What is it?"

"This Draconis is a European. He nailed the kid on the boat during the cruise over, but he could no more find a stranger at night in an unfamiliar city of seven million than you could."

"I beg your pardon!" said McGuire, drawing himself up to his full if unimpressive height.

"Damn it, Bats! You know who we looking for, you live in the city, and you didn't come up with a damned thing. Draconis is a stranger, he's probably got some handlers from the reading—I'm sure they paid his way across and want their money's worth—and he's got to be on stage at eleven. What if he actually caught the kid and couldn't find his way back? He has to figure the kid has told at least a friend or a relative what happened to him. I've been looking at this wrong. I figure that either Draconis hasn't given the kid a thought since he landed or else right now he's damned near as scared as the kid was."

"Scared?" repeated McGuire. "Of what?"

"I won't know that until I talk to him." Mallory sighed. "In the meantime I'll get over to the morgue, ID the body, and see what *did* kill him. It's always possible the cop was wrong. The fact that there are no marks on the neck doesn't mean somebody didn't drain his varicose vein."

"What a disgusting thought!" said McGuire. He paused and considered it. "But tasty."

"All right," said Mallory, stopping and staring down at the little vampire. "I don't know what I'm up against, and I have a feeling that I need all the protection I can get."

"Borrow your partner's Nitro Express," suggested McGuire.

"I can't walk through the streets of Manhattan carrying a high-powered rifle."

"Why not?" asked the vampire. "Hundreds of others do every day. Maybe thousands."

"Forget it."

"It's forgotten. But this is a very confusing conversation."

"I want you to think," said Mallory. "What are vampires most afraid of?"

"High cholesterol levels?" asked McGuire uncertainly.

"Come on, Bats," said Mallory irritably. "This isn't a school quiz and it's not a trick question. If a couple of vampires—let's stretch credibility and suggest that they're even more fearless than you—were coming at me, what one thing could hold them at bay?"

"Nothing. We're a pretty brave, gritty lot."

"There is *nothing* that every vampire fears?" persisted Mallory. "Crosses, garlic, anything?"

McGuire shook his head. "Not really. You have to understand: I'm much more sensitive and emotional than most of my kind."

A black cat shot out of the shadows and crossed their path.

"Omygod, omygod, omygod!" cried McGuire in panicky tones. "Let's turn around and go a different way."

"It's already crossed your path," said Mallory. "Any damage is already done."

"What are you talking about?" shrieked the little vampire. "It has claws, hasn't it? And teeth! And it can see better in the dark than a bat can!"

Mallory's eyes narrowed.

"And vampires don't like that?"

"We positively hate it! Let's turn down a side street. It might come back."

"There might be another one on a side street," suggested Mallory.

"You're ruining my digestion, and I haven't even eaten anything!" wailed the vampire.

"Thank you, Bats," said Mallory. "You've finally been a help."

"I have?" asked McGuire, blowing his nose on his sleeve.

Mallory nodded. "You've told me what kind of weapon I ought to have with me."

"Me? Really?" asked McGuire, his chest puffing up proudly. Suddenly he frowned in confusion. "What kind?"

"The inefficient kind," admitted the detective, "but it's the best I can do on short notice and limited information."

"Where will you find this weapon?"

"Unless I miss my guess, it'll be sleeping on top of the refrigerator in my office," said Mallory.

Mallory opened the door to his office and turned on the lights.

The first thing McGuire saw was the pair of Playmates (on which Winnifred had meticulously drawn undergarments with a Magic Marker) tacked to the wall behind Mallory's desk. Then there was the photo of Flyaway parading to the post; it was getting difficult to distinguish his features after the hundreds of times Mallory had thrown darts into it. There was the omnipresent *Racing Form* on the detective's desk. There were the fresh-cut flowers and the copy of Byron's poems on Winnifred's desk. But there was no Felina.

"Thank goodness she's gone!" breathed McGuire with a sigh of relief.

"No one else would put up with her," answered Mallory. "She's here."

"Now, you're *sure* she doesn't eat vampires?" asked McGuire nervously.

"Only when I'm hungry," purred a feminine voice from atop the refrigerator in the next room.

"Only when she's hungry," repeated Mallory.

"Is she hungry now?" asked McGuire, stepping hesitantly into the room while peering into shadows and corners.

"I'm always hungry," said the voice.

"That's it!" said McGuire. "Nice knowing you, Mallory, and I'm sure you'll get your man. Or bat. Or whatever."

He turned and started walking toward the door, but Mallory reached out and grabbed him by the back of the collar, pulling him back even as his short legs kept moving.

"Calm down," said the detective. "Felina, get over here."

"Beg me," purred Felina.

"I don't have to," said Mallory.

"Oh?" said Felina, puzzled. "Why not?"

"Because I'm on a case and I'm in a hurry, and if you don't come here right now I'm leaving, and there won't be anyone around to feed you."

"I'll just eat your friend."

"He's coming with me."

"And vampires taste terrible!" added McGuire urgently.

"Oh, all right," said Felina, and suddenly ninety pounds of feminine fur and sinew flew through the air, cartwheeled across Mallory's desk, and landed on her feet right next to him.

"He doesn't look very tasty," she opined, staring at McGuire. "Were they selling the runt of the litter?"

"His name is McGuire," said Mallory, "and he's working for us. I don't want you hurting him."

Felina walked once around the little vampire, who eyed her nervously.

"I can't hurt him?"

"That's right."

She studied him for a long moment. "It'll take all my skill, but I can do it."

"Do what?" asked McGuire uneasily.

"Kill you so fast it doesn't hurt."

"I don't believe you were paying attention," said Mallory, keeping his grip on the vampire's shirt as he tried to race to the door. "He's a friend. You will not hurt him. Do you understand?"

"Yes," said Felina.

"Good."

"No," said Felina. "Maybe. Perhaps. Possibly."

"Let me put it in terms you understand," said Mallory. "You hurt him and there's no milk for a week."

Felina studied the vampire, her pupils mere slits. "Even a little one like this could last more than a week."

"All right, then," said Mallory. "No milk for a month."

"It's not fair!" pouted Felina.

"Believe me, if things work out the way I think they will, there'll be plenty of things for you to hurt."

A huge happy smile. "You promise?"

"I said I *think* so."

"And I can play with them as long as I want?"

"Within reason."

"What does that mean?"

"It means until I tell you to stop."

She sniffed unhappily. "You always ruin everything."

"We're wasting time," said Mallory. "Felina, this is McGuire. Bats, this is Felina. Felina, you don't hurt him; Bats, you don't suck her blood. Has everyone got the ground rules straight?"

"Yes," said McGuire.

Felina turned her back on both of them and began licking her forearm.

"Felina?"

"Yes," she muttered.

"All right. It's All Hallows' Eve, every spook and spirit in the city is up and around, and we've got a killer to catch. Let's go."

He walked to the door, followed by McGuire. Felina leaped onto Winnifred's desk and sat down, her back still turned to him.

"Felina, let's go," said Mallory.

"I'm not coming," she announced.

"You're making a big mistake," said Mallory. "Think it through."

She turned and stared at him curiously.

"You're always saying that you'll desert me in the end, right?" said Mallory.

"Always," she agreed, nodding.

"Well, this is just the beginning," said Mallory. "It's too soon to desert me."

"You're right, John Justin!" she said happily, launching herself through the air and landing in his arms. "Let's go get the bad guys. I've got all night to desert you. I should wait until you're seconds away form a hideous death!"

"How thoughtful of you," said Mallory, setting her down on the floor.

The three of them walked out into the chilly October night.

CHAPTER 8

9:47 PM–10:26 PM

The morgue was five blocks away from Mallory's office. This meant that he had to pull Felina out of three grocery stores, a fish market, a lingerie shop, and a hunting boot store along the way, but eventually they made their way to the large bleak building.

The first hint they had that they were getting close was the pipe organ, which spewed Gregorian death chants into the night.

"I don't remember anything like that," remarked Mallory as they approached the morgue.

"They always bring the pipe organ out for All Hallows' Eve," said McGuire knowingly.

"Why?"

"It makes the corpses feel more relaxed."

"Aren't they all dead already?" asked Mallory.

"Absolutely," answered McGuire. "But not necessarily permanently."

"You know," muttered Mallory, "every time I think I'm getting the hang of this place, something like this happens."

"Yum!" said Felina, looking up at the roof where a flock of crows were eyeing all the new arrivals.

"You stay with me," Mallory ordered her.

"You didn't say anything about not eating crows," pouted Felina.

"I didn't say anything about not flapping your arms and flying to the top of the Vampire State Building either," said Mallory.

"Let's make a deal," offered Felina. "Let me eat two crows and I won't fly away."

"If I have to put you on a leash I will," said Mallory.

"Then I'll scream and tell everyone you're sexually abusing me."

"You don't even know what that means."

"No," she admitted. "But it always works."

"Around here they'd probably give me a prize."

"Would it be good to eat, I wonder?" asked the cat-girl.

"Felina, you're here to watch my back. Now, you do what you're told, or I lock you up in the office until this case is finished."

She hissed at him once, then walked behind him and stood still.

The pipe organ was joined by some truly bone-chilling wailing.

"What the hell is *that*?" asked Mallory.

"Unless I miss my guess, it's the Vienna Boys' Choir," said McGuire.

"They flew them all the way over here just for tonight?"

"No," said McGuire. "This is the eighteenth-century Vienna Boys' Choir. They show up *somewhere* every All Hallows' Eve. Lends atmosphere, don't you think?"

"Sounds eerie," said Mallory.

"Well, this *is* the City Morgue," replied McGuire.

Mallory looked around. "Where did Felina go?"

"I'm right here," said a voice from behind him.

"What are you doing?"

"I'm watching your back," she said. "But it's a really dull job. It just stays there between your head and your hips and doesn't do *anything*."

"Just make sure no one sneaks up on it," said Mallory.

They entered the building, found themselves in a small foyer, signed in at a registration desk, then signed statements that they were not dues-paying members in good standing of the Graverobbers Union. They were then ushered through the foyer and into a vast room, taking up almost a full city block. There were tables and slabs everywhere, orderlies rushing to and fro, the occasional pathologist examining the occasional corpse, and a huge coin-operated ice machine in one corner.

"They're not very well organized, are they?" remarked McGuire.

"What do you expect?" replied Mallory. "They're a bureaucracy. Look around and see if you can locate where they dumped the kid. You know what he looks like, right?"

"Yes."

"Take the left side of the building, I'll take the right." Mallory turned to Felina. "You stick with me."

She leaped lightly to his back. "Yes, John Justin."

"Not that close."

"You ruin everything," she said, sliding back down to the floor.

They began walking among the slabs. One housed a coffin, and a woman with chalk-white skin, a black dress, and bright red lipstick was standing next to it, arguing with an orderly.

"I don't care what quality the soil is," she was saying. "It's from the wrong country."

"Beggars can't be choosers," shot back the orderly. "You want a place to sleep tomorrow morning, you take what we've got. And I need five bucks up front."

"But I *can't* sleep in it!"

"Look, lady, that soil has been fertilized by the great Phar Cry himself. Soil like this, you'd have to pay three bucks a pound anywhere in the city."

"I don't care who crapped in it!" snapped the woman. "I need soil from my home in the Loire Valley!"

"Have you considered moving to Kentucky?" suggested the orderly.

"*No!*"

"Well, then, how about Yonkers?" said the orderly, moving to the next slab. "Now, this coffin is filled with the soil of beautiful downtown Yonkers and was fertilized less than four months ago by Harvey Melchik, who told me the entire shameful story in confidence and made me swear never to repeat it."

"You're hopeless!" snapped the woman.

"Maybe so," said the orderly with dignity, "but at least I know where I'm sleeping tonight."

Mallory continued walking. Felina looked like she was about to wander off, so he decided to hold her by the wrist.

"That hurts!" she complained.

"No it doesn't."

"Well, it would if I pulled and you twisted."

"So don't pull and I won't twist."

She smiled. "You think of everything, John Justin."

She made a sudden break for the back of the room. "*Ow!*" She glared at him. "I thought you weren't going to twist."

"I thought you weren't going to pull," said Mallory.

"Whatever gave you that idea?"

"Hey, Mister," said a goblin, sidling up to them. "You need some help beating up the little lady?"

"No," said Mallory.

"You sure?" said the goblin. "I come equipped with brass knuckles, blackjack, billy club, cattle prod, bullwhip . . ."

"Go away," said Mallory.

"What kind of talk is that?" said the goblin. "Here I make you an honest business proposition, and you tell me to go away. Where are your manners?"

"I left them in my other suit. Go away."

"Last chance," said the goblin.

"No."

"Okay, so I admit my equipment is a little out of date. But I have hobnailed boots back at my place. I can run home, get 'em, and be back in just three days' time."

"Forget it."

"Thumbscrews!" exclaimed the goblin. "How about thumbscrews?"

"I give up. How about them?"

"They do wonders on a recalcitrant cat-girl. I consider them a perfect balance to the red-hot pokers. Or (get this!), we tie her to a slab and I read every word of *Silas Marner* to her without taking so much as a single potty break. Can you think of a more excruciating torture?"

"Not for either of you," admitted Mallory. "If I do, I'll let you know."

"You will?" said the goblin, his face brightening. "Great! Shall we trade business cards?"

"Let's just remember," said Mallory. He gestured to the room. "You never know who might be watching or listening."

"Oh, right," said the goblin with a conspiratorial leer. "Catch you later." He headed off at a trot.

"They let just anyone into a morgue these days," muttered Mallory.

"You said it, Mac," agreed a nearby orderly. "We ought to charge double-time for zombies. They keep coming in, we stick 'em on slabs and put 'em in the deep freeze, and an hour later they're pounding on the door to get out."

"So use salt," said a second orderly. "You know the routine."

"There's a routine?" asked Mallory, curious.

"Sure," said the second orderly. "Everyone knows that. You get a zombie, you lay him out on a slab, you fill his mouth with salt, then you sew it shut."

"Must give him one hell of a thirst," commented Mallory.

"It glues him to the spot. Only way to make a zombie stay dead."

"The *mouth*, you say?" repeated the first orderly, frowning.

"Of course the mouth."

"*That's* what I've been doing wrong!" exclaimed the first orderly. "I thought it worked like with fawns. You sprinkle some salt on the tail, it nails 'em to the spot."

"Nah!" said the second orderly. "That's an old wives' tale."

"The hell it is!" snapped the first orderly. "I sprinkled some on *my* old wife. Didn't glue her anywhere. She took after me with an umbrella." He pointed to a scar on his forehead. "Three stitches to close it up. Old wives' remedy be damned." Suddenly he frowned again. "You know," he continued thoughtfully, "my next-door neighbor Amos has a gorgeous twenty-four-year-old wife. I wonder if it works on *young* wives? Maybe if I'd sprinkle a little salt on *her* tail when he's off at work . . ."

Mallory was about to comment when he had to step out of the way of what seemed a funeral procession. A gang of tough-looking trolls was carrying a dead troll on their shoulders, followed by a weeping gremlin girl and a gang of gremlins. Suddenly, as if by mutual consent, they all broke into dance.

"What the hell was *that*?" asked Mallory.

"Tony and Maria and their gangs," said a medic, who was examining a corpse at the next table. "They're here every night. They never got over that damned play."

"So they're just acting?"

"Not at all," said the medic. "Tony's as dead as a doornail."

"And they bring him by every night?" said Mallory. "He must not be turning into any nosegay."

"Oh, he smells all right," said the medic. "After all, he's only been dead for maybe half an hour."

"So all the other nights were just rehearsals for tonight?" asked Mallory.

"No, he was dead every night."

"What am I not understanding here?" asked Mallory.

"It's a mild case of death," replied the medic. "Hardly ever proves fatal. And it gives us a little entertainment, too. Believe me, we can use it in a place like this."

At just that moment the two gangs broke into song. A moment later Tony's corpse joined them.

"Fascinating," said Mallory, who in truth was getting more annoyed than fascinated with all the distractions of the City Morgue.

"Oh, we get a lot of theatrical types in here," offered the medic. "You see those three guys in the togas?"

He pointed across the room at the three men who were engaged in an animated conversation over a body that was stretched out on a slab.

"Yeah?" said Mallory. "What about them?"

"They're checking each corpse to see if its name is Caesar."

"Julius?" asked Mallory.

"Well, I'm sure they'd prefer Julius, but at this late date I think they'd happily settle for Augustus, or even Sid."

"What happens when they find him?"

"They each perform Caesar's funeral oration, of course," said the medic. "I think it's some kind of drama school assignment. The last time they found a Caesar, the guy in the middle was so magnificent that the corpse itself stood up and applauded." A pause. "By the way, you look exceptionally alive, as does your pet. Is there something I can help you with?"

"A young man was killed earlier tonight and brought here." Mallory flashed his detective's license. "I need to talk to the examining pathologist."

"I wish I could help you," said the medic, "but we're already nearing the thousand mark for the night. You'll just have to look around."

"That's what I've been doing. Would it help if I told you his name?"

"Will he answer to it?"

"No."

"Then it can hardly help, can it?" said the medic. "Keep a stiff upper lip, and best of luck to you."

The medic wandered off, and Mallory kept making his way among the beds and slabs.

"You don't get out of it this easily, Horace!" said a harsh feminine voice. Mallory turned and saw a woman who looked like the littermate to a pair of linebackers bent over a skinny, balding corpse that lay on its back with a peaceful expression on its face. "You promised to rake the leaves and paint the closets, and by God a little thing like a fatal heart attack isn't getting you off the hook. Are you listening to me, Horace?"

Horace lay motionless on the slab.

"I'm giving you one last chance, Horace!" she bellowed. "You get up right now, or we do it the hard way!"

Horace didn't respond.

"Okay," she said, "you asked for it!" She nodded to a lean man dressed in a robe and a conical hat, both covered with the signs of the zodiac.

The mage lit a candle at each end of the slab, rolled his eyes, and began chanting an ancient spell. He'd been at it for about thirty seconds when a second mage, dressed in similar patterns though different colors, emerged from the shadows and also began chanting.

The first mage stopped, surprised. "Bernie!" he exclaimed. "What are *you* doing here?"

"Hi, Sam," said Bernie. "How's the wife?"

"Just fine. Your boy still at college?"

"Yeah. He graduates next month." Bernie's face glowed with pride. "He's coming into the family business."

"*Mazel tov!*" said Sam. "As soon as I'm through bringing this poor son of a bitch back, let's go out for a drink."

"You talking about Horace here?"

Sam pulled a piece of paper out of his pocket and read it. "Yeah, that's his name. How'd you know it?"

"Because Horace hired me to let him sleep the Sleep of Eternity," said Bernie.

"He knew he was going to die?"

"If you were married to a *yenta* like that, wouldn't you figure your days were numbered—or at least hope they were?"

"Well, I like that!" bellowed the burly woman.

"Hey, lady, take a hike," said Bernie. "We're talking business here."

"You!" yelled the woman, pointing at Sam. "I hired you to bring him back from the dead! If you're not going to do what I've paid for, I want a full refund and I'll get someone who keeps his bargains."

"Lady, that suits me just fine," said Sam. He made a mystic sign in the air and the woman froze, motionless. Sam pulled a twenty-dollar bill out of a hidden pocket, walked over, and slid it between her lips. Then he turned back to Bernie. "Let the poor bastard stay dead. Who can blame him?"

"Sounds good to me," said Bernie. "Come on. I'm buying the first round."

The two mages walked off, arm in arm. As they reached an exit, Sam turned back and snapped his fingers, and the woman came back to life. She pulled the bill out of her mouth, stared at Horace's corpse for a moment, then cursed and shook her fist in the air. "You're not getting out of it that easily, you no-good deadbeat! I'll be back with another mage, and then another, until one of them finally does what I pay him to do. But one way or the other, Horace Neiderkamp, you're raking the yard and painting the closets, and that's all there is to it." She glared at him. "If you think a little thing like death is going to get you off the hook . . ."

She wandered off, still muttering threats and imprecations, and Mallory kept looking at corpses, some lying quietly on their slabs, some cursing a blue streak, some seeming to exist in a confused state midway between life and death.

"The kid *would* have to get himself killed on All Hallows' Eve," he complained, not even aware that he was speaking aloud. "It couldn't be some normal night when they only schlep a dozen or so corpses into this joint."

"Maybe we can come back on Some Hallows' Eve and it will only be half as crowded," suggested Felina helpfully.

"Thanks for the tip," said Mallory sardonically. "Hop up onto one of these tables and see if you can spot McGuire, and let me know if he's making any progress at all."

Felina leaped lightly to a table and peered across the room, then giggled.

"What is it?" asked Mallory.

"He thought he was pinching a real woman, but it was a witch," explained Felina. "Now she's beating him with her broom."

"Little bastard's really got to watch his appetites," remarked Mallory. "You never met Rupert Newton, did you?"

"No."

"Then there's no sense asking you if you can see him, is there?"

"Certainly there is," said Felina.

"Okay, can you see him?"

"I don't know," she answered. "What does he look like?"

Mallory resisted the urge to say that he looked exactly like a Rupert Newton. Instead he pointed to the floor. "Down."

She jumped down from the table, and they began walking again, until their way was blocked by a balding man in religious robes. A number of black-clad acolytes stood around him as he began chanting over the body of a well-dressed dead man.

"Thanks!" said the corpse, suddenly sitting up. "I feel ever so much better now."

"Be quiet," said the robed man. "I haven't finished commending your soul into Satan's hands yet."

"Well, now you don't have to," said the corpse. "The strength and purity of your belief has brought me back."

"Damn it, man," said the robed figure, "the black mass isn't *supposed* to bring you back."

"Well, it did," said the corpse. "I think we should drop to our knees and thank God."

"Blasphemy!" thundered the robed man.

"Second race at Belmont," called a voice from across the room. "Ten to one if it comes up muddy."

"What are you talking about?" demanded the robed man irritably.

"Weren't you just asking for the odds on Blasphemy? He's running at Belmont tomorrow."

"Leave me alone. I'm a high priest and I'm conducting a black mass."

"Well, strictly speaking, I think it's probably a gray mass, now that I'm alive," said the corpse.

"Silence!" said the high priest, sounding like he might burst into tears any moment. "All right, I've said the prayer, now I'm lighting the candles. What comes next? Ah, yes, the vessels of lust—where are Jezebel and Lilith?"

"Right here," said a lovely young girl wearing a black cloak.

"But we have to talk," said her equally pretty companion.

"There's nothing to say," replied the high priest. "Remove your cloaks and assume your position on the altar."

"That's what we have to talk about," said the second girl. "If this is only a gray mass, then we're only going to be *semi*-naked sacrifices to Satan."

"Right," said the first girl. "Fair is fair."

"There is nothing fair about a black mass!" thundered the high priest.

"*Gray* mass," the corpse corrected him.

"Besides, the candle dripped wax all over my hair the last time," said the first girl.

"And it smells bad," said the second.

"Worse than me?" asked the corpse.

The girl sniffed at him, then at the candle. "Yes."

"I *knew* I was alive again!" said the corpse happily, swinging his feet over the side of the table. "What say we all go out for something to eat? Dying can be pretty hungry work."

"You're ruining everything!" whined the high priest.

"Oh, come on now," said the corpse. "There are bodies all the hell over here. Go perform your mass on one of them."

"But they aren't my parishioners!" complained the high priest.

"What better way to add to the membership?" said the corpse, standing up and walking off with an arm around each girl.

"By Satan, I never thought of that!" said the high priest. He turned to his acolytes. "Come on. Let's find a rich one!"

Mallory stood aside as they marched off in pursuit of a new parishioner—and almost bumped into a gray-skinned uniformed policeman with two bullet holes clean through his skull. He had his arms folded across his chest, and his jaw jutted out pugnaciously.

"Oh, come on, Clarence, be reasonable," said a man with City Planning Commission credentials clipped to his vest pocket. "We're offering you a monument, an eternal flame, consecrated ground, and a round-the-clock uniformed guard."

"I don't care," said Clarence. "My job is catching villains, not lying there in that damned tomb so people can pay their respects to me. I mean, hell, they won't even know who I am."

"That's the whole point of the Tomb of the Unknown Policeman," explained the official.

"But I'm *not* unknown! I'm Clarence Weatherbee IV, and I want them respecting *me*, not some poor slob who got shot breaking up a card game in the City Council's executive bathroom."

"I don't think you get the idea at all," said the official in frustrated tones.

"Of course I get it," snapped Clarence. "That's why I climbed out and ran away."

"Look, Clarence, we're consecrating the ground, we're giving you an eternal flame, we're . . ."

"I heard all that. The answer is no."

"Is there no way you'll reconsider?" asked the official.

Clarence narrowed his eyes in thought for a moment. "Okay," he said at last. "Here's a list of my nonnegotiable demands."

"I'm listening."

"Listening only counts in horseshoes. Pull out your pen and write this down."

"All right," said the official, producing a pen and a small notebook.

"I like marigolds. There have to be marigolds around the tomb every day of the year."

"But they're not in bloom year-round."

"I don't care where you get 'em from. I've got to have them. Now, do I continue, or are we through already?"

"We'll find them, even if we have to force them in the conservatory. What's next?"

"I want a chapter of my favorite book to be read in front of the tomb every day at high noon."

"Easily done," said the official. "Something by Whitman, I'm guessing? Or perhaps Thoreau or Emerson?"

"I don't know who wrote it, but there's a copy of it in my desk back at the office."

"And the title?"

"*Meter Maids in Bondage.*"

"I beg your pardon?"

"You heard me. Do I continue?"

The official sighed wearily. "Go on."

Clarence went through forty-three more demands, including his own monthly comic book to be called *Superhero Cop vs. the Underworld Scum of Manhattan*. Finally he couldn't come up with any more demands.

"All right," said the official. "I'll get cracking on your list, and we should have you entombed again within forty-eight hours. I assume I can find you here at that time?"

"Right here," confirmed Clarence. As the official started off, Clarence called after him, "It gets mighty lonely down in that tomb."

"Surely you aren't suggesting that we kill you a female companion!" demanded the official.

"Nah," said Clarence. "This place is loaded with them. I'll have one chosen by the time you get back."

"This is most irregular!"

"No one will ever know," said Clarence. "Unless, of course, you'd prefer to change the inscription to read the Tomb of the Unknown Policeman and His Current Ladyfriend."

"*Current?*" said the official in shocked tones.

"Eternity's a long time," said Clarence. "And it's a small tomb. Tastes change."

The official glared at him for a long moment, then turned on his heel and stalked off.

"Bureaucrats!" said Clarence to Mallory with a contemptuous snort. "They always give in. Hell, if he'd stood his ground, I could have done without the mah-jongg set and the Norman Rockwell print." Clarence turned and began surveying the room. "Excuse me, pal, but I got to go select a running mate."

"Are you sure that's the term you want?" asked Mallory.

Clarence shrugged and smiled. "What's the fun of catching 'em if they don't run a little?"

"I don't know what you're catching," said Felina, "but leave the mice alone."

"I promise, cat-girl," said Clarence, heading off.

"And the birds," she called after him. "And the fish. And the rabbits. And the squirrels. And—"

"Enough," said Mallory. "We've still got work to do."

"Still?" repeated Felina. "Were we working?"

"One of us was," said Mallory. Suddenly something near the back wall caught his eye. "And I think it just paid off."

"What do you mean?"

He pointed to the body of a young man, lying alone and isolated in the darkest corner of the immense room.

"I think I finally spotted Rupert Newton."

CHAPTER 9

10:26 PM–10:43 PM

"Hey, Bats!" hollered Mallory.

Twenty-seven vampires turned to face him.

"McGuire!" yelled Mallory, ignoring them. "I found him!"

The little vampire signaled the detective that he'd heard him and began making his way across the huge room. So did seven other vampires, each with a lean and hungry look.

"Felina," said Mallory, "hop onto this table and flash your claws at them."

"Do I get to eat them?" she asked, leaping atop a nearby slab.

"You can do whatever you want to any of them that gets within reach of me."

"Including *him*?" she said, pointing to McGuire.

"No," answered Mallory. "He's on our side."

The other vampires saw the cat-girl displaying her three-inch claws and decided that whatever Mallory was summoning McGuire for, it wasn't worth the effort to join the proceedings.

"Okay," said Mallory. "Hop down."

"I like it up here."

"Hop down anyway."

"You never let me have any fun," she sniffed, jumping lightly to the floor.

"My heart bleeds for you," said Mallory.

A corpse with overdeveloped eyeteeth suddenly sat up and stared hungrily at him.

"A figure of speech," explained Mallory. "Go back to sleep."

The corpse muttered something, then lay back down.

"You found him?" asked McGuire, approaching them.

"Yeah," said Mallory. "Off in the corner there."

"It doesn't look like anyone's examined him yet," said McGuire.

"They're not as well organized as they might be."

"Well, let's go have a look at him," said McGuire eagerly.

"Bats, you're drooling again," said Mallory.

"I'm sorry," said the little vampire. "But it's like being locked in a candy shop."

"Don't they have to be alive to appeal to you?"

"Around here it's hard to tell the difference, if you know what I mean."

"I know exactly what you mean," said the detective. "But this is Winnifred's kin, and no one touches him without severe consequences, if *you* know what *I* mean."

"I get the point," said McGuire.

"I hope so," said Mallory. "Because if you try to take a bite of the kid, you're going to get ten more points." He jerked a thumb in Felina's direction. "*Hers.*"

Felina smiled in anticipation. "Yum!" she said.

Mallory began walking toward the slab that held Rupert Newton's body. When he was about thirty feet away, he found his way blocked by a leprechaun, an elf, a goblin, a gremlin, and a troll.

"That's far enough, pal," said the leprechaun.

"I want to examine the body," said Mallory.

"Yeah, that's what they all say."

"Then they do terrible, hideous, grotesque things to them," said the goblin.

"But fun," admitted the elf.

"We're wasting time," said Mallory. "I need to see that body."

"No way, Mallory," said the troll. "We're under orders. No one examines the corpse until the pathologist gets first shot at it."

"If you know my name, you know I'm a detective. Why don't you just stand aside and let me get to work?"

"Big tough guy!" sneered the first leprechaun. "You don't scare us!"

"Right!" said the elf. "Take another step and we'll tear you limb from limb!"

"We'll kill you with such skill and finesse that we'll be awarded both ears and the tail!" added the troll.

"Uh . . . I hate to be a spoilsport," said the goblin, "but he doesn't have a tail."

"Don't hassle us with details when we're working ourselves into a killing rage," said the leprechaun.

"Right!" said the elf. "You're a walking dead man, Mallory. Turn around and maybe we'll let you make it to the exit."

"Otherwise, we'll hit you so hard it'll kill your grandchildren!" said the troll.

"You did it again," complained the goblin. "Excuse me, Mallory, but would you clarify a point before we rip you to shreds?"

"What point?" asked Mallory.

"Are you a father?"

"No," said Mallory.

"See?" said the goblin furiously. "How can we kill his grandchildren if he doesn't have any?"

"He just said he didn't have any children," said the troll defensively. "He never mentioned grandchildren."

"Maybe he adopted some children," offered the elf.

"Would they let him?" asked the leprechaun. "After all, he's in a dangerous profession. I mean, here we are about to kill him, and we've only known him for maybe a minute and a half."

"Enough talk," said Mallory, starting to lose his patience. "I came here to examine that corpse, and that's what I'm about to do."

"Don't interrupt!" snapped the elf. "We're having a serious discussion here!"

"Have it somewhere else," said Mallory, taking a step forward.

"That's it, Mallory!" snapped the leprechaun. "Take one more step, even a little one, and my partner here will kill you."

"Uh . . . which partner was that?" asked the goblin nervously.

"You," said the leprechaun.

"I can't," said the goblin.

"Why not?"

"You know," replied the goblin uneasily. "My *problem*."

"What the hell does an enlarged prostate have to do with dismembering a detective?" demanded the leprechaun.

"I never know when I might have to run to the bathroom."

"Then kill him quick," said the leprechaun. "What's another ten seconds, more or less?"

"I'd love to kill him, really I would," said the goblin. "But I never know when this thing will act up, and I hate to start something and not finish it."

"No problem," said the leprechaun. "Just start, and if you have to run off to answer a call of Nature, Herbie here can finish it for you."

"Me?" said the elf.

"Yes, you," said the leprechaun. "You hate humans, don't you?"

"Yes, of course I do, but . . ."

"Then pull his arms and legs out of their sockets, rip his head off, and spit down his neck."

"Why did you have to say that?" demanded the gremlin. "Now I'm going to be sick!" He wandered off into the shadows, making retching noises.

The elf looked up at Mallory, who towered above him. "There's nothing I'd rather do than pull his limbs from his body," he said. "But my lumbago has been acting up . . ."

"I thought you had rheumatism . . ." said the leprechaun suspiciously.

"I do."

"Then what's this lumbago crap?"

"I can't spell rheumatism," said the elf defensively.

"What a bunch of wimps!" snapped the leprechaun. "Okay, Phil—kill the sonofabitch."

"But he's my friend," said the troll, putting an arm around the elf's shoulders.

"The *other* sonofabitch!" yelled the leprechaun.

"That's almost too easy," answered the troll. "Let's outsmart him instead."

"I don't care if you behead him or dazzle him with your wit, as long as he's just as dead at the end of it," said the leprechaun.

"Watch this now," said the troll confidently, pulling out a cigarette. "Hey, cat thing, I'll bet you ten to one that you can't kill Mallory before I finish smoking this cigarette."

"Ten whats?" asked Felina curiously.

"You name it."

"Whales," said Felina.

"Aw, come on, cat thing—be reasonable," said the troll. "Where am I going to get ten whales at this time of night? Especially in October?"

"I guess you're going to have to dazzle me some other way," said Mallory.

"You keep out of this," said the troll. "You're just the victim."

"You like bets, I'll make you one," said the detective.

"Yeah?"

"Yeah. I'll bet you two hundred to one that if you try to stop me from examining the corpse, I tell Felina to slash your face down to the bones."

"Make it three hundred to one," said the leprechaun, reaching into his pocket for his wallet.

"Hey!" complained the troll.

"Felina," said Mallory. "You want to give him a sample?"

"Wait! No! Stop!" cried the troll, backing away. "You're cheating!"

"What are you talking about?" said Mallory.

"Trolls are terrified of cat-people! You're taking unfair advantage of my genetic shortcomings!"

"Are trolls afraid of vampires?"

"Certainly not!" said the troll with dignity. "We're a race of warrior heroes. Except for this one tiny flaw in our makeup, we fear nothing and no one."

"Bats," said Mallory, "are you feeling thirsty?" He pointed to the troll. "Have a drink."

"Wait!" cried the troll as McGuire took a step toward him. "Let's consider this like civilized men."

"You're not a man, you're a troll," said Mallory. "And about to become a dead one."

"You can't scare my buddy!" said the leprechaun. "You heard him: Trolls fear nothing and no one."

"Well, now, that wasn't entirely true," said the troll nervously as McGuire took another step. "We don't like to mention it, but we have an innate fear of IRS audits, high blood pressure, blondes named Hortense, one-eyed giants with battle-axes and steel teeth, Ford Pintos . . ." The troll rattled off about fifty more things trolls were afraid of.

"But you're not afraid of vampires?" said the leprechaun.

"No."

"So stand your ground."

"There's one more thing we're afraid of," said the troll, still backing away.

"Just one?" said the leprechaun. "What is it?"

"Pain!" yelled the troll, turning and running off across the room.

McGuire turned to the elf.

"Uh . . . boss, I'd better go after Phil and make sure he's okay," said the elf, breaking into a run.

"Well," said Mallory, "I guess it's just you and me, now. Are you going to let me examine the body?"

"Only after a battle to the death," vowed the leprechaun.

"That suits me fine," said Mallory.

"It's a deal," said the leprechaun. "I'll take the cat thing, you take the ugly little bloodsucker."

"What are you talking about?"

"The battle to the death," responded the leprechaun. "If she wins, you get to examine the corpse. If he wins, you apologize to Phil and Herbie and promise to go home."

"You got it all wrong," said Mallory. "The battle to the death is between you and me."

"What are you talking about?" shrieked the leprechaun. "I can't indulge in battles to the death! I've got a wife and three kids and a mortgage and car payments and . . ."

"Then step aside," said Mallory.

"I'll tell you what," said the leprechaun. "My cousin Vinny gets out of stir in February. If you could just go home and come back then, I guarantee *he'll* be happy to battle you to the death, as long as he gets choice of weapons. And since he only weighs fifty-seven pounds, I think we should make you carry extra weights on your shoes or your sword arm or something."

"Forget it."

"Where's your sense of fair play?" demanded the leprechaun. "What kind of fiend are you, Mallory?"

"An impatient one. Felina, if he doesn't stand aside, he's all yours."

The cat-girl grinned and displayed her claws.

"Quick question," said the leprechaun. "Are prostate problems contagious?"

"I don't know. Why?"

"'Cause I gotta go to the bathroom!" he said, racing off.

Mallory walked over to Rupert's body, but before he reached it a middle-aged man in a white lab coat appeared. He had wild unruly hair, even wilder eyes, and a stethoscope, which struck Mallory as an extraneous instrument in this particular place, hung down from his neck.

"You're the pathologist?" asked Mallory.

"Maximillian," he said, extending an ice-cold hand. "Maximillian Mabuse, late of Vienna, Berlin, Paris, Prague, Budapest, Bucharest, and Great Falls, Montana."

"Dr. Mabuse," said Mallory, frowning. "I think I read something about a Dr. Mabuse somewhere."

"Lies, all lies, spread by enemies and jealous colleagues," said Dr. Mabuse. "Besides, she said she was seventeen." He turned to Rupert Newton's body. "Now, what have we here?"

"I need to know what killed him," said Mallory.

"Society," said Dr. Mabuse promptly.

"What the hell does that mean?"

Dr. Mabuse shrugged. "I don't know. But it sounds good in interviews and usually buys me a few seconds to come up with my next answer." He turned Rupert's head to a side and studied the bite marks on his neck. "He was definitely turning, but he hadn't joined the undead yet. Another bite or two and he'd have been indestructible."

"Really?"

"Well, that's a generalization, of course," said Dr. Mabuse. "Actually, there are one hundred thirty-seven known ways to kill a vampire, and that doesn't include being eaten by piranhas or succumbing to untreated social diseases." He continued examining the body. "No bullet holes, no knife wounds. Clearly he hasn't been gored by a rhinoceros. I wouldn't entirely rule out sunstroke, but it *has* been cloudy for the past week." Suddenly he ran his hands over Rupert's head. "Ah!"

"You found something?" asked Mallory.

"One hell of a dent," said Dr. Mabuse, leaning over and studying the wound. "Yes, this young man was clubbed with a blunt instrument."

"Any idea what kind?"

"I just told you: the blunt kind."

"Thanks," said Mallory. "What happens to the body now?"

"The morgue will hold it for a week. If it hasn't been claimed or walked away on its own power by then, we'll dispose of it."

"How?" asked McGuire, trying to hide his eagerness.

"It'll be claimed before the time is up," interjected Mallory.

"Hey, Doc," called an orderly from about thirty yards away. "Come on over here. We got a real stinker for you. Six arrows in his chest, a hatchet in his back, two bullets in his heart, and he keeps claiming his wife poisoned him."

Dr. Mabuse left to attend to the corpse in question, and Mallory headed toward an exit, accompanied by Felina and McGuire.

"So does this eliminate Draconis?" asked McGuire.

"Not necessarily," replied Mallory. "Vampires have superhuman strength, too." He looked at his undersized, balding companion. "Most of them, anyway. Maybe this one was just mad, not hungry. Maybe he was afraid the kid would expose him; after all, he's here as a poet, not a vampire. Who knows?" He paused and checked his watch. "It's almost a quarter to eleven. We'd better head over to the Garden and have a chat with Aristotle Draconis."

"I suppose so," agreed McGuire. "It's about a five-minute walk."

"Good," said Mallory. "That gives me a little time."

"For what?"

"I've spent damned near an hour of All Hallows' Eve here and haven't turned up a thing, except that the kid wasn't bitten again. It's time to consult an expert."

"On vampires or All Hallows' Eve or murder?" asked McGuire.

"Yes," said Mallory.

10:43 PM–10:47 PM

They left the morgue and turned in the direction of Madison Round Garden, which was about half a mile away. As they reached the corner, Mallory stopped and looked around. When he found what he wanted, he headed off to his right until he came to a hotel with a series of enormous swords forming a covered path to the front entrance.

"I thought we were going to the Garden," said McGuire, confused.

"We are, but like I said, there's someone I have to talk to first."

"And he's at this hotel?"

"He will be."

They entered the plush lobby, and Mallory walked right up to the registration desk.

"Good evening," said a clerk. "Welcome to the Sword Arms, formerly the Tudor Arms."

"Why Sword?" asked Mallory curiously.

"Old man Tudor lost his arm in a croquet accident and had it replaced with a three-foot-long sword blade," answered the clerk. "Damned impressive, especially when he's wearing his old military dress uniform, the one with all the medals for valor in the Patagonian campaign. Just don't be standing on his left if he turns suddenly." He smiled. "Now, what can I do for you? You look like a man who'd like a double single."

"What the hell is that?"

"A double room with a single woman, of course."

"That's not what I'm here for."

"Well, for an extra fee, we could arrange a single room with a double woman."

"I just want to know where the men's room is."

"Oh," said the clerk, pointing toward a door across the lobby and promptly losing all interest in the detective.

Mallory turned to McGuire as he began walking. "Bats, you got a cell phone?"

"Who would ever call a vampire after dark?" replied McGuire.

"Scout around the place and see if you can find one. I'll be in there," he concluded, pointing to the men's room.

"What about *her*?" asked the vampire, jerking a thumb toward Felina.

"Let me worry about her. You just find me a phone."

McGuire sighed and set off on his quest, and Mallory reached the door. He opened it, saw that the room was empty, and turned to Felina.

"Except for McGuire, no one enters. You got it?"

"Got what?" asked the cat-girl. "And is it good to eat?"

"Do you understand what I said?"

"When?"

"Just now."

"Yes, John Justin," said Felina with a happy smile. "You asked if I understood what you said."

"Before that."

"No one enters except McGuire."

"Right."

"Or maybe it was: Except for McGuire, no one enters."

"I'll accept that as a separate but equal right answer."

"I knew you would." She turned her back to him. "Skritch between my shoulder blades."

"Later."

"Okay," she said. "I'll invite everyone from the lobby into the men's room."

"Fine," said Mallory. "And I won't feed you until June."

"If I only invite half the lobby, will you feed me before we go to see Aristotle Draconis?"

"Let me put it in terms you understand," said Mallory. "If you let anyone into the men's room except McGuire, you're fired as the office cat. You will have no home, no place to go, and no one to feed you."

She counted on her fingers. "No home, no place to go, no food. That's three things I won't have."

"Right."

"What if I only let two men in?" continued the cat-girl. "Does three go into two? Or is it two into three? And how many lumps of sugar are left over?"

"I'll tell you what," said Mallory. "Don't let anyone in and you won't have to do the math."

Her face brightened. "Thanks, John Justin. That's your best idea all night. Well, since the last time you skritched me, anyway."

"All right," said Mallory. "I'm going into the men's room now. Remember: Don't let anyone in except McGuire."

"What if it's Aristotle Draconis?"

"He's an exception."

"I *like* exceptions," said Felina happily. "What if it's Warren G. Harding? Or Tom Mix? Or Mary Queen of Scots? Or Jackie Robinson?" She paused. "Wait a minute. I'm just being silly."

"You get no argument from me," said Mallory.

"Mary Queen of Scots wouldn't use the men's room."

"Just McGuire," grated the detective.

"And Draconis," she said. "Don't forget Draconis."

"And no one else," said Mallory, finally entering the men's room.

It was a large room, with a dozen sinks running down one wall, a dozen stalls on the opposite wall, and a row of urinals lining the back wall. The floor was tiled, and the walls were tastefully papered above a ceramic trim. Mallory paced the room impatiently for a moment, and then the door opened and McGuire entered.

"Here," he said, thrusting a cell phone into the detective's hand. "Make your calls fast, and maybe I can stick this back in the old broad's purse before she notices it's gone." A quick smile. "I'll keep the sawbuck that came with it."

"Thanks," said Mallory. "I'll just need it for a couple of seconds."

"Phone calls take longer than that," said McGuire.

"I'm not phoning, I'm summoning," said Mallory, opening the phone and activating it.

"I'll bet the ten bucks I just stole that I don't want to ask the next question, do I?" said McGuire nervously.

"Probably not," agreed Mallory. He looked at the phone, then carefully punched out G, R, U, N, D, and Y. "Thanks," he said, tossing the phone back.

"Did you just call who I am mortally afraid you called?"

Before Mallory could answer, there was a flash of light and a puff of smoke, and he found himself facing a tall creature that stood a few inches over six feet, with two prominent horns protruding from his forehead. His eyes were a burning yellow, his nose sharp and aquiline, his teeth white and gleaming, his skin a bright red. His shirt and pants were crushed velvet, his cloak satin, his collar and cuffs made from the fur of some white polar animal. He wore gleaming black gloves and boots, and he had two mystic rubies suspended from his neck on a golden chain. When he exhaled, small clouds of vapor emanated from his mouth and nostrils.

"You have summoned me at an awkward time," he said in a deep voice. He turned and pointed to McGuire. "What is *that*?"

"Bats," said Mallory, "I want you to meet the—"

"Can't!" said McGuire nervously, backing up to the door. "Big hurry! Gotta use the men's room."

"You're *in* the men's room," said Mallory.

"Some *other* men's room," whimpered McGuire, feeling behind him for the door. He found it and pulled it open. "*Any* other men's room!"

He was gone a fraction of a second later.

"You'll have to forgive him," said Mallory. "He's not used to being in the presence of Evil Incarnate."

"I have explained to you time and again . . ." began the Grundy.

"Fine," Mallory cut him off. "At least you don't deny that you're the most powerful demon on the East Coast."

"Deny it?" said the Grundy. "I revel in it. And this, of course, is my busiest night of the year."

"I find that odd," said Mallory. "I'd have thought that on a night when every ghost and ghoul and creepy-crawly in the city is up and around doing your work for you, you'd be home relaxing, maybe drinking a beer and watching a football game."

"Would you stay home if Flyaway was running?" shot back the Grundy.

"Touché," admitted Mallory. "You know why I've summoned you here, of course?"

"Of course."

"You know who killed the kid, also of course?"

"Certainly. Nothing happens in my domain that I am not aware of."

"You want to make my life easy and tell me?"

"Making your life easy isn't part of my job description," said the Grundy.

"Well, I had to ask," said Mallory. He checked his watch. "I hate to kiss and run, but I don't want to be late over at the Garden."

"You won't be," said the Grundy, making a mystic sign in the air with his right hand.

"What did you do?"

"I have frozen time for the rest of the world," answered the demon. "It will proceed as normal in here, between the two of us. For everyone and everything else, it has come to a halt until one of us leaves the room."

Mallory studied the Grundy, frowning. "Why?"

"I beg your pardon?"

"You've already said you're not going to give me the name I want, so why freeze time at all? Why not just vanish in a puff of smoke like you usually do?"

Suddenly the Grundy shifted his weight uncomfortably. "A whim."

"Bullshit," said Mallory. "You're a creature of pure logic. You don't act on whims."

"All right," said the Grundy. "As strange as it seems, given that we are mortal enemies and it is my destiny to kill you in the end, I find that I enjoy your company."

"Should I be flattered or terrified?"

"You are the one person in the world who is totally unafraid of me," said the Grundy. "That is part of your fascination for me."

"Why should I be afraid of you?" responded Mallory. "Hell, I've even done a couple of jobs for you—the Quatermain Cup and that old Chinese guy with the pegasus."

"I know," said the Grundy. "No one else in the world would have done it."

"Maybe you should try paying them instead of terrifying them."

"It is my nature to terrify things."

"I thought it was your nature to bring balance to worlds," replied Mallory. "At least, I've heard that song and dance often enough."

"It is," said the Grundy. "Where I find order, I bring chaos, and where I find chaos, I bring order."

"Sounds good," said Mallory. "You ever actually *found* any order, or are you still looking?"

"You see?" said the Grundy. "That is another reason I enjoy your company. You keep me on my mental toes."

"Why don't you thank me for all that by telling me who killed the kid?"

"That would contradict everything I am," said the Grundy, almost apologetically.

"So you won't, or you can't?"

"I can't."

"I feel sorry for you, Grundy," said Mallory.

"For being the most powerful being within thousands of miles?" said the Grundy, surprised. "Why?"

"Because if I want to do something silly, or foolish, or boneheaded, I can do it. Even if it is clearly against my best interest, if I make up my mind to say or do it, I can. And that means I have more free will than you."

"How can you, if I am the more powerful?"

"Power isn't everything," said Mallory. "An elephant can kill a lion, tear down a house, pull over a tree—but can he peel a grape?"

"I shall have to give this some thought," said the Grundy.

"Let me give you one more thing to ponder."

"Yes?"

"You've said on previous occasions, and again tonight, that making my life easier, or words to that effect, isn't part of your job description."

"That is correct," the Grundy assured him.

"And you're all-powerful, right?"

"In essence."

"Okay, who wrote it?"

"Who wrote *what*?" asked the Grundy, confused.

"Who wrote your job description?" said the detective. "Who's pulling your all-powerful strings?"

The Grundy suddenly smiled, the smile of a scientist who has stumbled onto a new and complex problem he can't wait to solve. "*Fascinating!* Thank you, Mallory."

"Why not thank me by giving me the name?"

"You are the first human I have thanked for anything in nine hundred and fifty-four years. Isn't that enough?"

"Evidently you think so," said Mallory. "But then, you're blinded by your nature."

"I have enjoyed our conversation, John Justin Mallory," said the Grundy, "and you have given me much to consider. I cannot give you the name you want—or at least, I don't know if I can or not; I shall have to delve deep into the ethics of it—but ask me any other favor, and it is yours."

"You know my partner?"

"The fat one with gray hair."

"The *stocky* one with gray hair," Mallory corrected him. "She's assembled her trolls and is out hunting for Draconis and her nephew. One's dead, and unless she's on her way to the Garden right this minute, she's not going to find the other."

The Grundy stared off at some fixed point that only he could see. "She is in Central Park, surrounded by a gang of goblins intent on robbing her."

Mallory couldn't resist a smile. "Boy, have they got a surprise coming." Then: "Can you get word to her that Rupert is dead, and she can claim him at the morgue?"

"That is the favor you want?"

"Yeah—and while I know you'd love to take the blame for it, tell her I'm after the killer, that it wasn't you."

"As you wish," said the Grundy. "I shall be there in seconds."

Mallory held up a hand. "Give her five minutes to teach those assholes a lesson. *Then* go."

"As you wish," said the Grundy, becoming first translucent, then transparent, and finally nothing at all.

Mallory checked his watch and found that not a second had passed since he'd entered the men's room. He walked to the door to leave. Just as his hand reached out for it, he heard the Grundy's disembodied voice.

"A word of warning, John Justin Mallory, from one almost-friend to another," it said. "This case is much more complex than you can imagine."

"Thanks a heap," muttered Mallory, walking out into the lobby.

They reached Madison Round Garden—the marquee proclaimed "We're not for squares!"—and entered the lobby.

"There must be thousands of people here," noted McGuire. "I had no idea poetry was that popular."

"It's not," said Mallory.

"Then what are they all doing here?"

"It's a big building," said the detective. "There's lots going on—a basketball game, a lot of other stuff."

As he said so, a goblin passed by, selling hatpins for fifty cents apiece.

"Do ladies still wear hats?" asked McGuire.

"You don't come here very often, do you?" said Mallory.

"Never."

Mallory smiled and pointed to three elderly women in print dresses. Two had canes, one was using a walker. All three were buying hatpins.

"But they don't have any hats," said McGuire.

"That's not what they're for," said Mallory. He gestured to the poster on a nearby wall: Horrible Hector vs. Gordie the Ghoul.

"Wrestlers?" asked McGuire.

Mallory nodded. "And they've also got a Tasmanian Tag Team match on the bill. *That's* what the hatpins are for."

"They stick them into the wrestlers?"

"Right."

"But that's . . . that's *barbaric*!"

"So is wrestling, when you get right down to it," said Mallory.

"But it's *fixed*, isn't it?"

"Of course. They're wrestling matches, aren't they?"

"Then no one gets hurt."

"That's why we buy the hatpins," said another little old lady, who happened to be passing by. "If we're going to pay good money to watch a little healthy carnage, it's only fitting that *someone* gets hurt." She smiled. "That's how I met my first husband."

"He stuck pins into wrestlers too?" asked McGuire.

"Certainly not. He was the Boston Behemoth. Evil Eye Eric had tossed him in my lap. Our eyes met as he was pulling my hatpin out of his left buttock, and it was love at first sight."

"Your *first* husband, you say?"

She nodded. "I left him for the Butcher of Belgrade, and then along came Vicious Vincent, and then . . ."

"How many husbands have you had?" asked McGuire.

"Eleven."

"All wrestlers?"

"All but one. Milton was a banker. I decided I liked my dishonesty up front and in the open, so I went back to wrestlers." She checked her watch. "I have to run. The match starts in another minute, and I promised Horrible Hector that I'd be waiting for Gordie the Ghoul with *this*." She held up a gleaming hatpin.

"Hector's a friend?"

"Hector's number eleven," she replied with a smile as she scurried off to the arena.

McGuire stared at her retreating figure in awe. "When you get right down to it, I suppose she's just a kind of collector."

"Hey, Mac!" yelled a voice. "Is that cat-girl yours?"

Mallory looked around and saw a very distressed candy salesman gesticulating wildly at Felina, who was perched atop a cotton candy machine.

"Yeah, she's mine."

"Better get her down from there before she falls in."

Mallory walked over and stood next to the salesman. "Felina, what the hell are you doing up there?"

"I can see all the way across the lobby," she said happily.

"Come down."

"I like it up here."

"Buddy," said the salesman, "you got twenty seconds to get her off my machine. Then I whack her with a mop, and she falls in and becomes just so much more spun sugar."

"Felina," said Mallory, "come on down and I'll buy you a candy bar."

"And three canaries and a mouse," said Felina.

"Just a candy bar. You've got ten seconds."

"And a swordfish," said Felina.

Mallory turned to the salesman. "She's all yours," he said in a loud voice. "I'm off to find another cat for the office."

No sooner had the words left his mouth than ninety pounds of cat-girl hurled itself through the air and landed on his back.

"I forgive you, John Justin!" she purred. "Give me two goldfinches and we'll forget this ever happened."

"Off," said Mallory.

"Okay," said Felina, dropping to the floor and holding out a hand. "One macaw."

"Forget it."

"How about one of those?" she asked, pointing to a small chimera with a jeweled collar. It was walking on a leash next to its owner, who was wearing a tuxedo. As they passed by, Mallory noted a numbered armband on the owner's left sleeve.

"It's a show," said Mallory, looking around. Finally he saw a sign proclaiming that the Chimera Club of Manhattan was holding its annual conformation show on the third level of the building, starting at 11:00 PM.

"Isn't eleven o'clock a little late to start a dog show or a wrestling match?" said Mallory.

"On most nights, yes—but not on All Hallows' Eve," answered McGuire.

"I want a necklace like that one," said Felina, pointing to the chimera's collar.

"Behave yourself, and maybe I'll pick one up for you tomorrow."

"I promise," she said, holding her right hand up in the air. "Do you really mean it?"

"About the collar?" asked Mallory.

"Yes."

"Do you really mean you'll behave?"

"Well," she hedged, "I meant it when I said it."

"Good," said Mallory. "Then we have a deal."

"Kind of," said Felina.

McGuire looked around. "So where's the poetry reading?"

"Probably one of the side rooms," said Mallory. "After all, it's cultured, erudite, and educational, with no bloodletting or naked women, so it doesn't figure to draw a twentieth as well as wrestling."

He began walking past a row of vendors.

"Shrunken heads!" yelled a burly woman with a half-smoked cigar in her mouth. "Shrunken heads, direct from Omaha!"

"Get your garlic here!" hollered a goblin. "Is your daughter dating one of the undead? Is your wife making eyes at that mailman who only delivers after midnight? Drive 'em off with genuine garlic, grown exclusively in the gardens of failed divinity students and almost-virgins!"

"Forget all those phonies, pal," said a leprechaun, sidling up to Mallory. "I have here a genuine Kiwanee talisman, guaranteed to ward off mad Turkish rabbis, insidious Oriental menaces, and rogue elephants. Six bucks takes it away."

"I'll scare all the rogue elephants away for free," said McGuire. "*Boo!*" he yelled. "See? No elephants."

"I want your name and driver's license, fella," said the leprechaun. "I'm reporting you to the Unfair Business Practices Committee in the morning."

"Do they stop them or perform them?" asked Mallory.

"Keep your nose out of this, Mac," said the leprechaun. "This is between me and the twerp here."

Mallory reached down and picked the leprechaun up by his neck.

"You're going to leave us alone now, aren't you?" said the detective.

The leprechaun, his eyes bulging, nodded his head rapidly.

"See the grinning young lady with the claws?" continued Mallory, turning him toward Felina. "If you bother us again, I'm going to give you to her to play with."

"Hi, Toots," grated the leprechaun. "What games do you like: Spin the Bottle or Pinch the Hostess?"

"You'll see," promised Felina with an evil grin.

"You wouldn't really hurt someone as sweet as me, would you?"

"Only for two or three hours," answered Felina. "Maybe seven."

"Okay," said Mallory, setting him down. "Take a hike."

The leprechaun stared at the talisman, shook it vigorously, and tapped it against a wall. "The damned thing's battery must have run down."

"It doesn't have a battery," said Mallory.

"Well, *something's* wrong with it. It's supposed to protect me from monsters like you."

"Felina?" said Mallory.

She took a step toward the leprechaun.

"I'm outta here!" he screamed, bowling over a pair of hucksters as he made a beeline for the far end of the lobby.

The detective surveyed the area, finally located a sign directing him to the poetry reading by Aristotle Draconis, and walked over to the door, which led to a small amphitheatre holding about two hundred seats, of which perhaps forty were filled.

"Doesn't draw quite as well as wrestling, does it?" noted McGuire.

"Maybe he should add some dirty limericks and a couple of belly dancers to his routine," said Mallory, sitting down on a chair. Felina was about to wander up to the stage when he grabbed her wrist and pulled her into the chair next to his. McGuire sat down, and a moment later a pudgy man with reptilian skin walked out onto the stage.

"Ladies, gentlemen, and others," he said, "it is my privilege to present to you, the one, the only, the great Aristotle Draconis, who has come from his ancestral home across the sea to be with us tonight."

Then Draconis came out on stage, wearing tie and tails, an incredibly tall, cadaverous figure with sunken cheeks, hollow burning eyes, canines that Mallory could actually see pushing against his lips, and a neatly coiffed head of coal black hair. One finger sported a ring with a huge, bloodred ruby. The backs of his hands were covered with matted hair, and his nails extended more than half an inch beyond his fingers.

"He sure as hell looks the part," whispered Mallory.

"He's terrifying, even to me," said McGuire.

"I like his ring," purred Felina.

Draconis stood at center stage, staring at his audience, member by member. Everyone but Mallory dropped their gaze; the detective looked back into the vampire's strange eyes, which seemed to consist of wall-to-wall pupils.

"I appreciate your coming out on such a special night to greet a stranger to your shores," said Draconis in a deep, slightly accented voice. "I shall endeavor to make you feel that the effort was not wasted."

And with that, he began reciting his poetry, all eldritch and foreboding, filled with vivid images of unclean things and unholy practices. After twenty minutes he stopped, the audience applauded politely, and he took a single bow and left the stage.

"What do you think?" said Mallory.

"He's terrifying," said McGuire. "In fact, he's everything *I'm* supposed to be. What do *you* think?"

"I think he doesn't have to immobilize his victims," replied Mallory. "He can bore 'em to sleep first."

"You're not afraid?" asked McGuire, amazed.

"Only of an encore," said Mallory, getting to his feet.

"Where are we going?" asked the little vampire apprehensively.

"Backstage. I've got to talk to him."

"Just talk?"

"At first."

"And then?" asked McGuire.

"And then, if he's guilty, I'll have to figure out what to do next."

"You're just saying that, right?" said McGuire, his words coming faster and faster. "I mean, you wouldn't really try to use force on something like *that*, would you? You're just trying to work up your courage, or to impress me, or—"

"Calm down, Bats," said Mallory. "You don't have to come if you don't want to."

"Well, of course I want to," said McGuire.

"Good."

"But he may have confederates lurking in the shadows," continued McGuire nervously. "I'd better stay outside the room and protect your back."

Suddenly Felina turned and hissed at the little vampire.

"What was *that* about?" demanded McGuire.

"*I'm* protecting his back!" she said. "You can protect his elbow or his left knee."

"You were just supposed to help me until I found the kid or the killer," Mallory told McGuire. "Well, we found the kid, and maybe we've found the killer. Your obligation is over."

"I don't know," said the vampire unhappily. "I'd feel like such a coward, deserting you in your time of need."

"Bats, you *are* a coward," said Mallory. "You can't help it any more than you can help being a vampire."

"But it sounds so . . . so *naked* when you just come out and say it."

"I haven't got time to sugarcoat it," said Mallory. "I have to see Draconis."

"I'll wait right outside the door, ready to burst in and save the day," offered McGuire.

"Whatever makes you happy," said Mallory. He walked up to an aging troll in a guard's uniform. "Hi, Pops," he said, flipping him a quarter. "Where's Draconis's dressing room?"

The old troll put the quarter in his mouth and bit down on it.

"It's real," Mallory assured him.

"I know," said the troll unhappily. "You got any chocolate ones?"

"I'm fresh out," said Mallory.

"Oh, well," said the troll with a shrug. He pocketed the quarter. "Third door on your left."

"Is he alone?"

"How the hell would I know?"

"Okay," said the detective, heading off toward the door. "Thanks, Pops."

"You're welcome, and the name is Thucydides."

"Really?"

"Nah . . . but it sounds better than Etherbert."

Mallory stopped when he reached the door, then turned to Felina. "You come with me." Then, to McGuire: "You wait out here."

He knocked on the door. There was no answer. He turned the knob and pushed it open.

Suddenly a voice rang out: "Not one step farther if you want to live."

CHAPTER 12

11:22 PM–11:43 PM

Mallory took a step into the room, holding his hands in front of him, palms up.

"I'm not armed," he said. "I just want to talk."

"Of course you're armed," said the sibilant voice. "You've got two that I can see, and who knows how the hell many more you've got hidden beneath that trenchcoat?"

Suddenly a reptilian creature emerged from a darkened corner of the room. Its skin was green, rough, and scaled, it had a pair of wings on its back, its hands were clawlike, its feet were actual claws, and its face was a cross between a snake and a crocodile. It wore a leather harness and carried a spear.

"You know," said Mallory, staring at it, "if someone were to ask me whether you were animal, vegetable, or mineral, my only answer would be: Probably."

"Keep a civil tongue in your head, Jack," said the creature. "You and your cat are in deep trouble."

"All I want to do is talk to Aristotle Draconis," said Mallory.

"Yeah, that's what they all say. And the next day there's an interview in the paper, and he's misquoted six ways to Sunday, and who gets blamed for it? *We* do."

"Who are you?"

"I'm part of the group that paid his way over and booked his tour," answered the creature.

"What do you guys call yourselves?" asked Mallory.

"The Dragon Writers, of course."

"Your club is composed entirely of dragons that write?"

"It's a *guild*. And Draconis is our spiritual leader."

"And you're all poets?"

"Certainly not," said the dragon. "We've got a science fiction writer, a Western writer, two espionage writers, and thirty-seven romance writers."

He wrinkled his nose. "Dragons don't seem to sell. I wish I knew how other-wise talented writers could find so many love stories about vampires."

"And what kind of writer are you?"

"Me? I write hard-boiled private eye stories. Did you ever hear of Wings O'Bannon? He's my character."

"No, I'm afraid not."

"Damn!" muttered the dragon. "What's the good of being the greatest prose writer alive if you only sold six hundred and fifty-one copies of your last book—and half of *them* went to relatives?"

"So how come you're not busy writing?" asked Mallory.

"Got to make a living," answered the dragon. "Writing's all very well, but my publisher is three years late with my check, and he's one of the faster ones." He paused. "We're getting off the subject here. You want to tell me who you are and what you're doing here before I rip you limb from limb and paper the walls with what's left of your pet?"

Mallory pulled out his license. "My name's John Justin Mallory, and I just want to talk to Draconis for a few minutes."

The dragon stared at the license. "That's for real, right?" he said excit-edly. "I mean, you didn't pick it up in a novelty shop?"

"It's real."

"Oh my goodness—a real shamus!" exclaimed the dragon. "I've never met one before. We have to talk! I've got my new book in the next room. It's only about eight hundred pages so far—I'm not quite halfway done with it. Could you look it over and give me a couple of hints?"

"I'm not a writer."

"Writers are a dime a dozen," said the dragon contemptuously. "Every idiot and his brother is a writer. I need to talk to a real private eye." He extended a claw. "Scaly Jim Chandler at your service."

"Scaly Jim Chandler?" repeated Mallory, taking his claw and trying not to wince as the nails dug into his skin.

"Well, that's my pen name," said the dragon apologetically. "Actually, I'm Nathan Botts. But who ever heard of a hard-drinking, womanizing, tough-guy writer called Nathan Botts?"

"Well, Nathan . . ."

"Scaly Jim," the dragon corrected him.

"Well, Scaly Jim," said Mallory, "I'd love to look at your manuscript, but I'm right in the middle of a case, and Aristotle Draconis may hold the key to it."

"A case?" The dragon's homely features lit up. "Is it . . . *murder?*"

"Yeah."

"Goddamn, that's exciting!"

"The victim would disagree with you."

"Look, Mr. Mallory . . ." began Nathan.

"Just Mallory will do."

"Yes, right, of course—no shamus wants to be called 'Mister.' Look, Mallory, I can make up mysteries with the best of them, but I've never been out in the field, so to speak." He paused, shifting his weight uncomfortably, staring at the floor. "And I was wondering . . . that is, if you wouldn't mind . . . could I . . . uh . . . ?"

"Tag along?" suggested Mallory.

"Yes."

"If there's still a case after I talk to Draconis, I don't see why not," replied Mallory. "What the hell, I need all the help I can get."

"Great!" cried the dragon enthusiastically. Then: "I thought private eyes liked to work solo."

"*This* private eye likes to live to the end of the case and isn't too proud to accept help whenever it's offered."

"Come on, now," said the dragon disbelievingly. "Next you'll be telling me you don't have an oversexed secretary called Velma."

"I don't."

Nathan frowned. "Well, that cuts a quick three hundred pages of gratuitous sex and violence out of the book," he said, trying to hide his disappointment. "I thought you guys were more self-sufficient."

"Only in novels."

The dragon sighed. "I've got a lot to learn."

"And the sooner I see Draconis, the sooner you can start," said Mallory.

Nathan stood aside and pointed to a door behind him. "Right through there, Mallory."

"Thanks, Jim."

"Scaly Jim."

"How about just Jim now that we're going to be friends?"

"We are?" The dragon's homely face lit up. "You know, my girlfriend calls me Cuddles."

"Let's stick to Jim," said Mallory. "It's more professional."

"Right. We're colleagues, aren't we?"

"As soon as I talk to Draconis."

"You want me to sit in on it while you grill him?" asked Nathan. "Maybe add a little muscle if it's needed?"

"Not just yet."

"Okay. I'll be right out here."

Mallory turned to Felina. She was curled up the floor, snoring peacefully.

"When she wakes up, tell her I'll be out in a minute," said Mallory. "You hear anything that sounds like furniture or people being knocked around, both of you come in on the double."

"Got it, partner."

Mallory opened the door and walked into a dressing room. Aristotle Draconis sat at a table that held the evening's readings. He was dabbing some sweat from his forehead with a silk handkerchief. Above the table was a mirror. Draconis himself left no reflection, but he saw Mallory standing behind him and turned to face him.

"I saw you in the audience," he said. "You were the only one who met my gaze. I admire that." He paused. "You should know that I only give autographs by prior arrangement."

"I'm more interested in when you give hickeys," said Mallory, flashing his credentials.

"I beg your pardon?"

"You're a vampire."

"I don't deny it," said Draconis. "There's no law against being a vampire."

"No, there isn't," agreed Mallory. "But the last time I looked, there's a law against murder."

"I haven't murdered anyone."

"That's what we have to talk about," said Mallory. "You came over here on a ship."

"Yes, the *Moribund Manatee* out of Liverpool," Draconis confirmed.

"There was a young man on the same ship," continued Mallory. "His name was Rupert Newton."

"Ah, young Newton. A very engaging fellow. I spent a few pleasant hours playing canasta and rummy with him."

"He was a very engaging fellow when he boarded the boat," said Mallory. "He was well on his way to becoming a very engaging vampire when he got off."

Draconis nodded his head. "Yes, I know. Terrible pity. I assume you know him?"

"He's my partner's nephew."

"Give him my regards."

"That'll be a little difficult," said Mallory. "He's in the morgue."

"And you think *I*—?"

"That's what I want to know," said Mallory. "You bit him on the boat. He was scared to death that you were following him around the city. And now he's dead."

"You have it all wrong, Mr. Mallory," said Draconis.

"Tell me why."

"I didn't bite that boy."

"He says he saw you leaving his stateroom right after he'd been bitten."

"That is true," said Draconis. "I was trying to *prevent* his being bitten. I was too late. What he saw was me chasing the creature that *did* bite him."

"You want to expand on that?" said Mallory.

"I am a poet. That has been my whole life. Like many others, I was initiated into the legion of the undead, but unlike most, I did not accept my new station in life. My entire existence revolves around elevating people, not harming them. I have never bitten another human being, not once."

"How do you stay alive?"

Draconis walked over to a small, portable refrigerator and opened it. "Do you see these half-gallon containers, Mr. Mallory? Each is filled with blood. This is my own private supply. It travels with me, and I am never without it."

"Whose is it?"

Draconis smiled. "It comes from my private herd of cattle," he replied.

"I raise them not for meat or milk, but as blood banks. I have that in common with the Maasai of Africa."

"I thought you had to drink human blood," said Mallory.

"It is more nourishing, to be sure, but it is not essential. After all, my kind takes its name from the vampire bats of South America, and what do they live on?"

"Cattle," said Mallory.

"That is correct."

"Then why don't more vampires do what you do?"

"Many lose their moral compass when they are bitten," answered Draconis. "Others cannot stand the constant hunger, for as I have said, the blood I drink is not as satisfying as that which flows through your veins. And for some, it is simply not practical. Where are you going to find an unprotected herd of cattle in New York City?"

"Makes sense."

"Then you accept my story?"

"For the moment," said Mallory. "But if you didn't bite the kid, who did? You must know, if you were trying to save him."

"I don't think you'll believe me," said Draconis.

"Perhaps not," said Mallory. "But why don't you tell me and let me decide?"

"He was bitten by the worst of our kind, a terrible, centuries-old creature from Transylvania itself."

"And his name?"

"Vlad Drachma."

"Where can I find him?"

"Take my word for it, Mr. Mallory, you don't want to," said Draconis sincerely. "Rupert Newton is already dead. Why should you join him?"

"You were willing to go up against this Drachma. Why shouldn't I?"

"I am already dead," answered Draconis. "What further harm can he do me?"

"Just tell me where he is," said Mallory.

"I can't give you an exact location," replied Draconis. "He travels with his own coffin, of course. There are places—very specialized mortuaries—that rent out space to traveling vampires. Your best bet is to try one of them, and your best hope is that you never find him."

"Thanks," said Mallory, walking to the door. "If you're telling the truth, we probably won't meet again. If you're lying, you're going to find out just how long the undead can suffer."

"Fair enough," said Draconis. Then, just as Mallory reached for the door, he added: "What did you think of my poetry?"

"I think H. P. Lovecraft would have admired it," said Mallory. *And probably seven other people in the world*, he added mentally.

Draconis smiled for the first time. "Thank you, Mr. Mallory. You have made my night. I just hope I haven't unmade yours."

Mallory walked into the outer room.

"Do we still have a case?" asked Nathan Botts the dragon.

"Yeah," said Mallory. "Look, if you have to stick around and guard Draconis . . ."

"To hell with that," said Nathan. "He's got fifty times my strength and even better teeth. Let's go."

Mallory nudged Felina gently with his toe. "Wake up."

"I wasn't sleeping," she said defensively, getting to her feet.

"What *were* you doing?"

"Resting my eyes," she said. "And my arms, and my legs, and my back, and my ears, and—"

"Skip it," said Mallory, leading them out into the corridor, where McGuire was waiting nervously.

"Bats, say hello to Scaly Jim Chandler," said Mallory. "He's joined the team."

"Hi," said the little vampire.

"Good evening," replied the dragon. Suddenly he looked embarrassed. "Excuse me—hiya, pal."

"Bats," said Mallory, "where do you sleep?"

"In a bed, of course," answered McGuire.

"I thought you guys had to sleep in soil from your homeland."

"Manhattan *is* my homeland," said McGuire.

"And the soil?"

"So I don't change the sheets," said McGuire defensively. "It works."

"Okay, but if you were traveling with a coffin, where would you park it for the night?"

"Why don't you just ask Draconis where *he* sleeps?"

"We're not after him," said Mallory. "We're after a vampire who's probably left his coffin at some mortuary that caters to the undead. Which is the likeliest one?"

"Ah!" said McGuire, his homely face lighting up. "I know just the place." He headed off toward the Garden's main exit. "Follow me!"

CHAPTER 13

11:43 PM–Midnight

"So where is this place?" asked Mallory as McGuire led their mismatched party of four down Madison Avenue.

"Not far," answered the vampire. "It's just off the corner of Death and Despair."

"Are those local streets?" asked Mallory, frowning. "I never heard of them."

"They have different names in the daytime," answered McGuire.

Suddenly Felina stopped and began sniffing the air.

"What is it?" asked Mallory.

"There's something dying in the alley," she said. "Something small and fat and tasty."

"Leave it alone," said Mallory. "We've got work to do."

"One of them can protect your front and one can protect your back," she said.

"I can't waste any more time," said Mallory. "Come or stay, it's up to you."

"I'll catch up with you," said Felina.

"You don't know where we're going."

"I'll follow your scents," she said. She pointed toward the dragon. "This one really stinks. He'll be easy to follow."

Nathan turned to Mallory. "I don't know if I've been complimented or insulted."

"Let's let it be one of life's little mysteries," said the detective. "Come on, Bats—let's get moving."

"Right," said McGuire.

They walked a block in silence, then turned right, right again, and right a third time.

"You know if you turn right again we're going to be back where we started," said Mallory.

"Only in daytime," answered McGuire, making a fourth right.

Mallory looked around, frowning. "Where are we, and what happened to Madison Avenue?"

"We're at the corner of Death and Destruction," said the vampire. "Despair is the next street down."

They began walking toward Despair. Only one building was lit, right at the corner. A flickering, buzzing neon sign, clearly in need of repair, told the world that this was Creepy Conrad's Cut-Rate All-Night Mortuary.

"And this is where all the vampires go?" asked Mallory.

"Of course not," answered McGuire. "There are thousands of us in Manhattan. This is just the likeliest spot."

"What makes it the likeliest spot?"

The vampire offered a weak smile. "It was the only one I could think of."

"Well, we're here," said Mallory. "Let's go in and see what they've got."

"Don't you want to case the joint first?" asked the dragon.

"We're looking for a vampire," explained Mallory. "The only way we'll know if this is where he's holed up is if we find his coffin, agreed?"

"Right," said Nathan.

"Do you see any coffins outside?"

"Ah!" said the dragon. "Good thinking, Mallory."

"Praise from on high," muttered Mallory. "Okay, let's go in."

They entered the mortuary, which was illuminated by a few hundred candles. A morbidly obese man in a tuxedo that was four sizes too small for him waddled up to them, his hands clasped together in front of his chest. Mallory wondered if his arms were long enough to clasp his hands in front of his stomach, and decided they weren't.

"Good evening, dear friends," said the man, "and welcome to Creepy Conrad's in your hour of need and suffering." He looked around. "May I ask where the deceased is?"

"We haven't decided where he should lie in state," answered Mallory. "We came by to see your facility."

The man nodded his head knowingly. "Of course," he said. "And what kind of service will you require?"

"We're not sure," said Mallory. "What kinds do you offer?"

"We run the entire gamut," said the man.

"Are you Conrad, by the way?"

"Oh, no, dear friends. Creepy Conrad has passed to another plane of existence, though he does come back and visit us for Scrabble on Tuesday evenings."

Suddenly the stillness of the night was broken by the sound of gunshots and screeching rubber.

"Excuse me, dear friends," said the man, "but I have a feeling that I shall soon have to preside at one of our short-term services. You are welcome to accompany me if you wish."

He abruptly turned and waddled down a darkened corridor, and Mallory's party followed suit. A moment later they emerged at a large picture window, and seconds after that a car, its body studded with bullet holes, skidded up.

"Good evening, dear friends," said the man, pressing a button that closed a gate in front of the car. "Welcome to our drive-by service window. Would you like the three-minute funeral with all the trimmings?"

A police siren began wailing.

"No time," said the driver, and Mallory could see that there was a bullet-riddled corpse in the back seat. "Just take him."

The fat man pushed a button and a drawer six feet long, three feet wide, and two feet deep shot out. The driver and another passenger lowered the back window and managed to shove the corpse onto the drawer.

"Our one-minute service is a bargain at only two hundred dollars," said the fat man.

Bullets began raining down on the car.

"Perhaps our ten-second special for fifty dollars?"

The driver threw a fifty on top of the corpse.

"Our father who art in heaven, here comes another one," intoned the fat man, releasing the gate and pulling the drawer in as the car peeled off. An instant later a police car raced by in hot pursuit.

"Our drive-by funerals are always a bit on the awkward side," commented the man as a crew of gnomes and elves suddenly appeared and began carting the body off. "Still, it's a necessary adjunct to our business."

"Yeah, I can see that," said McGuire.

"Now, dear friends, perhaps you can tell me something about the deceased, so that I can show you the proper line of coffins and services available."

"Well, it's a bit awkward," said Mallory.

"Not to worry, my good sir," said the fat man. "I'm sure no court in the land would find you guilty."

"That's a definite comfort," replied Mallory dryly. "But I'm afraid the problem is that our friend is not dead at the moment."

"You plan to commit the heinous deed this evening?" asked the fat man. "I understand completely. Not to worry, sir. My lips are sealed."

"Try not understanding me so fast," said Mallory. "My friend is one of the undead."

"Certainly," said the fat man, studying the undersized McGuire with an expert eye. "We can even save you some money with a child's coffin."

"Not him," said Mallory. "The friend in question is out on the prowl right now, but he's going to need a place to stay come morning."

"Will this be a long-term or a transient arrangement?"

"Long term," said Mallory, and the fat man inadvertently licked his chops. "First I have to make sure the accommodations are suitable."

"I shall be happy to show you around."

"We'll want a tour of the place, of course," said Mallory. "But there's something we have to address first."

"No problem, my good sir," said the fat man. "We accept dollars, pounds, francs, yen, rubles, drachmas, zlotys, rupees, gold, silver, diamonds, platinum, bearer bonds, and all major credit cards."

"Fine," said Mallory. "But we still have something to address."

"And what might that be?"

"My friend comes from Transylvania . . ."

"Ah!" said the man, rubbing his hands together. "The old country!"

"And his coffin is still in transit."

"As I said, we have an full line of coffins—wood, metal, even Styrofoam for those who awake in the middle of the endless sleep feeling claustrophobic and must get out right away."

"I don't think you see the problem," said Mallory. "The soil from his native land is also in transit. Have you any Transylvanian soil here? He assures me he'd just need to borrow a couple of cups of it to mix with American soil until his coffin arrives. He'll sleep uneasily, but at least he'll be able to sleep."

"I see," said the fat man, frowning. "I'll have to check our records."

"Are you boarding that many vampires?"

"Well over a hundred, sir," said the fat man. "Excuse me a moment while I go to my office and see if we can accommodate you."

He turned and left, and McGuire spoke in a low voice. "You can't just add a scoop of native soil. Drachma would never get to sleep."

"Doesn't matter," said Mallory. "I didn't know it, and more to the point *he* doesn't know it, so he'll give us the answer we need."

Nathan pulled a notebook and pen out of his leather harness and began scribbling furiously.

"What's that about?" asked McGuire curiously.

"I'm just taking notes on how a real pro bluffs the enemy," answered the dragon.

"He's not an enemy," said Mallory.

"Ah! Right! You'd call him a civilian, wouldn't you?"

"Why not?" asked Mallory. "He *is* one."

"I wonder why he's so secretive about his name?" persisted the dragon.

"If you want to know his name, why not just ask him?" said Mallory.

"Is that what you'd do?" replied Nathan.

"How else are you going to find out?"

"I don't know," said the dragon. "Lift his wallet. Get his license plate and check it out with headquarters."

"The direct way is usually the best," said Mallory.

"Let me write that down," said Nathan. "Direct way . . . best. Got it."

The fat man returned. "I do believe we can be of help to you, sir," he said. "Right now we are providing sanctuary for two different borders from the old country."

"Have they got names?"

"Certainly, but of course it is against our policy to give them out."

Nathan immediately began scribbling again, then tore the sheet out of his notebook and handed it to Mallory, who read it:

Do you want me to coldcock him when his back is turned and then go through his files?
Mallory crumpled the paper and stuck it in a pocket.

"I was just wondering if either of them might be friends of his," said Mallory. "It would make him much more eager to come here if he knew some of the residents."

"I see," said the fat man with a knowing smile. "I can't break our policy, but if it will help, you can tell him that they are a couple of roguish bits of fluff who are always looking for a good time with gentlemen of their particular persuasion."

"I'll pass the word to him," said Mallory. "Thank you. You've been most helpful, and I'm sure we'll be in touch with you again shortly."

He shook the man's pudgy hand, then walked out into the night, followed by Nathan and McGuire.

"Okay," said Mallory. "At least we know where Vlad Drachma *doesn't* keep his coffin." He turned to Nathan. "You weren't really going to crack him on the head and rummage through his office, were you?"

"Wings O'Bannon would have," replied the dragon defensively.

"Maybe that's why you only sold six hundred copies of his last book."

"Six hundred and fifty-one," said Nathan defensively.

"Let me ask you a question," said Mallory. "How many times does Wings O'Bannon get shot or knocked on the noggin in the course of one of your books?"

"At least once a chapter."

"Must have a hard head," said the detective.

"He has excellent recuperative powers," said Nathan.

"Obviously."

"All the gorgeous blondes who fall into bed with him remark on it," continued the dragon.

"I can imagine."

"Is that how it is with your women?"

"*My* women?" repeated Mallory.

"Are they slavishly devoted to you?"

"It's hard to say," replied Mallory. "One of them's off on a safari with her team of trolls in Central Park, and the other's killing something helpless in an alley two blocks from here."

"No I'm not," said Felina.

Mallory looked around, but couldn't spot her.

"Up here," she said from her perch atop a lamppost.

"I trust you enjoyed your meal?" said the detective sardonically.

She wrinkled her nose. "It begged and pleaded all the way down, and then after I'd eaten it, it began cursing a blue streak." She paused. "I just hate it when they do that."

"I probably would too."

"Curse, or hate it?" she asked curiously.

"A little of each. Come on down."

"I like it up here."

"Come down anyway. It's getting near time to rendezvous with Winnifred."

"I can see all the way to the next block." Felina looked thoughtfully down at him. "You wouldn't like it up here, John Justin."

"Heights don't scare me."

"I know," she said. "But what's coming up the street in this direction will."

CHAPTER 14

Midnight–12:26 AM

"I don't suppose you'd like to give me a hint?" said Mallory.

There was an earsplitting bellow.

"Never mind," said the detective.

"What the hell was that?" asked McGuire nervously.

"Something *big*," said Nathan, hefting his spear. "Whatever it is, I'm prepared for it."

Mallory looked up the street. "I don't think so," he said.

The vampire and the dragon both turned in the direction the detective was facing.

"My God!" exclaimed Nathan as a huge carnivorous dinosaur lumbered into sight. "He's even bigger than *T. rex!*"

"Uh . . . aren't they supposed to be extinct?" asked McGuire, stepping behind Mallory and peeking out around his hip.

"Goddammit, Grundy!" said Mallory. "Call him off!"

"You're just speaking in a normal voice," complained McGuire. "Shouldn't you be yelling to attract the Grundy's attention?"

"He can hear me," answered Mallory. "If I yell, I'll give you three guesses whose attention I'll attract."

"Whisper!" said the little vampire urgently.

"Put your spear down, Nathan," said Mallory.

"Scaly Jim, damn it!"

"Sorry. Put it down, Jim. You can't kill him."

"This is a pretty hefty spear, and I was second in the javelin throw in high school," replied the dragon.

"Believe me, it won't do any good," said Mallory. "He's already dead."

"He looks pretty alive to me."

"He's from the Natural History Museum," said Mallory. "He's dead, all right. He just doesn't know it." He stared at the approaching dinosaur. "It happens every night. They've been so expertly preserved that they don't know they're dead, so once the place is closed and the lights go down, they start flexing their muscles and moving around."

"And this is the Grundy's doing?"

"No," said Mallory. He finally raised his voice. "But he can freeze time and make it stop."

"If he freezes time, won't it stop for all of us?" asked Nathan.

"He can do it selectively."

"Why should he?" whimpered McGuire. "From what I hear, you're his greatest enemy."

"I'm going to be his deadest enemy in a minute," said Mallory. "Come on, Grundy. I thought we had an understanding."

The dinosaur saw the trio and altered his stride to approach them.

"*T. rex* hell!" said Nathan in awestruck tones. "He's *U. rex*, or maybe even *V. rex*!"

"And he hasn't eaten in sixty-five million years," added McGuire. "He's got a lean and famished look to him."

"Let's prepare to sell our lives as dearly as possible," said Nathan, clutching his spear.

"Put it down," said Mallory. "You'll just make him angry."

"Angry, hungry, what's the difference?" said McGuire. "Somebody *do* something!"

The dinosaur opened its mouth and bellowed again.

"I can smell his breath all the way from there," said Felina from her perch atop the lamppost. "He doesn't brush after every meal," she added helpfully.

"He's going to reach us in another twenty seconds!" stammered McGuire. "*Do* something, Mallory!"

"Why don't you just turn into a bat and fly off?" said Mallory. "You too, Scaly Joe. You've got wings."

"They're just for show, and to attract cheap bimbos," answered Nathan. "I can't actually fly."

"I can—but I can't change when I'm this scared!" whined McGuire.

"Well, at least let's spread out so he has to choose between us," suggested Mallory, "and maybe the other two can scramble to safety."

They did as he said, and the dinosaur watched them curiously for a moment, then continued approaching. It quickly became clear that he had singled out Mallory as his prey. He was perhaps two strides away when he opened his mouth and Mallory found himself looking down the black abyss of the monster's throat.

"I just hate magic!" the detective muttered as he prepared to be swallowed whole.

"Do you indeed?" said a familiar voice, and suddenly the dinosaur froze, its saliva-flecked jaws less than four feet from Mallory's head.

"Don't tell me," said Mallory to the disembodied voice. "You were in the bathroom."

"I admire your sense of humor, John Justin Mallory," replied the Grundy.

"I don't admire yours," said Mallory. "Why did you send this thing after me?"

"I didn't," answered the Grundy.

"Come on," said Mallory irritably. "We're three miles from the damned museum. Are you saying he got loose and then sought me out from among all eight or nine million residents?"

"Such ingratitude," said the Grundy. "Didn't I just save your life?"

"After endangering it," said Mallory. "I'd call it a wash."

"I assure you I did not bring the dinosaur to life or set him free."

"No, you just directed him to this spot so you could have a little fun. I'm surprised McGuire didn't wet himself."

"Yes I did," said the vampire softly.

"You can spend the next four minutes and nineteen seconds arguing with me," said the Grundy, "or you can spend it putting some distance between you and the dinosaur, but that is all the time you have before he returns to life."

"All right, we're gone. Did you contact Winnifred Carruthers?"

"Yes," said the Grundy. "She has taken possession of her nephew's body. And thank you, Mallory."

"For what?"

"For telling me to wait five minutes before contacting her. I haven't seen such carnage in centuries."

"You're damned lucky you didn't send the dinosaur after *her*," said Mallory. "My partner is one tough lady."

"Three minutes and twenty-six seconds," intoned the Grundy.

"We'll talk later," said Mallory. He turned to his companions. "Come on." He looked up at Felina. "You too."

She leaped lightly to the ground. "It's broken," she said.

"What is?" asked Mallory, hoping against hope that she hadn't damaged an ankle and that he wouldn't have to carry her.

"The dinosaur," she said. "Its battery ran down."

"Its battery is recharging right now," said Mallory, heading off to the north. "Let's go."

They ran to the corner, turned so they'd be out of sight, and slowed to a rapid walk. The dinosaur roared once, and then, a moment later, roared again; the second was much softer and more distant.

"You know," said Nathan, "if there's one thing I hate running into on the street at midnight, it's a *W. rex.*"

"Put him in your book," said Mallory.

"I never thought of that!" said the dragon. Suddenly he frowned. "But will anyone believe a dinosaur in a detective novel?"

"If they believe that Wings O'Bannon can get shot every fifteen pages and still bed three dozen women by the end of the book, they'll buy a dinosaur in Manhattan."

"Do you really think so?" asked Nathan, his face brightening.

"Absolutely," replied Mallory.

"I could set it on an alternate world, I suppose," continued the dragon.

"I come from an alternate Manhattan," said Mallory. "Trust me, tyrannosaurs are even rarer in that one."

"What was your Manhattan like?" persisted Nathan.

"Not all that different from this, when you get right down to it," answered the detective. "People still broke the laws, cops still arrested them, cheap shysters still got them back on the street before the cops could file their reports, judges still suspended sentences if you slipped then a quick twenty. We didn't have any animated dinosaurs, though."

"How was the troll problem?"

"No worse than here," said Mallory.

"How many species of dragon live in your former Manhattan?"

"I never counted," replied Mallory.

"Got anything as evil as the Grundy?"

"Some would say yes, and some would say absolutely," answered Mallory. "Mostly they run for office." He turned north again. "What the hell am *I* leading the way for? McGuire, you're the one who knows where the Belfry is."

The little vampire increased his pace, and within ten minutes they had reached Central Park. Suddenly McGuire paused, looking around with a confused expression.

"What's the problem?" asked Mallory.

"I did something wrong," said McGuire. "This is the corner of Fifth Avenue and Fifty-ninth Street."

"I know."

"Well, it's not supposed to be. We'll have to backtrack."

He walked south for a block, turned west for a block, then north, and then east. Somehow Mallory wasn't surprised when the street signs told him that they were now at the corner of Eerie and Eldritch.

They heard a flutter of wings overhead and looked up to see a harpy flying just above them.

Felina leaped up and tried to snare it with her claws, but it was too high.

"Nevermore!" cackled the harpy, banking and heading off to the Upper West Seventies, where ecologists and preservationists set food and even blankets out on all the balconies and lived in as close to a state of Nature with the harpies, banshees, and other winged denizens of the night as possible in the big city. (And on those occasions that the winged denizens relieved themselves on balconies or in rooftop pools, the residents would call in all the Second Amendment absolutists who lived in the West Nineties, and a mildly different state of Nature would be quickly and noisily restored.)

"You see any sign of Winnifred and her trolls?" Mallory asked his companions.

"I don't even know what she looks like," answered the dragon.

"No," answered McGuire. "But bats don't see very well. Just a second." He put two fingers in his mouth and emitted a shrill whistle, which seemed to bounce and echo all across their surroundings. "Nope. Either she's already in the Belfry, or else she hasn't arrived yet."

"All right," said Mallory. "Let's go into the Belfry and find out."

"You haven't asked *me* if I've seen any sign of Winnifred," sniffed Felina.

"Would you tell me?"

"Yes, John Justin," she said. Then: "Probably." Then: "No." Then: "Perhaps." And finally: "Maybe."

"It's comforting to know that you're as helpful as ever," said the detective.

"I knew that would make you happy, John Justin," said Felina.

A banshee circled high above them, screeching something they couldn't quite make out. Two harpies screamed back, an owl hooted, and before long they were surrounded by a cacophony of sound.

"Bats, lead the way," said Mallory. "I'm surprised they didn't bring their own drummer."

The little vampire led them halfway down Eldritch, crossed the street, and walked back to the corner of Eerie.

"Here we are," he announced.

"I'd have sworn this building wasn't here before," said Mallory.

"It's shy," explained McGuire. "You just have to know how to approach it."

Mallory studied the structure, which resembled a small Gothic castle. "There's nobody here, Bats. All the light are out."

"Not all of them," answered McGuire. "The club's in the basement."

"You'd think there'd at least be a sign out front."

"Why? Anyone who wants to find it knows where it is."

McGuire pushed against the door, which creaked as if it hadn't been opened or oiled in years.

"This way," he said, descending a dimly lit staircase that spiraled off to the right. Mallory, Nathan, and Felina followed him.

For five minutes no one spoke, and finally McGuire announced that they were almost halfway there.

"Halfway?" repeated Mallory. "Bats, we must be five hundred feet down."

"The club was built to withstand earthquakes, hexes, floods, curses, nuclear devices of less than eight megatons, and termites," replied McGuire. "It takes some getting to, but once we're there, you'll be secure in the knowledge that you're totally safe."

"Unless I want to get out in a hurry."

"No problem," answered the vampire. "All the chairs have ejector seats."

"How does that help if the room has a ceiling?" said Mallory.

"I never thought of that," admitted McGuire.

"Somehow I'm not surprised."

"You will be, though," said Felina.

"Why?" asked Mallory.

She learned forward and sniffed the cool, damp, underground air. "There are dead things up ahead."

"You mean like vampires?"

She shook her head. "No, vampires are undead. What I smell is *dead*."

"Permanently?" asked Mallory.

"Yes."

"That's a relief," said the detective. "You're sure, now—all the dead things you can smell are permanently dead?"

"Yes, John Justin," said Felina. "Absolutely. Certainly. Positively."

"Thanks."

"I have a question, John Justin." she continued.

"Yeah?"

"What does 'permanently' mean?"

"You'd think a joint called the Belfry would be *up*, not down," remarked Mallory as they finally came to the end of the stairs.

"It used to be," replied McGuire. "In fact, it was at the top of the Rockefeller Rectangle (which should actually have been called the Rockefeller Demipolytetrahedron, but let it pass)."

"So what happened?"

"Harpies kept begging at the tables, so they enclosed the place, and then new vampires who hadn't adjusted to flying by sonar began flying into the windows and bouncing off, and some of the patrons found that they couldn't drink and look down at low-flying clouds without getting sick, and then the elevators stopped working every time there was a brownout, and—"

"Okay, I get the picture," said Mallory.

The entry foyer was small and dimly lit. The entire club was built to give the impression of a cave, with ersatz stone walls, floors that looked damp but weren't, and indirect lighting. There were tunnels leading to the various dining rooms, and Mallory decided that if a bat couldn't find a perch in a belfry, it would probably be comfortable in his current surroundings.

A waiter, dressed in a tux and a red velvet cape and sporting truly impressive canines, approached them. "May I help you?"

He noticed Mallory staring at him and Nathan tightening his grip on his spear. "It's standard dress uniform for employees, sir," continued the waiter, removing his eyeteeth. "It makes the customers feel more at home."

"Has a Winnifred Carruthers shown up yet?" asked Mallory. "We're supposed to meet her here."

"I really couldn't say, sir," replied the waiter. "Perhaps if you could describe her?"

"Stocky woman, gray-haired, probably wearing khakis and carrying a Nitro Express."

The waiter smiled. "Ah! The lady with the wicked-looking rifle. Yes, she's waiting for you in the next room." He turned to the dragon. "Would you care to check your spear, sir?"

"I never let it out of my sight," answered Nathan.

"And you, sir?" he said to Mallory. "We have a small kennel on the premises where a number of wizards and witches leave their familiars, if you would care to place your cat there while you're eating." Felina hissed and flashed her claws. "Perhaps not," said the waiter smoothly without missing a beat. "If you will follow me, then. . . ."

He headed off to an adjoining room, and a moment later Mallory and his party were standing in front of Winnifred's table.

"I'm sorry about Rupert," said Mallory, sitting down and nodding to the others to do so too. "The Grundy told me he got word to you."

She nodded. "The poor boy. At least he's really dead. Another bite or two and that would have been denied him. Have you found Aristotle Draconis yet?"

"He didn't do it."

She looked dubious. "Can you be sure?"

"Pretty sure."

"I was with him all evening," chimed in Nathan.

"And who are you?"

"Scaly Jim Chandler at your service, ma'am," replied the dragon.

"The mystery writer?" asked Winnifred.

The dragon's face lit up. "You've *read* me?"

"*Kiss the Blood Off My Shoes*," she said. "Not bad."

"Wait'll you read the sequel!" said Nathan enthusiastically. "Wings O'Bannon has to solve a crime in high society."

"I'll look for it," promised Winnifred. "What's the title?"

"*Kiss the Blood Off My Spats*."

"You ever been around high society?" asked Mallory.

"No, but—"

"Maybe you ought to write about what you know."

"*Kiss the Blood Off My Manuscript*?" said Nathan. He frowned. "I think it lacks a little punch."

"Excuse me for getting back onto the subject," said Winnifred, "but if the killer isn't Aristotle Draconis, who is it?"

"Right at the moment, it looks like a transplanted Transylvanian named Vlad Drachma."

"I've always had a strict rule," said Nathan. "Beware of Transylvanian vampires named Vlad."

The waiter stopped by the table just then. "May I take your orders, please?"

"Give the lady anything she wants," said Mallory. "The rest of us are just here to visit."

"*I'm* not," said Felina. "I want three parakeets, two mice, a guinea pig, a trout, four salamanders, a water buffalo, a whale, and some catnip."

"No dessert?" asked Mallory sarcastically.

"More catnip."

"She'll have a small glass of milk," Mallory told the waiter.

"And a straw," added Felina.

"And a straw," said Mallory.

"Made of hummingbird," said Felina.

"Quit while you're ahead," said Mallory. He turned to Winnifred. "Where did you park your trolls?"

"They're in the bar," she said. "They'd rather drink than eat."

"And they haven't even spoken to Felina yet," said Mallory. "Amazing."

"So have you any leads on this Vlad Drachma?" asked Winnifred.

"Not really," said Mallory. "We know he's a vampire, we know he was on the *Moribund Manatee*, we know he's the one who bit Rupert—or at least we think we know it. We know that Draconis actually chased him out of Rupert's room and was the kid's secret protector. And we know he's got to have a coffin filled with Transylvanian soil somewhere in Manhattan."

"Do you have a description of him?"

Mallory shook his head. "Just that he's a vampire."

"That's not much help," replied Winnifred. "Mr. McGuire here is a vampire, and he doesn't look a thing like vampires are *supposed* to look."

"I take that as a high compliment," said McGuire.

"So what's our next step, John Justin?" asked Winnifred. "We've got no description and it's a big city."

"Well, he probably thinks he's safe, since we don't know what he looks like and he's not aware that I've spoken to Draconis. He won't be looking out for us, so that's to our advantage."

"But we have no idea what he looks like, and that's to *his* advantage."

"Bats," said Mallory, turning to the little vampire, "where would a vampire go to celebrate?"

"Celebrate what?" asked McGuire. "Killing young Rupert or getting away with it?"

"Either."

"Well, the Zombies' Ball is probably in full swing by now. If you want to mingle with the undead—vampires, zombies, ghouls, whatever—that's the place to be."

"But we still don't know who we're looking for," protested Nathan.

"That's not so," replied Mallory. "We just don't know what he looks like."

"What's the difference?"

"If we try to describe him, none," said Mallory. "But if we start asking around for Vlad Drachma, maybe someone will point him out to us."

"To a shamus?" said Nathan dubiously.

"I won't tell them if you won't," said Mallory. "Of course no one will ID him for a detective, at least not unless we cross their palms with more silver than we can lay our hands on—but they might point him out to a guy who's selling the security codes to the blood bank over on West Hades Street."

The dragon considered it. "You know, they might at that." He smiled apologetically. "I'm so used to Wings O'Bannon just beating the information he needs out of cheap punks, or seducing it out of beautiful women . . ."

"Don't plain women ever have any information?" asked Winnifred.

"Plain women don't travel in the same circles as O'Bannon," explained Nathan. "After all, there are hallowed traditions to be upheld. I mean, you'd never write a romance in which the hero wasn't a wildly attractive vampire, or a horse race story in which the winner wasn't a long shot that everyone except a little girl and her grandpa wanted to sell or shoot as a yearling, or a fantasy novel that doesn't have a magic sword and goes less than two pounds . . ."

"Price?" asked Mallory.

"Weight," explained Nathan. "So, since all serious fiction is so rigidly defined, you can't really expect me to write a mystery where Wings takes a normal-looking woman to bed."

"Or fails to perform like a combination of Don Juan and Secretariat?" suggested Mallory.

"Precisely," replied the dragon. "After all, these books go to discriminating readers."

"Sorry," said Mallory. "Every now and then that truism escapes me."

"May we get back to the subject at hand?" suggested Winnifred.

"Hard-boiled mystery stories?" said Nathan as the waiter arrived with Felina's milk. The cat-girl threw the straw away, leaned over, and began lapping it up with her tongue.

"Vlad Drachma," replied Winnifred. "I suppose we should continue to split up and cover more ground, but we need a plan."

"It's only about half an hour past midnight," said Mallory. "That gives us maybe six or seven hours to find him before daylight. I suppose I'll start at the Zombies' Ball. You might get a list of mortuaries that'll board a coffin, so to speak—and you can skip Creepy Conrad's. We've been there."

"He could leave his coffin *anywhere*," protested Winnifred. "It doesn't have to be a mortuary. It could be an abandoned building, a rented house, anything."

"All right, then," said Mallory. "Why don't you see if you can trace his movements after he left the *Moribund Manatee*? I'll start hitting all the places a vampire might go for an evening's recreation."

"It makes sense," she said, as they all rose from the table. "Do you want my trolls? I don't think I'll need them."

Mallory looked at his little party—a dragon, a vampire, and a cat-girl. "I think I'll attract more than my share of attention without a crew of trolls. Keep 'em for protection."

"*I* protected *them* from a gang of muggers not an hour ago," said Winnifred.

"Sorry," said Mallory. "I lost my head."

"No," said Felina, finishing her milk. "That comes at the Zombies' Ball."

CHAPTER 16

12:39 AM–1:08 AM

The Zombies' Ball was held in the vast ballroom of the L. Gonquin Hotel, which, it was pointed out on signs and placards throughout the premises, had nothing to do with the Algonquin Hotel but was named after Lamont "High C" Gonquin, the first musician to plug his instrument into an electric socket. His charred remains were no longer on display but could be seen at the Museum of Screech and Shout, a subsidiary of the Museum of Rock and Roll.

Mallory and his party walked through the plush foyer of the hotel. There were dirt-covered men and women in tattered rags, mummies wrapped in bandages, pale men in capes, elves, leprechauns, goblins, gremlins, even the occasional normal-looking man or woman.

"I see an awful lot of different types here," said Mallory. "Are you sure we're in the right place?"

The strains of "The Second Time Around" came to their ears.

"We're in the right place," McGuire assured him. "That's their theme song."

They followed the music to its source and were soon in the ballroom, where they ran into even more nightmare creatures, most of them dancing, a few standing and chatting, a handful drinking at the makeshift bar at one end of the room.

"They're sure not sparing any expense," noted Nathan. "You see that band up there at the front of the room?"

"You know them?"

The dragon nodded his head. "That's Charlie the Harp and the Dead Enders."

"Never heard of them," replied Mallory.

"Their CD of 'The Graveyard Gavotte' went platinum last month," said Nathan.

Mallory took a good, hard look at the band. There were two zombies, a winged monster of some type, a dragon that looked like a distant relative of Nathan's, and a goblin, each playing an instrument Mallory had never seen or heard before. Leading them was a man with wild, unruly red hair and a pair of white feathered wings that stuck out through the back of his tuxedo.

The band finished its number, and then a small, dapper man stepped out, carrying a microphone. He had regular features, he was well dressed, he moved with a certain grace, and it was only after Mallory had been studying him for a moment that he realized that the small man's throat had been slit, though no blood was coming out of it. A few seconds later he saw the bullet hole just above the man's left eye.

"Thank you, Charlie," he said, "for starting off our ball in fine fashion." He turned to the audience. "I'm your host, Third Chance Louie, and I want to welcome you to the Zombies' Ball. We have an evening of very special entertainment in store for you. Three of the meeting rooms on the mezzanine level have been converted into a small theater, and in just thirty minutes you'll be able to see the first performance of *Rebirth of a Salesman*, which they tell me is even better than last year's world premiere of *Life Takes a Holiday*. We have lots of other treats in store for you as the night goes on, so enjoy yourselves and let's not let this evening die too soon. Charlie, why don't you and the boys put them in the mood with your wonderful rendition of 'The Termination Tango'?"

Charlie the Harp stamped his foot, waved his baton, cursed at it as it turned into a snake, slapped it on the side of its head, waited for it to hiss once and become a baton again, and began leading the Dead Enders in a tango that sounded more like a Brazilian dirge to Mallory.

"I think we'll get a lot more accomplished if we split up," suggested the detective.

"And do what?" asked McGuire.

"See if anyone knows where we can find Vlad Drachma."

"That could be dangerous," said McGuire. "You tell something like *that* that you're looking for him, and he just might decide to go looking for you instead."

"Let's hope so," said Mallory. "It'll save us a lot of work."

"I think I just resigned from the detective business," said McGuire. "I can't just walk up to these people and tell them my friend wants to jail Vlad Drachma and could they please tell me where he's hiding?"

"Let him come," said the dragon, hoisting his spear. "I'm ready for him."

"Put it down," said Mallory. "You're not going to hurt him with a spear."

"Will bullets hurt him?" asked Nathan.

"I very much doubt it."

"Then maybe McGuire has a point. We could just tell your partner that the young man died of heart failure, or maybe a social disease. I could write you such a brilliant speech that she'll never see through it, or my name isn't Scaly Jim Chandler."

"Your name *isn't* Scaly Jim Chandler, and I never lie to my partner," replied Mallory.

"All right, then," said Nathan. "I stand ready to battle him to the death."

"Whose?" asked McGuire.

"His, I hope," answered the dragon. "But if it's mine, at least I'll die in a noble cause."

"What's so noble about annoying a vampire when he wants to be left alone?" persisted McGuire.

"Whose side are you on, anyway?" snapped Nathan.

"Ours. But I have a unique ability to see the vampire's point of view."

"Cut it out, both of you," said Mallory. "You're not going to have to face Vlad Drachma. That's *my* job."

"It is?" said McGuire, his face brightening noticeably. "Then I'm back on the case."

"Fine. What I want you to do is pass the word that I'm looking for him."

"Right," said McGuire. "Tell him that a detective is looking for him in connection with a hideous murder."

"No," said Mallory, trying to control his temper. "You will tell anyone who'll listen that I'm a lawyer, that Drachma's inherited a lot of money and some real estate, and that I need to meet with him so that he can sign for it and I can turn it over to him."

"Who died?" asked McGuire.

Mallory simply stared at him.

"Oh, I see," said McGuire, who definitely did not see.

"All right," said Mallory. "Spread out." He turned to Felina. "Not you."

"But there's food on that table!" she protested.

"Later."

"All you ever say is Later," grumbled Felina.

"I'm a man of few words."

"And I know them all," protested the cat-girl. "They're 'Later' and 'No' and 'Stop' and 'Flyaway's running today.' That's not even true," she pouted. "Flyaway doesn't run. He plods."

"Surely I say something else from time to time."

"Just 'Look at the knockers on that Playmate,'" answered Felina.

"All right," said Mallory. "If we get you something to eat, will you stick around and keep quiet?"

"Probably."

"I guess you're going to go hungry."

"Yes," she amended.

"You're sure?"

"Almost." He stared at her silently. "Yes."

"Okay, let's go over and see what they've got."

There was a long table at the back of the room, with a punch bowl at each end of it. In between were little finger cakes, cookies, brownies, and other sweets.

"Where are the fish?" said Felina, frowning.

"What you see is what you get," said Mallory.

She leaned over and sniffed at a frosted devil's food cake. "There's nothing dead here."

"I promise you that cake isn't going to get up and walk away," said Mallory. "It's one of the deadest cakes I've seen."

Felina tapped a zombie on the shoulder. "Hey, Mister," she said, "where are the canaries?"

"The one who killed me is buried in about five different places," answered the zombie. "I can't speak for any of the others."

"I don't like this place," said Felina. "There's nothing to eat here."

"I wish I could help you," said the zombie. "But the only person I know here is my lawyer."

"What's a lawyer, and can you eat one?"

The zombie shook his head. "It'd take you forever to clean it first."

He wandered off, and when she turned back to Mallory, she saw the detective handing a five-dollar bill across the table to one of the servers on the other side and receiving a small box in exchange.

"What's that?" asked Felina.

"It's for you," said Mallory. "Animal crackers."

She sniffed at the box. "They're just cookies."

"True," he admitted. "But you can bite each of their heads off. That ought to keep you happy for a while."

She opened the box and pulled out a cookie shaped like an elephant, then bit off its head. She flashed Mallory a huge smile, and then proceeded to bite the heads off a lion, a zebra, and a rhinoceros.

"You'll behave yourself now?" said Mallory.

"These are *fun!*" said Felina, decapitating a gorilla.

"You didn't answer me."

"Yes, I did. You said, 'You'll behave yourself now?' and I said, 'These are fun.'"

"You didn't answer the question."

"That's not part of the rules," said Felina.

"It's part of *my* rules," said Mallory, taking the box back.

"Yes, I'll behave myself," said Felina.

"Well or badly?"

"One or the other."

"I didn't quite hear that," said Mallory, pulling the box back out of reach as she grabbed for it.

"Well," said Felina.

Mallory handed her the box. "Don't eat 'em all at once," said the detective.

"I won't," promised Felina. "I'll eat them one at a time, right after each other."

Mallory felt a heavy hand on his shoulder and turned to face its owner. He almost wished he hadn't.

Confronting him was a tall, burly man, though Mallory thought "men" might be more accurate, since he seemed to be composed of numerous disparate parts, each sewn together with the stitching still visible. He had one blue eye and one brown, one cauliflower ear and one small delicate one, a huge skull with a tiny chin, one arm longer than a basketball center's, the other shorter than a jockey's, and equally mismatched legs and feet. He was dressed all in black, with a turned-around collar.

"Good evening, friend," he said in a deep voice. "Billy-Bob Lazarus is the name—the Reverend Billy-Bob Lazarus, to be precise. You look to me like a man who longs to be born again."

"I haven't gotten over being born the first time yet," said Mallory.

Billy-Bob Lazarus threw back his head and laughed. "That's a good one!" The laughter stopped as suddenly as it had begun. "Now, friend, are you *sure* you don't have a secret driving desire to join my Born Again Brigade?"

"If I do, it's so secret it hasn't informed me yet," said Mallory.

"Would you like to discuss it?"

"My secret desire or your brigade?"

"Don't make light of being born again, friend. We all do it, each in our own way."

"Hard to argue that, given the crowd here," said Mallory. "But I'm afraid I'm not interested."

"Is there anything I can say to make you change your mind?" said Lazarus.

"Yeah, there is," said Mallory. "Tell me where I can find Vlad Drachma."

"Room 666 of this hotel," came the answer. "Now, how much would you like to contribute to our poor box?"

"He's right here at the Gonquin?"

"Damned if I know," said the Reverend. "Personally, I never heard of this Drachma before."

"But you just told me he was in this hotel," said Mallory irritably.

"You said you'd join my Born Again Brigade if I told you where to find him. You never said I had to be right."

"Go away."

"Hey, we have a deal!" protested Lazarus.

"I never said you had to be right. You never gave me a time frame. I'll join in another eighty-three years."

"I'll hold you to that," promised Lazarus, walking off to hunt up fresh blood. *Or*, thought Mallory, *exceptionally old, tired blood.*

Mallory began circulating through the room, passing himself off as a lawyer with an inheritance for Vlad Drachma, but no one knew the vampire in question, or at least no one was willing to admit to knowing him. He'd spent about twenty minutes when the music stopped and Third Chance Louie came out again, microphone in hand.

"Thank you, Charlie," he said. "That was just what the coroner ordered. Revelers, let's all give Charlie and his Dead Enders a hand."

Most of the revelers applauded politely. Three of them threw severed hands in the direction of the band, which bowed and walked off the stage.

"That's just the beginning, folks. Coming up in a few minutes, all the way from Bucharest, is the hottest band on the Continent, Igor and the Graverobbers." More applause. "But first, fresh from his record-breaking run at the Shady Glen Memorial Home, here's Morty Pickman, the funniest comic hanged!"

A pudgy zombie walked out, the remnants of a noose around his neck, wearing a tux that was a little too tight and a little too old, and took the microphone from Louie.

"Good evening, and thanks for that introduction, Louie," he said. "I used to be the funniest comic unhanged, until they caught me with my hand in the till . . . Well, it wasn't exactly my hand, and her full name was Tilly."

He waited for the audience to laugh. When it didn't, he waved Louie back onto the stage, handed him the microphone, and stalked off.

"Uh . . . Igor and the Graverobbers are still having a little refreshment out in the cemetery," said Louie, "so this might be a good time for our Fourth Annual Lee Harvey Oswald Look-Alike Contest. Would the contestants please step up here?"

Five *things* shambled out and stood shoulder to shoulder, facing the audience.

"But they're all moldering corpses!" said a voice Mallory recognized at Nathan's.

"Have you see Lee lately?" Louie shot back.

Mallory decided he'd seen enough of the contest, and he walked out into the lobby, followed by Felina. No sooner had he gotten there than he saw a lovely, dark-haired woman in a black evening gown, sitting on a chair, crying. She looked totally normal to him, the first normal person he'd seen since entering the hotel, and he walked over to her.

"I couldn't help noticing that you're crying," he said. "Is there anything I can do to help?"

"I doubt it," she said with what he took to be a Russian accent, tears still rolling down her face.

"Perhaps I could try, if you'd tell me what's wrong."

"It wouldn't help," she said. "Nothing helps."

"Why don't you tell me about it anyway?"

"My name is Natasha. I am Russian."

"I guessed as much."

"You guessed my name?"

"I guessed you were Russian."

"The crying," she said knowingly. "All Russians are morbid. All I want to do is die." She dabbed some tears away with a black handkerchief. "I take poison. I shoot myself. I jump off buildings. I run out in traffic. Nothing works. I am reduced to following Third Chance Louie and Igor and the Gravediggers and the others around, hoping whatever they have will rub off on me."

"You're saying that you're kind of a camp follower?" asked Mallory.

"Yes," said Natasha. "But it doesn't work. I am alive, and they want no part of me. Not even," she added confidentially, "the part men kill for." Tears began gushing out again.

Mallory had no idea how to respond. "I wish I could help you, ma'am," he said, "but—"

"No one can help me," she moaned. "Even Vlad Drachma could not bring me over to the Other Side, and if *he* couldn't . . ."

"Vlad Drachma?" demanded Mallory instantly. "What do you know about him?"

"I know he has his limitations," said Natasha. "He can kill dozens of men and women every day, but not only couldn't he break the skin on my neck, he couldn't even raise a hickey."

"When did you see him?" persisted Mallory. "Is he in the hotel?"

She shook her head. "I met him two hours ago. It was a brief affair. He gave up after half an hour."

"Where did you meet him?" said Mallory. "How did you know who he was?"

"If you just want to join the"—another sob—"undead, you don't have to go to the Gryphon's Roost. There must be twenty vampires in the ballroom who can accommodate you."

"The Gryphon's Roost?" repeated Mallory. "Is that where you met him? What is it?"

"A place for assignations."

"How did you know he'd be there?"

"Mary told me."

"Mary who?"

"The Roost is also a gambling den, and she's in charge of the slot machines. They call her Mary, Queen of Slots. She told me he's been showing up every night since he arrived in Manhattan."

"Where is it?"

"On Seventeenth Avenue, between Lust and Sloth."

"There isn't any Seventeenth Avenue," said Mallory.

"Yes there is," replied Natasha. "You just have to know how to find it."

"Thanks," said Mallory, starting to walk away.

"Mister?" she called after him.

"Yes?"

"If you see him, tell him I forgive him."

"I'll tell him," said Mallory, and silently added: *But I know two detectives who won't forgive him.*

He went back into the ballroom to collect Nathan and McGuire. Just as they were leaving, one of the revelers morphed into a huge wolf and began uttering a series of mournful howls.

"Boy, they'll let just *anyone* in here!" muttered a zombie, downing a drink that immediately ran out the eleven bullet holes in his chest.

"So you've got a lead?" asked Nathan eagerly.

"Yeah," said Mallory. "I met a woman who saw him just two hours ago."

"Can you trust her?" asked McGuire. "I mean, she belongs to *him* now."

"Not her," said Mallory. "She only wishes she did."

"I don't understand."

"It's a difficult story to believe, even in *this* Manhattan," said Mallory.

"So where are we going next?" asked Nathan.

"It could be a little problematical," said Mallory. "Do either of you know how to get to Seventeenth Avenue?"

"It sounds like it's under the river," said Nathan.

"Fifteenth Avenue I could probably find," added McGuire. "But Seventeeth?"

"I know where it is," said Felina.

"Why do I anticipate a negotiation?" said Mallory dryly.

"Two cockatoos and a killer whale," said the cat-girl.

"One hot dog from Greasy Gus's stand on the corner," countered Mallory.

"And a hippopotamus," said Felina.

"One hot dog."

"Wrapped in a bald eagle."

"One hot dog."

"Oh, all right," she sniffed. "But you're mean to me."

As if on cue, Igor and the Gravediggers began playing "Mean to Me," as Mallory and his unlikely team walked out past the "Many Happy Returns" placards and headed off toward Seventeeth Avenue.

It took Felina five minutes to choose between hot dogs—there were two of them, identical in every way as far as Mallory could tell—and another five minutes to lead them through winding streets the detective never knew existed to the tall building that housed the Gryphon's Roost on its top floor.

"Nathan," said Mallory, "I want you to stay down here and guard the door, just in case he's inside and makes a break for it."

"Only if you call me Scaly Jim."

"Sorry, Jim. My mistake." He looked at McGuire. "Bats, you might as well stay here too. If Drachma tries to get out, give Jim a hand. If he tries to get in, sprout your wings, fly up there, and give me a little warning."

"It's not that easy," said McGuire. "I have to get out of my clothes first, or I can't flap my wings." He grimaced. "The last time I did that, I was arrested for indecent exposure before I could make the change."

"Find a way," said Mallory. "Come on, Felina."

"Why are you taking *her*?" asked the little vampire.

"Because I've never found anything she's afraid of, except maybe missing a meal."

Mallory entered the building, held the door open for Felina, and the two of them walked to an elevator.

"Where to?" asked the uniformed operator.

"Up," said Mallory, looking at him as if he were a few bricks shy of a load.

"Let me rephrase that. What floor?"

"The one with the Gryphon's Roost."

The elevator shot up, forcing a startled grunt from the detective. Felina just grinned and purred. "I like elevators," she confided.

"I can't imagine why," said Mallory. "You can't eat them."

"Sixty-sixth floor—the Gryphon's Roost," announced the elevator operator as the doors slid open.

Mallory and Felina emerged into a large foyer, paneled with dark wood. To their left was a bar, to their right a casino. Mallory went to the casino, followed by the cat-girl. A large fat man with a bushy mustache had pushed all his chips to the center of a craps table. "Ah, what the hell," he said. "I feel lucky." He then proceeded to add his diamond ring, his Swiss watch, and his ruby tiepin to the pot.

"I'll match that," said a sullen-voiced green-skinned ogre standing at the foot of the table.

"I'm not done," said the man, starting to climb out of his clothes. As he removed each item, he folded it neatly and placed it next to his pile of chips. The ogre studied the clothes, then pulled out a five-hundred-dollar bill and added it to the pot. The now thoroughly naked man picked up the dice and began shaking them above his head. "Baby needs a new pair of shoes!" he cried.

"Shoes are going to be the least of baby's needs if it comes up snake eyes," noted Mallory.

The man rolled the dice. They immediately vanished under his pile of clothes. He raced around the table, pulled up a shirtsleeve, and announced that he'd hit a seven and was the winner.

"Let me see that!" said the ogre, walking to the side of the table.

"Too late!" said the man, picking up the dice.

"*How* late?" said the ogre in a thundering voice, as his body began expanding. Suddenly he was fifteen feet tall and staring down at the naked fat man.

"I believe it's just after one o'clock, sir," said the fat man meekly. "I'll tell you what: Why don't I just roll the dice again?"

"I'll tell *you* what," said the ogre. "Why don't you tell me what you really rolled?"

"Twenty-seven, sir," said the fat man.

"They only go up to twelve."

"I'm seeing spots before my eyes. It must be the height. Why don't we just call the game off? I'll take my clothes and money and go home, and the table's all yours."

"You can go," said the ogre.

"Thank you, sir," said the fat man. He reached out for his pants and the ogre slapped his hand away.

"I said *you* can go. Everything else stays here."

"At least let me take my shorts. It's chilly out there."

"You can have one sock," said the ogre. "I wouldn't want it said that you went home with nothing."

The fat man seemed about to argue, then sighed, grabbed a sock, and made a beeline for the elevator.

"What are *you* staring at?" said the ogre to Mallory.

"I was just wondering why someone hasn't signed you up as a power forward," answered the detective.

"Why should they?" asked the ogre, suddenly shrinking back down to six feet in height.

"Beats the hell out of me," said Mallory. "Forget I asked."

"You here to shoot craps?" asked the ogre.

"No. I don't even carry a gun."

"A comedian," snorted the ogre, suddenly losing all interest in Mallory.

The detective looked around the casino. There were poker and roulette tables, plus some games he'd never seen before that seemed to draw their share of elves and goblins. Finally he saw a pretty woman in her late twenties or early thirties emptying a slot machine. She had long dark hair, a nice but not exceptional figure, and she wore a lavender pants suit. Mallory walked over to her.

"Yes?" she said, staring at him.

"Excuse me, but are you Mary, Queen of Slots?"

"That's me."

"Good. My name is Mallory. A friend of yours told me you might be able to help me."

"If you want a loan, go to a bank."

"I want information," he said. "A woman named Natasha said you might be able to tell me something about Vlad Drachma."

She stared at him. "You a cop?"

"No, I'm private."

"You working for Natasha?"

He shook his head. "No, she just told me that he hangs out here."

She nodded. "Every night."

"What can you tell me about him?" asked Mallory.

"He's one of the undead."

"What *else?*"

"He's old," she said. "*Very* old."

"Can you be a little more specific?" said Mallory. "Fifty? Sixty? Seventy?"

"Try a few thousand," she replied.

Mallory frowned. "How does he get around?"

"He's manages," said Mary. "There's just something about him that says you shouldn't mess with him."

"What does he look like?"

"It varies. If he hasn't eaten . . . well, drunk . . . he looks like a dried-up old man of ninety, but he's still got that air about him."

"And when he *has* drunk?"

She shrugged. "He's still old, but a few of the wrinkles are gone, and his color's a little better. He could pass for seventy."

"Does he bring his dates here, or pick them up here?"

"He always comes in alone," said Mary. "Sometimes he's alone for the whole time. Sometimes someone—usually a woman, but not always—will walk over to his table and visit with him. He doesn't ever invite anyone, but they seem, I don't know, *attracted* to him."

"Hey, Mister!" called a voice from the bar. "If you can't control your cat, the both of you are gonna have to leave."

"Excuse me," said Mallory to Mary. He turned, walked out of the casino, and entered the bar. The bartender, a balding, burly man, merely pointed at the ceiling. Mallory looked up and saw Felina perched on a crystal chandelier.

"Felina," he said, "come down from there."

"I like it up here," she said, shifting her weight and making the chandelier sway. "Listen to it jingle."

"*Now!*" said the detective firmly.

"You never let me have any fun," she pouted.

Mallory turned to the bartender. "Can you make a brandy alexander?"

"Yeah. Why?"

"She'll have one without the alcohol."

"That's just cream," said the bartender.

"Right."

The bartender shrugged, reached behind the bar, pulled out a glass, and filled it with cream. Mallory set it on the bar.

"Come down in the next five seconds and you can have it," he said, gesturing to the cream.

Felina leaped into the air, did a triple somersault, and landed lightly on the bar right next to the glass, which she picked up and began lapping.

"No animals on the bar," said the bartender.

She hissed at him, but jumped to the floor before Mallory could take the cream away.

"Sorry for the inconvenience," said Mallory, slipping the bartender a bill. "Keep the cream coming and she'll behave." The bartender pocketed the money. "As long as I'm here, maybe you can tell me a little about one of your customers."

"Who?"

"Vlad Drachma."

"He's a strange one, that old guy," said the bartender. "Looks like a strong wind could blow him over. But one night a bunch of trolls came here after a bowling tournament—I think they were using gremlins as the pins—and somehow or other one of them challenged him to an arm-wrestling match. I thought the troll would bust his arm in half in less than a second, but damned if he didn't win, and then beat every other creature in the house." The bartender shook his head in wonderment. "Strange old guy."

"How long has he been coming here?" asked Mallory.

"Just a few days, but we're his regular place now." He pointed toward an empty booth. "That's his."

"You mean that's where he usually sits?"

"That's his for the next year. He put five thousand dollars down to rent it. It's reserved for him, and no one else can use it. That's what I mean when I said we're his regular joint."

"What does he order to eat or drink when he's here?"

"Nothing. He just sits there with a glass of water. Far as I know, he's never taken a sip."

"What does he talk about?"

"It varies. He knows a little something about everything, but nothing seems to interest him. Strange old guy. Looks harmless enough, but there's something about him, something that says no matter who you are, no matter how tough, you'd better not mess with him. Probably he's made up in wisdom what he's lost in vigor. You don't live to be as old as him without being pretty damned sharp."

"Any chance he'll be back tonight?" asked Mallory.

The bartender shook his head. "He was already here earlier tonight. He doesn't show up twice in the same night."

"Thanks," said Mallory. He walked over to Drachma's booth. "Felina, stop playing with your cream and come over here."

The cat-girl turned her back to him.

"If I have to come get you, I'll pour the rest of it out."

She walked over to him with a sullen expression on her face and a death grip on her glass.

"No one's sat here since Vlad, right?" said Mallory to the bartender.

"Right."

"Felina, crawl around on the booth and see if you can get the scent of the man who was here last."

"I don't have to," replied the cat-girl. "I can smell him from here. He's very old."

"You'd recognize that scent if we find it again?"

"Yes."

"And if we pick up his trail, could you follow it?"

"If you bought me two sparrows, a dove, and a buffalo."

"We'll negotiate later. But you can identify his scent, and if you find it again you can definitely follow it?"

"Yes."

"Let's put you to work right now. Can you follow it to the elevator?"

She took a few steps toward the elevator, then stopped. "He didn't go this way."

"Is there a set of fire stairs around here?" Mallory asked the bartender, who pointed to an Exit sign just past the foyer. "How about there?" asked Mallory, pointing the way to Felina.

As before, she took a couple of steps and stopped. "He didn't go this way either."

"I think I'm going about this ass-backward," said Mallory. "Why don't you follow his scent and tell me how he got out of here?"

She sniffed the air a few times, then walked toward an open window. "This way," she said.

"The son of a bitch *flew* here!" said Mallory. "Damn. So much for following his trail."

He walked back to the casino and approached Mary, Queen of Slots.

"Does he have any other hangouts that you know about?" he asked.

She shook her head. "He's been in the country less than a week," she said. "How many could he have found?"

"Has he ever mentioned a particular mortuary?"

"No."

"Damn," muttered the detective. "There must be dozens in town. I guess I'll have to do it the hard way."

"Not necessarily," said Mary.

"Oh?"

"It's possible that there's another way to go about this," she said.

"I'm willing to learn," replied Mallory. "Enlighten me."

"You're wondering where a dead thing goes," said Mary.

"Right."

"But that's only part of his character," she continued. "It's true that he's one of the undead. But he's more than that." Mallory frowned, trying to follow her line of reasoning. "I saw you just dope it out over in the bar. He's also a bat—and where would a bat go to relax and hang out?"

"To a zoo?" asked Mallory, sure he was wrong and feeling rather foolish.

"Some detective!" she snorted. "You live in Manhattan, don't you? Now *think*."

"Of course!" exclaimed Mallory. "The Battery!"

They caught a bus that took them south. Mallory sat down on a seat with a torn cushion. Felina stood on the adjacent seat, studying the pornographic graffiti with a mystified expression on her catlike face. Nathan, whose wings prevented him from sitting, stood stoically on one foot, leaning on his spear.

"You look like you're going to fall over, Scaly Jim," offered McGuire, who was seated across the aisle from Mallory.

"I saw this in a book," answered the dragon. "The Maasai do it all the time."

"Must be an obscure book," said McGuire. "This is the first I've seen of it."

"You ought to read more about the Maasai. They were drinking blood long before Aristotle Draconis was born."

"But not before Vlad Drachma, if we're to believe what we're told," shot back the little vampire.

"Do you?" persisted Nathan. "Believe it, I mean?"

"Absolutely. As old as the hills are, he's older."

"You sound terrified of him."

"I am."

"Then why are you still with us?" asked the dragon.

"I just *hate* questions like that," muttered McGuire.

"He's here because he said he'd help," interjected Mallory, "and he's a man of his word."

"But is he a bat of his word?" asked Nathan.

"So far."

Nathan shrugged, and his posture made it clear that he didn't have much use for *any* vampire, even undersized balding ones.

The bus slowed down, caught in traffic. Cars started honking, which didn't make the traffic any faster but did make it appreciably louder.

"Where the hell do they all come from?" muttered Mallory. "There's eight zillion cars out tonight, and I don't know a single New Yorker who drives."

The bus made slow headway, but after another few minutes it let them off in the Battery, the area at the southern end of Manhattan where the city was first settled.

"Maybe this wasn't the greatest idea in the world," said Mallory. "We could do a house-to-house search and not finish by Memorial Day."

"I smell him," said Felina.

"Where?" asked Mallory, suddenly alert.

She pointed to her left. "That way."

"That's Battery Park," said Nathan.

"Figures," said Mallory. "Let's go. Felina, don't get too far ahead of us. This is a dangerous customer."

"It makes sense," said McGuire thoughtfully.

"What does?" asked the dragon.

"Battery Park," replied McGuire. "The Battery itself is filled with apartments and offices, but no one enters the park at night. Well, no one but bats and a few small animals," he amended.

"That doesn't make as much sense as you think," said Mallory.

"Why not?" asked McGuire, puzzled.

"I thought he had to have his native soil. He's not going to find it in a New York park, and I doubt that he's parked his coffin here."

McGuire shook his head. "He won't be sleeping here. Don't forget—he sleeps by day."

"Okay, what *is* he doing here?" asked Mallory.

"Luring victims, having romantic assignations with your kind or mine, or maybe just relaxing among his own species."

"But by dawn he's got to be back in his coffin?"

"Well, in his soil," answered McGuire. "The coffin's just a container, so to speak."

"Wings O'Bannon wouldn't depend on a cat creature to track his prey," offered Nathan. "He'd roust a couple of vampires out of their nests and beat the information out of them."

"Would he, now?" said Mallory.

"That's what hard-boiled private dicks do."

"Even when they're surrounded by hundreds, maybe thousands, of the vampire's bloodsucking friends who know that the cops never go into the park at night?"

"What makes you think they never go into the park at night?" asked Nathan.

"We're in the park," said Mallory. "You see any cops?"

"Well, now that you mention it . . ." said Nathan. He frowned. "We're at a dead end, with no one to question."

"That's your considered opinion?" asked Mallory.

"Yes."

"I'm surprised your last book sold as many as six hundred copies."

"What other options are there?" asked the dragon.

"Felina can keep following Vlad Drachma's scent until we catch up with him. We can interview some of the residents of the park; you'd be surprised how reliable their information can be, especially if you cross their palms with money instead of kicking the shit out of them. We can hunt for Drachma's coffin."

"It won't be here."

"I agree," said Mallory. "But there are half a dozen freighters at the dock over there." He gestured to the pier that seemed to terminate just short of the park.

"Well, yes," agreed the dragon, "I suppose you *could* try all those things. They just don't occur to hard-boiled men of action."

"That's probably why so few of them live past thirty," replied Mallory. "How big is this damned park, I wonder?"

"I'd say about twenty-one acres," answered McGuire.

"That looks about right," agreed Mallory.

"It should," said the little vampire. "I read it in a guide book."

As they walked deeper into the park, Mallory was able to see that there were thousands, possibly even millions, of bats sleeping in the trees. Most were small, normal-looking animals, but a few were quite large, and he decided that they must be vampires.

They came to an all-night lemonade stand, run by two goblins, who for some reason seemed to have more economic get-up-and-go than any other species, including Man.

"Get your lemonade here! Only six dollars a cup!"

"That seems a little high for a paper cup of lemonade," said Mallory.

"You find anyone selling it for three bucks a cup, we'll lower our prices. This is a seller's market, chum!"

"Of course no one's undercutting you," said Mallory. "It's October. No one else is crazy enough to sell an iced drink."

"See?" said one of the goblins. "If you want an ice-cold lemonade, you have to come to us."

"But I don't want one," said Mallory. "It's so cold I can see my breath."

The other goblin pulled out a pair of glasses. "Polarized lenses!" he exclaimed. "You can see right through your frigid breath with them."

"Fine, but I still don't want a lemonade."

"How about iced tea with lemon?" said the first goblin. "Of course you'll have to imagine the tea."

"Forget it," said Mallory. "How about helping me with what *I* want?"

"This ain't a good year for radical ideas . . ." said the first goblin dubiously.

"Still, it can't hurt to listen," said the second. "Especially since we're stuck here with seventeen barrels of lemonade that nobody wants."

"I'm looking for a vampire," said Mallory.

"You've come to the right place!" said the first goblin enthusiastically. "I can introduce you to a nineteen-year-old: beautiful body, perfect teeth, hardly digs her nails in at all when she holds your hand."

"You talking about Vera?" asked his companion.

"Right. What a honey!"

"Vera Cruz is fifteen."

"Well, she's a *mature* fifteen," said the first goblin to Mallory. "What do you say, pal?"

"I say I know who I'm looking for."

"Then why are you asking us for an unforgettable night of sin with an underage vampire girl?"

"Beats the hell out of me," said Mallory. "How about helping me find the one I'm looking for instead?"

"Well, it's not as much fun, but what the hell, who is it?" said the first goblin.

"A vampire named Vlad Drachma."

"That sounds like a man's name."

"It is."

"We don't keep track of that," said the goblin. "You want a specialist."

"A specialist in *what*?" asked Mallory.

"In male bats." He put two fingers in his mouth and emitted a whistle that was so high-pitched Mallory was sure the fillings were about to fall out of his teeth.

"Hey, have a little consideration," growled something that was neither man nor bat. "Some of us are trying to sleep here."

"Some of you are too cheap to rent a room," shot back the goblin.

"We don't *all* trade in nine-year-old girls," said the voice. "Some of us have legitimate professions."

"Yeah, you field-test benches in the park every night," said the goblin.

The voice uttered a curse and Mallory could hear a heavy body getting to its feet and stalking off.

"What the hell was that?"

"Billy Bitchum."

"Billy Bitchum?" repeated Mallory. "Didn't he used to be a gossip columnist a few years back?"

"Yeah."

"So what happened to him?"

"All the dirt he imbibed turned him into *that*," said the goblin, pointing toward a not-quite-human figure shambling off across the park. "After a while all the slime he spread made his paper so slippery no one could hold it. It kept sliding out of their hands. So he lost his job. Of course, he tried to borrow money, but he'd slandered every person he knew, and no one would give him a penny, not even to move to another continent. So he wound up here, sleeping on a different bench every night. When he's hit every bench, I suppose he'll move on to Grammercy Park."

"Why can't he just choose one and stay put?" asked Mallory.

"Slides right off by morning," answered the goblin. "He may not write anymore, but once a slimeball, always a slimeball." He paused. "Are you sure I can't sell you a pack of nicotine-free cigarettes?"

"Have they finally made one that's really nicotine-free?"

"*These* are," said the goblin. He handed one to Mallory, who stared at it and frowned.

"This is just the paper," said the detective. "There's nothing inside it."

"See?" said the goblin. "One hundred percent nicotine-free."

"It's one hundred percent tobacco-free."

"Right. Not a single carcinogen in the pack."

Just then a small man, his arms morphed into wings, walked up. He was wearing a colorful flowing satin shirt, a brocaded vest, skintight pants, and pink ballet shoes. His nose seemed to want to extend well beyond his face, and the tip of it was almost black.

"It took you long enough to get here," said one of the goblins. "Didn't you hear me whistle?"

"You know it takes me time to make myself presentable," said the man. "I'm here now, so what do you want?"

"This fellow here"—the goblin indicated Mallory—"has some questions for you."

"I'm five foot eight, I don't each sushi, and I adore Xavier Cugat," said the man.

"Those weren't my questions," said Mallory. "You got a name?"

"Raoul."

"Hello, Raoul. I'm looking for a vampire who goes by the name of Vlad Drachma. You know anything about him?"

"Does he dance? Is he a Johnny Mathis fan? Does he mix blood with his latte?"

"I don't know."

"Is he a fruit bat at all?"

"I don't know. He comes from Transylvania, if that helps."

"Is that anywhere near Guadalajara?"

"Nine, ten thousand miles," said Mallory.

"Why would *I* know anything about him?" said Raoul. "Not all vampires speak with accents and sleep in dirt, you know. I come from Ecuador. I only sip the blood of sweet young things—don't ask—and I sleep in a casket of ripe avocados while playing Charo's recording of 'Perfidia' on my Walkman."

"Sorry to have bothered you," said Mallory.

"That's all right," replied Raoul. "I'm used to it." He winked at Mallory. "Lose the three weirdos and we'll talk."

He wandered off, humming to himself.

"Care for a dozen long-stemmed roses?" asked one of the goblins. He held them up and studied them. "Well, three long-stemmed and nine short-stemmed ones. They'll pave the way to the little fruit bat's heart."

"At least the little fruit bat was honest with me," said Mallory.

"And are you any closer to finding your vampire?" shot back the goblin. "So much for honesty, which, along with sexual abstinence and betting on claimers who are moving up in class, is a greatly overrated virtue."

"If you're so smart, what are you doing selling lemonade at 1:30 AM on a chilly November morning?" said Nathan irritably.

"Well, we're smarter than a dragon who's walking around that same park at 1:30 AM with nothing to eat or drink."

Mallory suddenly realized that Felina was no longer standing next to him. He looked around and finally spotted her on the limb of a nearby tree, a dozen feet above the ground.

"Felina, what the hell are you doing up there?"

"*He* was up here," she replied.

"You're sure?"

She nodded. "He jumped."

"He's got the body of a ninety-year-old man," said Mallory. "He must have turned into a bat and flown."

She shook her head. "If he had, his shoes would still be on the grass."

Mallory frowned. "Are you trying to tell me this ancient guy actually *jumped* up there?"

Felina nodded and smiled. "It's not very hard at all."

"Jumping?"

"No, telling you."

"What did he do when he left the branch?"

"I don't know yet. I'll find out if you like."

"Yes, I would," said Mallory.

"For a goldfish."

"Okay."

"And a snail."

"Don't push it."

"And three zebras and a great white shark."

"Enjoy your tree," said Mallory. "We're out of here."

"Half a goldfish!" yelled Felina.

"Good-bye."

Suddenly Felina hurled herself through the air and landed on Mallory's back, sending him sprawling. "I'll protect you, John Justin!" she cried.

Mallory turned his head just in time to see Felina's jaws clamp down on the last mosquito of the season, which was simply flying by, minding its own business.

"Where would you be without me, John Justin?" she asked proudly.

"On my feet," muttered the detective.

"That was a killer mosquito," she continued, "doubtless infected with hepititamus. I saved your life, John Justin." She began purring. "Skritch my back."

"Do you two do this very often?" asked Nathan.

"Only when she's awake," said Mallory.

"I wasn't making fun of you," the dragon assured him. "But I think Wings O'Bannon needs a sidekick, and the cat thing not only provides you with an expert tracker who can see in the dark, but she's great comic relief."

"Hilarious," said Mallory grimly, pulling himself painfully to his feet.

"Hey," said McGuire, "I see an old friend!" The little vampire began waving his hands above his head. "Hey, Bubba! Over here! It's Bats!"

A large man with broad shoulders, a narrow waist, and the grace of an athlete began approaching them, a big smile on his face.

"Bats, you little bastard!" he called out. "How the hell are you?"

"Never better!" said McGuire. "Well, actually I've been better lots of times, but I'm kind of okay. Come on over. I have some friends I want you to meet. This is Scaly Jim Chandler, a mystery writer. This is Felina, a cat creature. And this is my pal John Justin Mallory, the world-famous detective."

"Provided that the world doesn't extend more than ten feet in any direction from my office," said Mallory, extending his hand.

"Pleased to meet you," said Bubba. "And I'm Bubba Preston."

"Didn't you used to be a fullback for the Mashers?" asked Nathan.

"Yeah," confirmed Bubba. "I was on my way to a thousand-yard season. I still remember the day everything changed. I was carrying the ball on what we called a forty-seven-spread-pound-right. I picked up about five yards, and then the Green Devils nailed me, and eight of 'em must have piled on me. Then I felt one of 'em sinking his teeth into my calf. Wasn't anything unusual; things like that happen on the bottoms of piles all the time. But as it turns out, I was bit by Jason Grim, and we all know what happened to him."

"Not quite all of us," said Mallory.

"They suspended him for a year for biting some guy in a night club. He decided he couldn't live without football, so he figured he'd end it all, and he jumped off the top of the Vampire State Building—but he didn't land. By the time he passed the fortieth floor, he'd shrunk out of his clothes and sprouted wings, and finally the press knew *why* he was always biting everyone. He must have cost eight or nine of us our jobs, because the league passed a new rule that each team could only have three vampires on its roster, and I was making more than three of the other guys he bit, so I was the one who had to go. They say it was a salary-cap move, and I said it was anti-vampire bigotry. The commissioner has turned down my application for reinstatement three times now."

"Gonna try again?" asked McGuire.

"Sure. Football's my life. But this time I have a new strategy. I'm tired of telling him how sorry I am and how much I want to play. This time I'm just going to tell him that I think he's got a really tasty-looking daughter." Bubba grinned. "If *that* doesn't do the trick, maybe I *will* find out just how good she tastes."

"Do you mind if we have lunch one day this week?" asked Nathan eagerly. "And can I bring a tape recorder along? I find your story fascinating. I think it'd make a great chapter in my next Wings O'Bannon book."

"Fine with me," said Bubba. "As long as you don't mind having lunch at three in the morning. I don't go out much in the daytime. These days I burn kind of easy."

"It's a deal," said Nathan.

"So what are you doing out here, Bats?" asked Bubba. "Are they . . . ah . . . *converts?*"

"No," said McGuire. "We're looking for someone, and we have reason to believe he's been here recently."

"Maybe I can help. What's his name?"

"Vlad Drachma," answered Mallory.

"Watch out for him," said Bubba, his expression suddenly apprehensive. "You don't want to mess with him."

"It's hard to imagine *you* being afraid of anything," said McGuire.

"He's just . . . *strange*," said Bubba. "Even other vampires don't want to cross him."

"Do you have any idea where he is now?" asked Mallory.

Bubba shook his head. "He never stays anywhere more than an hour or so. I think it's how he got to be so old. Never presents a stationary target."

"But he's got to come to rest at sunrise, doesn't he?" persisted the detective.

"What's the population of this island?" asked Bubba. "Seven million? Eight? And an equal number of offices and other rooms? The guy's got maybe sixteen million hiding places. How are you going to find him?"

"With brilliant detective work and deductive reasoning," Nathan chimed in. "That's why he's got the creator of Wings O'Bannon along for counsel and advice."

"He killed my partner's nephew," said Mallory. "I've *got* to find him, dangerous or not. Have you got any suggestions at all?"

"You absolutely insist on finding him?"

"Yeah."

"Okay," said Bubba. "The best advice I've got for you is: Get help."

"I've got a dragon, a cat-girl—"

"You need *real* help, Mallory," said the vampire, "not some hodgepodge made-up crew."

"Okay, who do I need?"

"The Wall Street Five, obviously."

"Do they work for the cops?"

Bubba chuckled. "They *own* the cops. Trust me, shamus—if you want a little protection when you finally go up against Vlad, you want the Wall Street Five."

"Where can I find them?"

"The Stock Exchange."

"They have offices there?"

"They own it."

"You got some names and numbers? This probably can't wait until daylight."

"They live there around the clock."

"In the Stock Exchange?" said Mallory dubiously.

"When you meet them it'll make sense to you," Bubba assured him. He looked off to his left. "Ah! Here come my dates."

A pair of very sexy girls in their twenties approached. It was only when the moonlight glinted off their teeth that Mallory could see that they, too, had highly developed canines.

"Mabel and Maxine, say hello to Mr. Mallory and my old friend Bats McGuire." The girls gave each a smile that started out charming and, once their teeth were exposed, ended up chilling. "And this here is Jack Chandelier, the mystery writer."

"Scaly Jim Chandler," the dragon corrected him.

"And I don't know what that thing up in the tree is, but she came with them."

"I'm looking for owls," said Felina from her perch ten feet above the ground.

"So you definitely don't know where Drachma is," persisted Mallory.

"I don't know, and I don't *want* to know," said Bubba. "And neither should you."

"Which way to Wall Street?" asked Mallory. "I'm all turned around."

"See that little kid with the saxophone?" said Bubba, pointing to a small boy who suddenly appeared about two hundred feet away. "Comes here every night, because his parents and neighbors won't let him practice at home. I hope he turns out to be good; I hate to see that much love and dedication go to waste."

"I'm surprised you haven't taken a bite out of him," said Mallory.

"Listen, shamus, there are enough bad eggs in the world; I don't need to crack any pasteurized ones."

"Well said," replied the detective. "We'd better be going. Thanks for the info."

"Smartest thing you could do is forget it," said Bubba. "Come on, girls. Let's go out for a snack."

They giggled and joined him as he walked off toward the buildings on the west side of the park.

"I thought vampires were afraid of cat people," said Mallory.

"Most of us are," answered McGuire. "But Bubba's a pro football player. All he's afraid of are fumbles and penalties."

"Felina, take a sniff and tell me which way he went," said Mallory.

She sniffed the air, jumped lightly to the ground, and walked in a broad circle, sniffing. "He flew away."

"He seems to change back and forth a lot," noted Mallory. "Bats, is that normal?"

"He's three thousand years old," answered McGuire. "Who knows what's normal for someone who's been a vampire that long?"

"I hope Winnifred is having better luck," said Mallory. "Let's go."

"Where?" asked Nathan.

"The Stock Exchange. Unless you think Bubba was lying to us?"

"No, he never lies."

"Then that's where we're going."

He started off, paused to stick a dollar bill in the boy's saxophone, then made a semicircle around a thick stand of bushes and came to a young woman who was leaning against a tree, weeping softly.

"Are you all right?" asked Mallory solicitously.

"I'm fine," she said, tears streaming down her face.

"What's the problem?"

"Ewen."

"Me?"

"No. I'm in love with Ewen." She exposed her neck, which had a series of bite marks on it. "I let him *convert* me to prove my love. We were going to be together for all eternity. I was meeting him here tonight—and he hasn't shown up! Now I'm all alone, *and* undead!"

She began crying again. Mallory felt totally helpless, and after making a few soothing noises, he began walking again.

They'd gone a quarter mile when they came to a small, gnarly man standing out in the open.

"Good evening, gentlemen," he said. "And kind-of lady. Lovely night, isn't it?"

"Beautiful," said Mallory warily.

"Still, it may not always be that way. Could rain, you know."

"What are you selling?" asked Mallory. "Umbrellas?"

"Protection," answered the man. "Anyone can insure your house or your car. But who can insure you against a rain of toads, or a spaceship from Sirius VII plunging into your house?"

"Let me guess," said Mallory.

"No need to guess," said the man. "Dimitrios the Disaster Agent at your service. No risk too small, no premium too large—or did I mean that the other way around? No matter. Here I am, your friend and savior."

"We're on the trail of a vampire," said Nathan.

"My specialty!" exclaimed Dimitrios.

"What'll you charge to insure us if we catch up with Vlad Drachma?"

"Did you say Vlad Drachma?" repeated Dimitrios.

"That's right."

"Nice knowing you gents," he said, shambling away. "Be sure to give him my regards. Just don't tell him my name."

Then he was out of sight.

"Guy's got a bit of a reputation," noted Mallory.

"Dimitrios?" replied McGuire. "I never heard of him before."

"Vlad," said the detective.

"I wonder if we *could* buy protection?"

"Not unless you're as rich as the men we're on our way to see," said Mallory.

They circled another bush and bumped into a distraught young man in a tie and tails.

"I'm sorry," he said. "I'm so upset I'm just not paying attention. I hope I didn't harm anyone."

"No."

"It's just not fair!" he said. "Nobody should be this miserable!"

"What's the matter?" said Mallory.

"I shouldn't burden you with my problems."

"My job is solving problems. Maybe I can help."

"No one can help. She's gone, and I'll never find her again."

"Who's gone?"

"The woman I was going to spend the rest of my life with." He exposed his fangs. "And that figures to be a *long* time. Now I'll have to spend it alone." He shook his head miserably. "She swore she'd wait for me right by the purple chrysanthemums in the park. What did I do to drive her away?"

"Would your name happen to be Ewen?" asked Mallory.

"How did you know?" asked the young man sharply.

"Oh, I know a lot of things," said Mallory. "For example, I know that you're standing next to a bed of purple asters."

"Purple asters?" repeated Ewen.

"Yeah. And I know there's a very worried young lady standing next to some purple chrysanthemums about a quarter of a mile in that direction," he added, pointing.

"I don't know how to thank you!" said Ewen, impulsively kissing Mallory on each cheek and resisting the impulse to take a little bite out of his neck. "You've saved my life. If I can ever return the favor, you've only to ask."

As he began running toward the girl and the chrysanthemums, Mallory said under his breath, "That might be sooner than you think."

Within five more minutes he and his team had reached the edge of the park and headed toward Wall Street.

CHAPTER 19

1:49 AM–2:01 AM

"The Stock Exchange," announced Nathan as they came within sight of it. "Now the plot begins to thicken."

"It wasn't thick enough for you already?" asked Mallory. "We've spent half of All Hallows' Eve looking for a vampire none of us has ever seen, and if we're lucky enough to find him, he's probably twenty times stronger than all of us put together."

"You don't understand how these cases work," explained the dragon patiently. "They have an ebb and flow to them."

"As long as it's not my blood that's flowing . . ." replied the detective.

"I'm trying to think of what Wings O'Bannon would do in this situation."

"From what you've told me, he'd probably seduce half the contestants in the Miss Nude Manhattan Contest while thinking of his next move."

"I take umbrage at that remark!" said Nathan.

"Do you deny it?"

"No, but I take umbrage."

"Don't take it too far," said Mallory. "We're almost there."

"I've been here before," said Felina, twitching her nostrils.

"I know," said Mallory. "If we're lucky, they won't remember."

"What did she do?" asked McGuire.

"It's a long story."

(Publisher's note: but a good one. Read about it in *Stalking the Unicorn*, available from Pyr Books.)

They stopped in front of the main entrance to the Exchange.

"Oh, boy—the intrigue that goes on here could fill half a dozen books!" said Nathan enthusiastically.

"And at least two thousand jail cells," added Mallory.

"So what's our next move?" asked the dragon. "Case the joint? Talk to one of our snitches?"

"We don't have any snitches," said Mallory, "and we don't have to case the American Stock Exchange. We'll just enter it."

"Just like that?" said Nathan dubiously.

"They've been watching us since we got here," said Mallory. "Third floor, sixth window on the left. If they don't want us to come in, the door will be locked." He turned to the cat-girl. "Felina, climb those stairs there and see if the door opens."

She soon reached the door, and before she could touch it, it swung inward.

"I guess that means they don't mind visitors," said Mallory. "Felina, do you smell the vampire here?"

The cat-girl sniffed the air and shook her head.

"Then it should be relatively safe," said Mallory. "Let's go."

He entered the building and found himself in the Grand Foyer. He waited for the other three to join him, then looked around. To his left was the floor of the Exchange itself, to his right a series of conference and media rooms.

"They seem to have pulled all the guards," remarked Nathan.

"You think so, do you?" asked Mallory.

"Yes, I do," said Nathan. "I mean, look at all the expensive electronic equipment on the Exchange floor. Tens of millions of dollars' worth. Only a fool would leave them unguarded."

"Unless there's something even more valuable to guard," said the detective.

"Are you just killing time, or did you have some point to make?" asked McGuire.

"Those things in the next room are just machines," said Mallory. "They break, you fix 'em or you build new ones. They compute, but they don't *think*." He paused. "But those people *upstairs* . . . them you can't rebuild, and they're the brains of the outfit, the ones that make the machines worth so much."

"You're talking about them like they're machines themselves," noted McGuire.

"They're moneymaking machines," answered Mallory. "And it's my guess that like any of their kind, their twin fuels are greed and corruption."

"Then why should they let a private eye and his award-winning biographer in here in the first place?" asked Nathan.

"You've won an award?" said McGuire, surprised.

"I will, now that I'm teaming with a real Marlowe."

"Mallory," the detective corrected him.

"So based on what you say, they've let us in because they can make a profit on us," said McGuire. *"How?"*

"I suspect that once you get the hang of it, you can find a profit in anything," said Mallory.

"Give me an example."

"Look at the oil companies," said Mallory. "The price of crude goes up halfway around the world, and tomorrow the price of gas at your local station is up fifteen cents a gallon. But that crude won't get processed and reach here for months. The stuff you're paying fifteen cents extra for was bought when it was cheaper and has been sitting at the gas station or the refinery for months."

"I never thought of that," admitted McGuire.

"Me neither," said Nathan.

"Somehow I'm not surprised," said Mallory. "You know, there's an old myth that seven financiers run the economy of the world in secret." He glanced at the ceiling. "I guess it's really only five. And I think it's time to go visit them."

"How do you suppose they can help us?" asked McGuire.

"I don't know. Maybe we'll let Wings O'Bannon's creator use his keen deductive mind and figure it out."

"Me?" said the dragon nervously.

"Why not?" said Mallory. "You're an award-winning author, aren't you?"

"Suddenly my stomach hurts," said Nathan.

"Don't worry about it," said Mallory. "I'll do the talking."

"Maybe we should just stay here and protect your back," suggested McGuire.

"From two floors away?" replied Mallory.

"You never know where danger might come from," said McGuire weakly.

"True," agreed the detective. "But I've got a pretty good idea where it's *not* coming from. I'll post the pair of you outside the door to their room, but you're not doing anyone any good here on the ground floor."

Mallory headed off toward an elevator, but Felina saw the escalator first and pounced on it.

"I like moving stairs," she confided at the top of her lungs.

"Thanks for yelling," said Mallory sardonically. "I wouldn't want our presence to startle anyone once we get off at the third floor."

"I'm thoughtful to a fault," replied Felina with a happy smile.

They reached the third floor without incident. The first thing they noticed was that the corridor was lined with uniformed guards. Only one office was lit, and Mallory began walking toward it. The guards scrutinized him and his group carefully, but made no move to stop them.

Mallory finally reached the door, then stopped and turned to McGuire and Nathan.

"Your choice," he said. "Come in, or stay out here."

"I'm coming in," said Nathan. "Do you think they'll mind if I take notes, or maybe record the conversation?"

"If they do, I'm sure they'll make their objections known to you," answered the detective.

"Well, I'm sure not staying out here alone," said McGuire nervously. "I'm coming in, too."

Mallory opened the door, and his party entered a plush, well-appointed suite. Four expensively dressed gray-haired men, each puffing on a cigar, were waiting for them, as was a young woman in a business suit who was seated at a huge mahogany desk.

"Good evening," said the detective. "My name is—"

"Skip the preliminaries," said one of the men. "Time is money."

"Right," said another. "You got a proposition for us?"

"In a manner of speaking."

"That's a very awkward manner," said the woman. "Explain yourself."

"I have a challenge for you."

"Do we look like Boy Scouts to you?"

"No," said Mallory. "Especially the young lady. In fact, what you look like is the Wall Street Five."

"You know who we are?" asked one of the men, surprised.

"I think everyone knows who and what you are," answered Mallory. "But I guess not everyone knows what to call you."

"Well, I'll be damned!" said one of them. "Who told you about us?"

"A friend."

"And why does this friend think we'd be interested in helping you?"

"He doesn't think you're at all interested in helping *me*," said Mallory. He paused meaningfully. "But he thinks you'd probably like to help yourselves."

"Explain yourself," said one of the men.

"My name is John Justin Mallory, and I'm a detective. I'm on the track of an incredibly powerful vampire who goes by the name of Vlad Drachma. This vampire is literally thousands of years old, seems to have near-super-human strength, and has been on a killing spree since he arrived here from Transylvania last week. He killed my partner's nephew earlier tonight. It's my job to bring him in, but so far I haven't had much luck."

"How do you think we can help?" asked the woman. "And more to the point, why should we?"

"You make your money by bilking the public," said Mallory bluntly. "Well, this particular vampire is fully capable of costing you twenty to thirty members of that public every week."

"Vampires all start out hot and energetic," said one of the men. "It's just a phase they go through."

"Vlad Drachma has been going through this particular phase since before Moses brought the Ten Commandments down from Mount Sinai," answered Mallory. He stared at each of them in turn. "I don't think any of you have a charitable bone in your bodies, so I won't appeal to your better natures or ask you to help me. But I think for people in your position selfishness is considered a virtue, or at least a survival trait, so I urge you to help yourselves."

"We will need a moment to confer," said the woman, getting to her feet. "We'll be back directly."

The five of them left the room.

"Well?" said Mallory.

"I thought you insulted them," said McGuire.

"They're beyond petty emotions like love and hate and fear and jealousy," answered Mallory with absolute certainty. "All they care about is profit and loss."

"I hope you're right."

"While you were studying each of them," said Nathan, "which one did you decide was the weak link?"

"Who knows?"

"But it's your job to know!" insisted the dragon.

"Right now my job consists of apprehending Vlad Drachma, and I'm grateful to anyone or any*thing* that will help me accomplish my purpose."

"How, exactly, can these five help?"

"Anyone who runs the world is probably not without resources," said Mallory with a smile. He was about to say something more when the Wall Street Five reentered the room.

"Well?" asked Mallory.

"Mr. Mallory, we have a deal," said the oldest of the men. "Allow me to introduce myself. I am John D. Stoneyfeller. If it flies, I own it. If it pulls freight, I own its tracks. If it's parked in your garage, it goes nowhere without my tires and my engine. And if it works for a union, you'll never find it in my employ."

"P. J. Morgan," said another. "I shortened it from Morganthau. I issued every credit card in your wallet. And all of your savings are on deposit in my bank, because regardless of the names they use, every bank is *my* bank."

"William Vandergilt at your service. Do you eat fried cicadas or choco-late-covered ants?"

"No," said Mallory.

"Then I can say without fear of contradiction that every piece of food you've eaten for the last thirteen years, be it animal or vegetable, has been *my* food, picked on my farms or dispatched in my slaughterhouses."

"And I am Andrew Boatnagie," said the fourth man.

"Transportation, money, and food seem to be spoken for," replied Mallory. "What do *you* control?"

"Control is such an insipid word, Mr. Mallory," said Boatnagie. "I am the czar of your leisure time. Not a movie gets made, not a play gets produced, not a sporting event takes place, not a book gets published, not a CD or DVD gets cut, until I greenlight it."

"And if the public doesn't like what you present?"

"Let them go to a competitor."

"Are there any?"

Boatnagie smiled. "Never for long."

"You're four captains of industry, to be sure," said Mallory. He turned to the young woman. "And you are . . . ?"

"Miss Subways," answered the woman.

"Miss Subways?" repeated Mallory. "Like in *On the Town?*"

"No," said Stoneyfeller. "Like she owns every subway in the USA, Europe, and Japan—the cars, the tracks, the stations, even the concessions."

"I assume you didn't inherit them?" said Mallory.

She smiled a chilling smile. "What fun would that have been?"

"So, Mr. Mallory," said Stoneyfeller, "our combined might is at your service. Not only that, but with a snap of our collective fingers, we can supply you with cannon fodder almost beyond calculation. How may we help you destroy this foul fiend who would dare interfere with our profit flow?"

"I'm going to have to give it a little thought," replied Mallory, "and decide how best to utilize you."

"Fine," said Morgan. "We'll be right here waiting, and woe betide the vampire that is foolish enough to match strength with us."

"He's pretty strong," offered McGuire.

"So are we," answered Boatnagie. "Economically speaking, that is—and when all is said and done, what other type of strength matters?"

Mallory walked to the door.

"You'll be in touch?" said Miss Subways.

"First chance I get," he promised her.

Then, followed by Felina, McGuire, and Nathan, he left the room, walked to the escalator, and a moment later emerged from the main entrance to the building.

"How does my nose look?" he asked McGuire.

"Why?"

"I just want to make sure it didn't grow six inches after I lied about getting back to them."

"Aren't we going to?"

Mallory shook his head. "No. It's a pity, too. There's not a drop of red blood left among the five of them. They'd be immune to Vlad Drachma's bite."

"Then why won't you use them, if you're so sure they could help us with Drachma?"

"Because," replied Mallory, "while I was listening to them, I realized that sometimes the cure is worse than the disease."

"So it's back to Square One?" asked McGuire.

"Not exactly," replied Mallory. "While I was listening to them, something they said gave me an idea . . ."

CHAPTER 20
2:01 AM–2:38 AM

"So what's your insight?" asked McGuire.

"Private eyes don't have insights," Nathan corrected him. "They have notions."

"Okay, what's your notion?" asked the vampire.

"Vlad's been living here for a few days, right?" said Mallory.

"I don't know if *living* is the proper word," said Nathan. "But go ahead with your notion."

"It's an expensive town. If he's in a hotel, or even in a mortuary, no one's giving it to him for free. Maybe he doesn't pay for the blood he drinks, but he hangs out at the Gryphon's Roost and for all I know a couple of other places. He's got to pay for whatever he's getting."

"Of course," said McGuire. "But everyone needs money, and everyone spends it. What's your point?"

"We're trying to find him, right?" said Mallory. "If he uses cash, where did he convert it from the currency he used in Transylvania? If he uses a credit card—well, you heard P. J. Morgan. He controls every credit card in the world. There's got to be a record of what he's spent, and more important, where he spent it."

"I thought you didn't want to work with Morgan and those others," said McGuire.

"I don't."

"Then how—?"

"We'll go back to the Gryphon's Roost," answered Mallory. "We know it's his hangout. If he's used any plastic, they'll have a record of it. Once we get his card number, we can always hunt up a hacker who can find out when and where he's using it."

"I don't know . . ." said Nathan dubiously.

"What's wrong with it?" asked Mallory.

"Wings O'Bannon never asks for help."

"That's a book," said Mallory. "This is the real world." He grimaced. "Probably a little less real than some . . ."

He heard a hissing sound above him and looked up to see Felina atop a lamppost, hissing at a banshee that had swooped down and flown off with a pigeon just before she could pounce on it.

"And a lot less real than others," added the detective. "Felina, come on down."

"I like it up here," she said. "I can see clear to the next block."

"Don't tell me," said Mallory. "Another dinosaur?"

"Just a lot of people taking off their clothes and dancing."

"Maybe we should just go take a quick look, in case Vlad's one of them," said McGuire, heading off in the direction Felina indicated.

"You do what you have to do," said Mallory, his voice heavy with disgust. "I'm going to the Gryphon's Roost. Felina, come on down or I'm leaving you behind."

"If you do, I'll never tell you what's waiting for you in that alley you're coming to," she said.

"If I don't leave, then it doesn't matter what's waiting, does it?"

"I never thought of that," said Felina, leaping lightly to the pavement. "All right, John Justin, let's go."

They began walking, followed by Nathan and McGuire. As they reached the alley, a goblin put his fingers into his mouth and gave them an annoying "Pssst!"

"What do you want?" asked Mallory in bored tones.

"Me?" said the goblin. "I don't want anything. But you look like a man who needs something unique, something that causes him to stand out in a crowd."

"And you don't think walking around with a dragon and a cat-girl will do that?" said Mallory.

"Not as much as *this*!" said the goblin enthusiastically, pulling a three-foot-long snake out of his pocket. "Just consider its uses. It makes the perfect belt. Skin it and you have the makings of a unique pair of shoes, provided that your size is eight and a half double-A or smaller. If you've grown tired of your pet rat, just leave it alone with the snake for a minute and your problems are over. Are you being pursued by an aggressive but morbidly obese redhead with a snake phobia? This is the answer to your prayers. Are you worried about being attacked in your sleep? Leave this snake on the floor by your bedside, and when you hear the revolting squishing sound of his being stepped on in the dark, you'll have up to three seconds to prepare your defense or race out the other side of the bed, provided that it's not pushed up against an open eighth-floor window. There is absolutely no limit to the number of uses to which this snake can be put."

"I hate snakes."

"No problem, sir. Feed him and he goes comatose for two months while he's digesting his meal. You won't have to walk him, play with him, groom him, or even acknowledge his existence. Even when he's awake he'll have no more fondness for you than you have for him, so unless you turn your back on him after abusing him, the two of you need never have any physical contact or social interaction at all. What more could a man want to treat himself to on All Hallows' Eve? And—get this!—the price is only three thousand dollars."

"Forget it."

"Two thousand."

"Go away."

"Seven dollars and ninety-three cents?"

"No."

"It's not fair!" complained the goblin. "Here I am, entering into an honest transaction, and you aren't holding up your end of the negotiation."

"I think that sums it up nicely."

"Okay, take him," said the goblin, holding out the snake. "He's yours."

"I don't want him."

"What has that got to do with anything?" whined the goblin. "This is a free-market society. I'm a merchant. You're a consumer. You're not fulfilling your function!"

"I thought the consumer was always right."

"That's an urban myth," replied the goblin. "All right, I'll pay you seventy-five cents to take the damned thing off my hands."

"No."

"Two dollars!"

Mallory began walking, followed by Felina, McGuire, and the dragon.

"Five dollars, and that's my final offer!" the goblin yelled after him.

"Good," said Mallory.

"Six fifty, and I'll throw in the August 1962 issue of *Playboy*!"

Mallory kept walking.

"What the hell am I going to do with a snake?" yelled the goblin. "It doesn't even like me."

"I can't imagine why," said the detective with a sardonic smile.

Then they were out of earshot.

"You know," said Mallory to his companions, "I think I liked goblins better back in *my* Manhattan, when all they did was scare the hell out of impressionable schoolkids. They seem to have become the merchant class in this Manhattan."

"But they never sell anything useful," noted McGuire.

"Neither do most the merchants back where I come from," answered Mallory. "Felina, we're going back to the Gryphon's Roost. You know how to get us there?"

"Yes, John Justin."

"Okay, lead the way."

"For six goldfish."

"No."

"Seven?"

"No."

"Then skritch my back."

"When we get there."

"What if I die of a hideous disease before then?" asked Felina.

"Then your back probably won't itch," said Mallory.

"I never thought of that," said Felina. She smiled brightly. "This way."

They followed her to the entrance. As before, Mallory left McGuire and Nathan just outside the building, while he and Felina took the elevator up to the sixty-sixth floor. When they got off they entered the casino, where Mallory sought out Mary, Queen of Slots.

"Back already?" she said.

"I need some information."

"Sure," she said. "Never draw to an inside straight." She waited for the laughter than was not forthcoming. "That was a joke."

"Hilarious," said Mallory without smiling.

"All right, shamus," she said. "What can I do for you?"

"You said Vlad Drachma comes here every night, right?"

"Yes."

"How does he pay his tab?"

"You'd have to ask in the bar," said Mary. "He never gambles, so he never spends any money here in the casino."

"Thanks," said Mallory. He left the casino and walked into the bar.

"Another cream for your cat?" asked the bartender.

"Yeah, why not?" said Mallory, shoving a bill across the bar.

"Hey, that's a sawbuck," noted the bartender. "For that she gets two gallons."

"We'll settle for one glass and some information."

The bartender filled a glass and handed it to Felina, who began lapping it noisily. "What can I tell you?"

"How does Vlad Drachma pay his bill?"

"He doesn't."

"I thought he was here every night," said Mallory, frowning. "Is he running a tab?"

"No. I suppose we'd let him run one if he asked, but after he shelled out five large, in cash, for the booth, he hasn't ordered a damned thing. Just asks for water and never drinks it."

"The cash," said Mallory. "Was it dollars or some other currency?"

"All we take is stuff printed in the good old USA," said the bartender.

"And he hasn't spent a penny since then?"

"Nope."

"Okay, thanks anyway," said Mallory. "Felina, finish that up and let's go."

"You didn't skritch my back yet," she said accusingly.

"I bought you the cream instead. Now finish it. We're in a hurry."

"Maybe I'll just stay here where I'm appreciated," she said. "Maybe I'll just live on cream and back-skritching."

"Fine," said Mallory, heading to the elevator. "I wish you a long and happy life."

He knew what was coming next, but the force of ninety pounds flying through the air and landing on his back still almost knocked him down.

"I forgive you, John Justin!" purred Felina.

"I can't tell you how thrilled I am," he grated as he reached the elevator.

"I knew it would make you happy," said Felina as the doors slid shut behind them. She turned to the elevator operator. "We're a team."

"Bully for us" was the reply.

"Isn't this the same elevator we took to the Gryphon's Roost?" she asked.

"Yes, it is."

"I have an observation," she said. "Whatever goes up must go down."

"Zounds," said Mallory. "I must wire Vienna immediately."

"I'm a genius, aren't I?" said Felina proudly.

"In every month that's got a K in it," answered Mallory.

McGuire and Nathan were waiting for them as they emerged from the building.

"Did you learn anything?" asked the little vampire.

Mallory shook his head. "He had some cash the first day he showed up and hasn't spent a cent since then."

"So we don't even know if he has a credit card?"

"That's right."

"And the cash he spent is untraceable?" asked Nathan.

"Probably."

"Then the money trail is a dead end," said the dragon.

"Not necessarily," said Mallory.

"I don't understand," said McGuire.

"The whole reason I'm trying to find him is because he bit Rupert Newton on the boat coming over, right?"

"Right," said Nathan and McGuire in unison.

"He had to have paid for his passage," said Mallory. "And perhaps it was with a credit card."

"I don't know," said McGuire. "We vampires are like royalty in Transylvania. Maybe they comped him."

"And maybe they were so glad to be rid of him they comped him," added Nathan. "This could be another dead end."

"You're both overlooking something," said Mallory.

"Oh? What?" asked McGuire.

"He wouldn't have come without his coffin, loaded with Transylvanian soil. Even if he was given free passage, my guess is that he'd have had to pay the cargo fee for the coffin. I mean, there's no way he could take it into a cabin with him."

Nathan had his notepad out again. "Wings O'Bannon couldn't have reasoned it out any better."

"I'm flattered beyond belief," said Mallory dryly.

"What's your next move?"

"We'll go down to the docks, find the ship that Rupert and Vlad arrived on, and learn out how Vlad paid."

"Very good," said Nathan, scribbling away. "Will you go in disguise?"

"Why?"

"Because I've never seen a private eye don a disguise before, and since Wings O'Bannon looks like a different person in every chapter, at least until he takes his pants off, I should see how it's done."

"I hate to disappoint you, but when you're asking questions and following leads, the very best disguise is to appear as a private eye," answered Mallory.

"And what if we find the right boat and the captain or the chief petty officer or whoever else you want to speak to tells you there's no record of payment, that it was made before the ship sailed?" said McGuire. "What then?"

"Then we interview every cargo hand."

"Why?"

"Because he had to have come with his own coffin, and I'll bet every cent I have that it's not still on board. And that means there's still another way to locate him—more dangerous, to be sure, but possibly also more effective."

"To find his"—McGuire gulped—"coffin?"

"Right."

"You know," said McGuire, "this is America."

"What's that got to do with anything?"

"It's a land of second chances," continued McGuire. "I think if Vlad apologizes and is really sincere in his contrition, perhaps we should all just forgive him, just like we forgive all the overpaid athletes and movie stars who apologize and tell us how sorry they are each time they get caught taking drugs and driving drunk, and go back to our normal everyday lives."

"He's not a quarterback or an actress, Bats," said Mallory. "He's killed people—including my partner's nephew."

"Maybe it was an accident."

"How do you accidentally bite someone in the neck, and then do it again the next night?"

"Nearsightedness?" said McGuire weakly.

"Look, Bats," said Mallory, "if you're scared, if you want to back out, now's a good time. I've got Nathan with me, and it's just a matter of detective work, at least until I catch up with him."

"I can't leave you!" said McGuire. "What kind of person do you take me for?"

"A frightened one."

"Besides that!"

"Bats, I'm just thinking of you."

"I've been thinking about me for forty-seven years," said the little vampire, "and all it's gotten me is anemia and an unemployment check. It's time I started thinking about something else."

"All right," said Mallory. "Let's go find this Transylvanian bloodsucker."

"I'm with you to the end," said McGuire.

"One for all and all for one," added Nathan.

"I'm hungry," said Felina.

Mallory and his team walked back through Battery Park, heading toward the dock. They had just about crossed it when Bubba appeared.

"Hey, Bats!" he called out. "Twice in one night. What gives?"

"We're still on Vlad Drachma's trail," answered McGuire. "This time it's leading us to the waterfront."

"Bats, this is an island," said Bubba. "Wherever you're standing, you're never more than a mile from the waterfront, and usually less."

"We have to get down to the docks," explained McGuire.

"There are docks all the hell over," said Bubba. "Why those particular ones?"

"Because . . ." McGuire stopped and frowned, then turned to Mallory. "Why those?"

"Because that's where the Never Sink Cruise Line unloads its ships," said Mallory.

"There's really a Never Sink Cruise Line?" asked Bubba.

"That's what the kid's aunt told me," said Mallory. "And she's pretty good on details."

"You sure you're looking for a vampire?" said Bubba. "We don't like the water much, you know. Shipwrecks scare the hell out of us. You want something worse than drowning? Be one of the undead whose ship goes down to the bottom of the sea and isn't salvaged for a few centuries."

"They can just swim to the surface," said Mallory.

"I can't swim," said Bubba. "I spent all my time crippling halfbacks and falling on loose balls."

"Besides, it's hard to push a coffin open under two hundred fathoms of water," added McGuire.

"So he's probably not going to be there," concluded Bubba.

"That's not a problem," replied Mallory. "We don't really expect to find him there."

"Makes sense," said Bubba, nodding his head sagely. "If I was after a dangerous killer from the old country, I'd spend all my time looking where I didn't expect to find him too."

"Why don't you tag along with us?" said Mallory. "We could use a big bruiser like you on our side—especially one who's already dead, so he can't be killed."

"That's a really tempting offer—risking my neck for a man I've met once for maybe three minutes and trying to capture or kill a creature of my own kind who never did me any harm." Bubba smiled in amusement and shook his head. "No offense, but I think I'll take a pass on it."

"Our loss, no doubt," said Mallory, starting to walk toward the docks again. His companions followed suit, he picked up the pace, and they reached their destination within ten minutes, despite Felina's tendency to stop and peer into every store window and then announce which five or six items she wanted Mallory to buy or steal for her.

When they reached the dock area, Mallory slipped the night watchthing a bill and found out that the Never Sink line owned only three ships, one of which, the *Moribund Manatee*, was docked there.

"Which one is it?" asked the detective.

"You can't miss her," answered the watchthing. "She's the one that's kind of rust colored."

"Funny color for a ship," remarked Mallory.

"Ain't as if rust comes in a lot of colors," said the watchman. "It's about the only thing holding the *Manatee* together."

"I think I see it now," said Mallory, looking down the dock. "Anyone aboard her?"

"She'll have a skeleton crew."

"Thanks for the information," said Mallory. "I guess we'll pay her a visit."

"Go ahead," said the watchthing. "I'll give a howl if anyone comes looking for you."

"Like who?" asked the detective.

"How should *I* know?" replied the watchthing. "Gangsters. Bill collectors. Revenue agents. Mesopotamian spies. Sweet young things who misconstrued your flights of poetic fancy as bona fide proposals of marriage."

"But no vampires?"

"Around here? They ain't much for water."

Mallory began walking down the dock, past one impressive cruise ship after another. When he came to the one that seemed to have no earthly reason for remaining afloat, he knew he had come to the *Manatee*.

A rickety gangplank led up to the main deck, and Mallory began walking it, followed by the others. When he had almost reached the top, a very strange-looking man with scaly skin and not-quite-concealed gills on his neck suddenly appeared.

"Who goes there?" he demanded.

"My name is Mallory," said the detective, "and these are my associates. We'd like to speak to someone in authority."

"That'd be the captain."

"Then that's who we want."

"Against protocol. You can't just walk up here and demand to see the captain. There's red tape galore. I'll need your birth certificate, proof of citizenship, union card if any, library card if any, blood sugar and cholesterol readings, death certificate if you are among the undead, voter registration card, and driver's license—and the same for all your friends."

"Or perhaps I could just slip you five dollars?" suggested Mallory.

"It'd save both of us a lot of time and trouble," agreed the man, extending his hand and grabbing the bill when Mallory offered it. "Welcome aboard the *Moribund Manatee*, flagship of the Never Sink Cruise Line."

Mallory looked around the decrepit main deck. "Why is this one your flagship?"

"It's the one that's still afloat," answered the man.

Mallory nodded. "Yeah, that's about the only answer that'd make sense. Where's your captain?"

"On the aft deck, disciplining a crewman" was the answer.

A moment later a trio of gunshots rang out.

"I think Captain Blight will see you now."

"Captain Blight?" repeated Mallory. "I seem to remember someone with a similar name."

"That'd be Captain Bligh of the *Bounty*," said the man. "They're like two peas in a pod, except for Captain Bligh being friendlier and more compassionate. Also, Captain Bligh went ashore from time to time. Captain Blight never leaves the ship."

"Why not?"

"Things die when he walks too near them."

"Things?" said Mallory.

"Plants, flowers, the occasional tree," answered the man. "Those sort of things."

"But not men?"

"They wouldn't have the guts to make the captain mad by dying while they were on duty. He'd follow 'em right down to hell and bring 'em back."

"Sounds like the kind of man who's sorry flogging at the mainmast went out of style," remarked Mallory.

"It fair broke his little black heart" was the answer. "Until he found out that flogging at the flagpole worked just as well, and could even be construed as patriotic."

A burly man dressed all in black began approaching them. He had a thick black beard that was starting to turn gray and was armed with two pistols, a sword, and a bullwhip.

"Captain Blight, sir," said the man, "these here gents would like a word with you."

Blight glared at them. "Are you ACFO?"

"I beg your pardon?" said Mallory.

"You heard me," snarled Blight. "Are you from the American Civil Freedoms Organization?"

"No, I'm John Justin Mallory of the Mallory and Carruthers Detective Agency," said Mallory. "These are my assistants."

Blight stared at each in turn. "But you're definitely not ACFO?"

"Definitely not," Mallory assured him.

"All right," muttered Blight. "You get to live—until I find out you're lying."

"Thanks," said Mallory.

"What can I do for you, as long as it doesn't inconvenience me in any way?"

"I've got some questions concerning one of your passengers on your recent trip from Europe."

"She said she was nineteen, *she* supplied the handcuffs, cattle prod, aqualung, and apricot preserves, and that's all I'm saying until I see my lawyer."

"A *different* passenger."

"He challenged me to a swordfight. It doesn't make any difference whether he was drunk or sober, he was the instigator. And besides, the ship's surgeon offered to sew them back on if anyone could find them."

"I'm talking about a passenger from Transylvania named Vlad Drachma."

"Can't help you out," said Blight. "Transylvania's not one of our ports of call."

"He probably got on in England."

"What about him?"

"Did he buy anything during the trip? And if he did, how did he pay for it?"

"How the hell should I know?" bellowed Blight. "You know the penalty for wasting the captain's time?"

"No, I don't," admitted Mallory. "But you're in Manhattan now. Do you know the penalty for withholding information in a murder case?"

Blight stared at him for a long moment. "Are you *sure* you're not from the ACFO?"

"I told you: I'm a detective."

"Then go detect something and leave me to run my ship!"

"Your ship's in port," said Mallory. "It's not running anywhere."

"There's cargo to load and unload, decks to swab, crewmen to discipline. You think a captain's life is easy? I've flogged so many crewmen on this latest voyage that I've damaged my rotator."

"Happens to pitchers all the time," remarked McGuire, not without sympathy.

"So are you going to tell me what I want to know," said Mallory, "or am I going to get a court order to impound the ship and everything in it?"

Blight glared at him again. "If I had a yardarm, can you guess who I'd hang from it right this minute?"

"Just tell me what I want to know and I'll be out of your hair," said Mallory.

"But *I* won't be," said a smooth, cultured voice.

They all turned and saw a very well-dressed man reaching the top of the gangplank. His suit was custom tailored and European, his tiepin held a huge diamond, and his shoes were handmade Italian.

"You again?" roared Blight.

"Me again," said the man, totally unflustered by Captain Blight's belligerence.

Blight turned to Mallory. "I was right! You're just his stalking horse!"

"I never saw him before in my life," said Mallory.

"Then you don't watch the news on television often enough," said the man. "I am Clarence Drummond at your service." He handed Mallory an embossed business card.

"You're goddamned ACFO, is what you are," muttered Captain Blight.

"My good man," said Drummond, "as long as you insist on keeping the cargo aboard ship, I shall continue to file legal briefs to force you to relinquish it."

"What's this all about?" asked Mallory.

"It's about seven thousand cartons of cigarettes in the hold of the *Moribund Manatee*," explained Drummond.

"What about them?"

"Captain Blight refuses to unload them."

"They were smuggled by a couple of crewmen who have since gone on to their rewards in Davey Jones's locker," said Blight. "That makes them mine, and I can get a better price in Patagonia. Now why can't the ACFO leave me alone?"

"Because American citizens have every right to smoke those cigarettes," answered Drummond.

"Maybe the Captain's doing them a favor," said Mallory. "That's a lot of cancer in the hold of the ship."

"The ACFO's position is that Americans have a constitutional right to contract cancer, and Captain Blight is standing in the way of their exercising that freedom," said Drummond. "I'd stay and explain our position in detail, but I just stopped by for a moment to see if he's changed his mind." He looked at his diamond-studded Rolex. "I really must run. I'm due in court in another twenty minutes."

"Another cigarette case?" asked Mallory.

"No," answered the lawyer. "This one involves a college binge eater who gobbled down thirty-four cheeseburgers and twelve chocolate malts in a single sitting."

"He must have been as sick as a dog," said the detective.

"That's beside the point," answered Drummond. "It was his legal right to order that meal."

"Then what's the suit about?"

"The American Civil Freedoms Organization is suing the short-order cook who filled the order and let him get that sick. Wherever there is suffering, there must be a culprit."

"Sounds like your organization has more business than it can handle."

"True, true," agreed Drummond. "Tomorrow we're defending two innocent souls who were prevented from exercising their freedom of self-expression at the Temple of All Saints."

"They weren't allowed to speak?"

"I didn't say freedom of speech. I said freedom of self-expression."

"What's the difference?" asked Mallory.

"They were suicide bombers."

"Well, it's sure comforting to know that you're out there protecting us from our worst tendencies," said Mallory.

"It's a dirty job, standing up for the poor and disadvantaged whether they want you to or not, but someone's got to do it," said Drummond. He turned to Blight. "I'll be back. You can't prevent the public from exercising its rights forever."

He turned on his heels, walked to the gangplank, and left the ship.

"So you really don't work for him?" said Blight.

"I really don't," said Mallory. "And if you'll tell me what I want to know, I'll tell you how to get him to stop bothering you."

"Really?"

"Really."

"It's a deal!" said Blight. "How do I make him go away?"

"Next time he comes by, tell him you'll only discuss releasing your cargo if he'll have a friendly smoke with you."

Blight frowned. "That's *it*? That's your whole plan?"

"Where I come from, the ACFO only protects *other* people's rights to kill themselves. They don't practice those rights themselves. This guy seems cut from the same mold."

"You know, now that you mention it . . ." said Blight.

"Okay, so now can you hunt up the information I need?"

"I'll have the purser get right on it," said Blight. "We had gambling, floor shows, all kinds of entertainments. I even had one of the strippers get semidressed and sell some of the cigarettes from the hold. He's got to have spent money on *something*."

Blight walked over to the ship's intercom and told the purser what he needed.

"It'll just take a minute or two," he said, returning to Mallory.

"While we're just passing the time of day," said McGuire, "I'm not without my contacts. Possibly we could do some business. Besides the cigarettes, what contraband do you carry?"

"Just the one," said Blight. "There are six of them, I think."

"Uh . . . I'm confused," said McGuire.

"The dance band," answered Blight. "A drummer, two trumpets, a sax, a clarinet, and a piano. Six Contras from Nicaragua. Or was it seven? I can't remember. There might have been a trombone, too."

"I guess maybe we'll do business some other time," said McGuire.

"I'll tell you, I'm glad this voyage is over," said Blight. "A captain's job is never done. I performed seventeen weddings, eleven divorces, three baptisms, a bris, and three funerals."

"Three funerals?" said Mallory. "That's a lot of people to die on a five-day voyage, isn't it?"

"I performed 'em all after we were in port here," said Blight. "It was after the ACFO lawyers began shooting at each other. Some disagreement about firearms control."

"Sounds like you've had an eventful week."

"Yeah, along with all that other stuff, we fired on two rowboats, a canoe, a humpback whale, and a Greek fishing vessel that were all blocking our way." He scowled. "Missed the canoe."

The purser approached them and handed a piece of paper to Blight, who looked at it and turned it over to Mallory.

"Here you are, shamus," he said. "This is your man's TransEx number."

"TransEx?" asked Mallory.

"Transylvanian Express card."

"Thanks," said Mallory. "Now it's just a matter of finding out when and where he might have used it in New York."

As Mallory began walking down the gangplank, followed by Felina, McGuire, and Nathan, Captain Blight called after him: "You really think it'll work?"

"Tracing the TransEx card? No reason why not."

Blight shook his head impatiently. "Insisting that Drummond have a smoke."

"Absolutely. He may care more about everyone else's rights than his own, but I guarantee he cares more about his own health, safety, and comfort than anyone else's."

"You sure about that?" asked McGuire softly, as they reached the pier.

"Some things don't change from one Manhattan to another," said Mallory. "Human nature is one of them."

CHAPTER 22

2:57 AM–3:20 AM

"So do we ask P. J. Morgan for help?" queried Nathan as they left the water-front.

"Not a chance," said Mallory. "You let one of that bunch into your life, you never get him out."

"Then what's our next move?" persisted the dragon. "I'm tired of being a spear carrier in this drama. I'm ready to become the hero."

"You *are* a spear carrier," noted Mallory, indicating Nathan's spear. "Let's hope you don't have to use it."

"I hate to interrupt," said McGuire, "but we seem to have lost the cat thing."

Mallory looked around and couldn't spot Felina.

"She can't have gone too far," he said. "Did you see a mouse shoot out from one of the shadows?"

McGuire shook his head. "No."

"Here she comes," said Nathan, pointing to a nearby alley, from which Felina was emerging.

"Where were you?" asked Mallory.

"I saw the cutest little dove," she replied. "Don't you think they're sweet the way they just coo lovingly at the whole world?" She smiled at him, and a pair of feathers fell out of her mouth.

"Are you going to stay with us now?" asked the detective.

"Yes," she said. "Perhaps. Probably." She smiled again and emitted a very unladylike burp.

"See that you do," said Mallory.

"So where are we going?" asked Nathan. "We've only got three or four more hours before it's light out and we've lost him."

"We've got to find him before we can lose him," McGuire corrected him.

185

"We need a hacker," said Mallory.

"A cabbie?" said McGuire. "What on earth for?"

"A computer hacker," said Mallory. "Somebody who can break into Transylvania Express's database and find out if Vlad has used his card recently."

"And where he's used it," added Nathan.

"And doubtless you have one on retainer that you routinely use in all your cases," suggested McGuire.

"We've never needed one before," replied Mallory. "But I think I know one who can help us. I did him a favor last year; he ought to be willing to return it."

"What favor?"

"I didn't turn him in to the cops," said Mallory.

"He was breaking the law?"

"Yeah."

"Then why—?"

"He was hacking into Vito Cherricola's bank account."

"You were working for Hot Lips Cherricola, the Mafia don?"

Mallory nodded. "I work for whoever needs a detective."

"Damn! I'm impressed!" said Nathan. "Why didn't you arrest this hacker?"

"I'm not a cop," answered Mallory. "My job is solving problems, not arresting people. I got him to stop dating Cherricola's daughter and return the money he'd stolen, and to promise not to do either again, so Vito was happy. And in exchange for the hacker's cooperation, I didn't turn him in, so he was happy. He owes me one now. I think it's time to collect."

"So how do we find him?"

"He lives just a block away from here," said Mallory.

"Has he got a name?"

"Everyone's got a name," answered Mallory. "He's probably got five or six for business purposes. The one I know him by is Albert Feinstein."

"Why do I think that doesn't have a ring of truth and honesty to it?" said Nathan.

"Truth and honesty are not his stock-in-trade," replied Mallory.

"But he's really good with a computer?" asked McGuire.

"That's why we're going to his place."

"Maybe when he's got the data you need, I can borrow him for a couple of minutes."

"What do you need him for, Bats?"

"There's this vampire porno site," said McGuire uncomfortably. "I gave them a bad credit card number, and they locked me out. Maybe he can get me back in."

"Why don't you just give them the right number?" suggested Nathan.

"Because I don't own a credit card," said McGuire.

"How did you buy your computer?"

"I didn't exactly *buy* it," replied the little vampire.

"You stole it."

"I had no choice," complained McGuire. "I blame it all on racism in high places."

"Racism?" repeated Nathan dubiously.

"You may think it's all fun and games being a vampire," said McGuire, "but let me tell you, our welfare checks are smaller than anyone else's. They say it's because we get more food stamps, but they know we can't use them! It's an outrage."

"And you were so outraged you stole a computer."

"I view it as a long-term loan," replied McGuire with dignity. "I have every intention of returning it just as soon as they come out with the next generation."

"Here we are," announced Mallory, stopping in front of a century-old apartment building.

"How do you know he'll be home?" asked Nathan.

"He's under house arrest."

"What for?"

"He forged letters of resignation from the whole City Council."

"So they lock him in his apartment with his computer," commented Nathan. "Maybe someone should have accepted all those resignations."

Mallory pressed the bell for Feinstein's apartment.

"This is the Super Secret Spy in the Sky Government Security System," said a harsh mechanical voice. "Hand over all your money or prepare to be defenestrated."

"Open up, Albert," said the detective. "It's John Justin Mallory."

"Mallory!" cried a human voice. "How the hell are you, and did you bring any jelly doughnuts or ripe naked women?"

"Fine, no, and no. Now let me in."

The door buzzed, and Mallory held it open until his three companions could pass through it. Then he led them up to the second floor, down a long corridor, and finally into Albert Feinstein's apartment, which was littered with books, magazines, computer manuals, and unwashed dishes.

Feinstein was waiting for them. He was a skinny man, not much taller than McGuire, with a head of unruly red hair and a handlebar mustache. He wore glasses with such thick lenses that they totally distorted the way his eyes looked behind them. He was stark naked except for a shopworn bowler hat.

"Dressed in rather a hurry, didn't you?" remarked Mallory.

"I work in the nude," answered Feinstein.

"What's the hat for?"

"There's always the chance that I'll get company. Like tonight. What can I do for you, Mallory?"

"What you do best," said Mallory.

"I can't," said Feinstein. "You didn't bring any women."

"All right, what you do second best."

"You're asking me to break the law and cause someone untold misery, just because you think I'm under some obligation to you, is that it?"

"Yes," said Mallory.

A huge smile spread across Feinstein's homely face. "I'll be delighted! Whose life are we out to ruin tonight?"

"No one's."

"What fun is that?"

"I need you to break into a secure database and get some information for me," said Mallory.

"Happy to," said Feinstein. "What am I breaking into? The Chase Manhattan Bank? The World Bank? Donald Trump's petty cash account?"

Mallory handed him the slip of paper with Vlad Drachma's TransEx account number on it.

"I want you to discreetly access the Transylvania Express database and find out if this card has been used in the past couple of days—and if so, when and where."

"Who does it belong to?"

"Does it make a difference?" asked Mallory.

"Only if I want to blackmail him at a later date."

"Do you have a single moral bone in your body?" asked the detective with a weary sigh.

"I used to," answered Feinstein. "I had it taken out when they gave me my hip replacement."

"You're a little young for a hip replacement, aren't you?"

"High Stakes Louie took my original hip when I couldn't pay off one of my bets, so I figured I might as well get a replacement."

"High Stakes Louie?" repeated Mallory. "I haven't heard of him in a couple of years."

"He's doing six thousand years in Leavenworth," said Feinstein with a satisfied smile. "Seems someone unearthed an almost-authentic computer transcript of his plans to assassinate the president and blow up the Capitol building, and sent it to the Justice Department. We can do perfectly well without a president and all those senators and congressmen, of course, but the building would cost a pretty penny to replace."

"Vito Cherricola, High Stakes Louie, the City Council," recited Mallory. "Don't you ever go after a small target?"

"Who would remember Saint George if he had only killed a dragonfly?" responded Feinstein. "By the way, are you ever going to introduce me to your gang?"

"They're my *friends*," said Mallory. "Bats McGuire, Scaly Jim Chandler, Felina, say hello to Albert Feinstein, the best and certainly the most immoral hacker in all of Manhattan."

"One does what one can," said Feinstein with false humility.

"So go to your computer and do your best."

"Are you in that much of a hurry?" said Feinstein. "I thought we could exchange dirty jokes for a few minutes, then describe our favorite sexual perversions, maybe make a couple of side bets on tomorrow's races (especially if you're still betting on Flyaway), and then around dawn we'd have some coffee and maybe a cheese Danish or two, and then I'd get your information."

"I need it now," said Mallory.

"So you're after a vampire," said Feinstein.

"Yes, I'm after a vampire. And the longer we talk, the less chance I've got of catching up with him."

"All right, all right," said Feinstein, walking to the desk that housed his computer, "don't make a federal case out of it." He sat down on a beat-up swivel chair. "Activate."

The computer suddenly glowed with life. "Ready, Darling," it said in a sultry feminine voice.

"Knock it off, Computer," said Feinstein uncomfortably. "There are people present."

"Computer?" whined the machine. "How come you never call me Cutie Pie anymore?"

"Just scan this credit card number and don't hassle me," said Feinstein.

"Not until you apologize for snapping at me," said the computer.

"All right, I apologize."

"And call me Cutie Pie."

"You're not the only computer in the world," growled Feinstein.

"I'm the only one for you, Darling."

"Are you going to scan the damned number or not?"

"Scanning . . . done. It's not as pretty as your eyes."

"You're embarrassing me in front of my friends," said Feinstein.

"Get rid of them," replied the computer. "I'm all you'll ever need."

"Concentrate on your work," said Feinstein. "You're driving me crazy."

"With passion?" giggled the computer.

"We'll talk later. Just access Transylvania Express's data files."

"Working . . . I'm locked out."

"What kind of security do they have?"

"Code 666."

Feinstein snorted. "I don't know why they all think that's impenetrable. Try breaking through it with a four-slash-L-slash-twenty-six strong left."

"You think it'll work?" asked the computer.

"It worked for Notre Dame against Michigan State back in 1973," answered Feinstein.

"Working . . . I'm in."

"I need to know if the card's been used in the past forty-eight hours, and if so, where," said Feinstein.

"Give me forty-five seconds, Darling."

Feinstein turned to Mallory. "We're even now, right?"

"We're even once she . . . make that *it* . . . gives me the information."

"You call me an *it* again and it'll be a cold day in hell before I retrieve it," said the computer.

Mallory resisted the urge to reply and waited silently while the computer scanned the TransEx database.

"I'll want a hard copy," said Feinstein.

"Working, Darling . . . here it is."

Feinstein reached out and took the paper.

"Oh!" exclaimed the computer. "You have such strong hands!"

Feinstein gave the paper to Mallory, who read it carefully.

"When did he use the card most recently?" asked Nathan.

"We're in luck," said Mallory. "Seventeen minutes ago."

"Where?"

"A drugstore in the Village." He frowned. "But I'll be damned if I can make any sense out of what he bought."

"What was it?" asked McGuire.

"Eye of newt. Powdered gorgon nails. Baking soda. Two harpy feathers. Baby aspirin. Bay leaves. Peach nectar. And peanut butter."

Feinstein turned to the computer. "Is there anything, any mixture, that requires all those elements?"

"Are you addressing me?" said the computer.

"You know I am."

"I have a name."

Feinstein sighed. "All right. Cutie Pie, is there anything that requires all those elements?"

"There sure is, Snookums," replied the computer. "It's an antidote."

"To what?"

"An anti-vampire spray."

"Somebody sprayed him?" said Mallory.

"Not necessarily," said the computer.

"Could you explain, please?" said the detective.

"Only if you call me Honey Bunny."

"Could you explain, Honey Bunny?" said Mallory, starting to feel some sympathy for Feinstein.

"Certain businesses hire pest control companies to spray their premises with a solution that repels vampires. The residue is enough to cause them serious discomfort. They don't have to actually be sprayed themselves."

"There must be dozens of pest control companies in Manhattan," said Mallory grimly. "This could take forever."

"Not necessarily," said the computer.

"Why not?"

"I didn't hear that."

"Why not, Honey Bunny?"

"The peach nectar is the giveaway," answered the computer. "The only antidote that uses it comes from Odd Peter's Pest Removal Service."

"Where are they located?"

Silence.

"Where are they located, Honey Bunny?"

"On the corner of Agony and Retribution."

"Where the hell is *that*?" said Mallory.

"It's in Greenwich Village," said Nathan. "I know the way."

"Thanks, Albert," said Mallory, shaking the hacker's hand. "Now we're square." He walked to the door.

"Just a minute, Mallory," said Feinstein. "I'd rather have you owe me one."

Mallory stared at him curiously.

"Cutie Pie, check out the owner of that TransEx card you just traced. He's got to have a Social Security number, or a passport, or *something*. See what you can find out about him. And make it a hard copy again."

"You got it, Sweetmeats," said the computer. "Working . . ."

"I've been awake too long," said Mallory. "I should have thought of that myself."

"Don't let it bother you," replied Feinstein. "We can't all be geniuses whose IQs measure right off the scale."

"I guess we can't all be that modest, either," said Mallory.

"Here you are, Darling," said the computer.

Feinstein pulled out the paper.

"That tickles!" giggled the computer.

"Well, now, this is really interesting," said Feinstein, reading the printout.

"What is?"

"The card is registered to a Vlad Drachma, but that isn't his real name."

"I have a horrible feeling I'm not going to like what you say next," muttered Mallory unhappily.

"His real name, or at least the one he's used for the past few centuries in Transylvania, is Vlad Dracule."

"Shit!" said Mallory. "I *knew* you were going to say that!" He paused. "Well, what else have you got?"

"I sure don't envy you, Mallory," said Feinstein sincerely.

"Oh?"

He held up the printout. "This Dracule has been a *bad* boy."

"So what's our next stop?" asked McGuire as they left Feinstein's apartment.

"I think that should be obvious, Bats," said Mallory. "Tell him, Felina."

"The fish market," said Felina.

"Well, maybe not as obvious as I thought," said the detective. "We're going to Odd Peter's Pest Removal Service."

"Why?" asked McGuire. "Clearly whatever solution he's using didn't kill Vlad."

Mallory stared at McGuire for a long moment. "When you become a vampire, do you lose half your brain?"

"I don't think so," said McGuire. "Why?"

"Just wondering," replied Mallory. "We're going to Odd Peter's on the reasonable assumption that he hasn't covered the whole of Manhattan with that stuff, which means maybe he can tell us exactly where he did apply it."

"I never thought of that," admitted the little vampire.

"I'm flabbergasted," muttered Mallory. He turned to the dragon. "Nathan . . ."

"Scaly Jim, damn it!"

"Okay, Jim," Mallory amended. "I think once you get me to Odd Peter's, you and Bats had better stay outside."

"You think he might make a break for it?" asked Nathan.

"Why should he? He's a legitimate businessman."

"Then why—?"

"Because dragons and vampires might be susceptible to some of the stuff he's got on the premises."

"You really think someone would pay him to get rid of dragons?" asked Nathan, surprised.

"Why not?"

"But we're so cute and lovable! Except for us masculine types who go armed and make war," he added quickly.

"Better safe than sorry," said Mallory.

"Better safe than dead," McGuire chimed in.

"Bats, you're already dead," said the detective.

"There's dead and then there's *dead*," replied the little vampire.

"What's the difference?"

"I don't know," admitted McGuire. "But there must be one, or why would I still be afraid of dying?"

"All right," said Nathan. "We'll stay outside, right by the front door."

"Stay half a block away," said Mallory. "If this stuff is in powdered form and a breeze comes along, who the hell knows what damage it can do to someone standing that close?"

"It makes us seem like cowards."

"You're no use to me dead," said Mallory irritably. "Will you just do what I say?"

"On one condition," said the dragon. He pulled a tiny tape recorder out of his harness and handed it to Mallory. "I want you to tape everything you and Odd Peter say so I can use it in my book."

"I thought you were just getting background on how a detective works," said Mallory.

"I was. But then I figured, what the hell, I've been tracking down clues with you all over the city, and I've been in on most of your interviews, so why not write *this* case up as a Wings O'Bannon adventure?"

"Let's hope he survives it," said Mallory.

"I've got confidence in you," said Nathan. He paused. "I don't suppose you've been to bed with anyone since Vlad killed your partner's nephew?"

Mallory just stared at him.

"No, I suppose not," continued the dragon. "Well, I'll just have to improvise. I don't suppose you and Felina ever . . . uh . . . ?"

"Try not to be disgusting," said Mallory.

"Right," said Nathan. "Forget I mentioned it. By the way, I never asked, but what kind of gat do you carry?"

Mallory pulled his gun out of his trenchcoat pocket and handed it to the dragon.

"No shoulder holster?" asked Nathan.

"They're uncomfortable."

Nathan studied the gun. "Looks new."

"It ought to," replied Mallory. "I think I've fired it three times in fifteen years."

"But Wings O'Bannon is a crack shot. How do you keep in practice if you don't go to the target range two or three times a week?"

"My name isn't Wings O'Bannon, and I never shoot anything that's more than six feet away," answered Mallory.

"No problem, I can fix that," said Nathan. "After all, I *am* a fiction writer."

"And you're really going to write up this case?" asked McGuire.

"More or less."

"Will *I* be in it?" continued the vampire.

"You're here, aren't you?" replied Nathan.

"Could you make me four inches taller and more attractive to women?"

"Sure," said the dragon. "They call it poetic license."

"They call it unrealistic exaggeration," said Mallory.

"Same thing," said Nathan with a shrug.

"And what do you plan to call this epic?" asked Mallory.

"*Stalking the Vampire*," answered Nathan. "Great title, don't you agree? Surefire best seller."

"I think it's been done."

"Not in *this* Manhattan," replied the dragon. "Ah, here we are." He pointed to the sign in a window that proclaimed that they had arrived at Odd Peter's Pest Removal Service.

"They're still open at three in the morning," noted McGuire. "Isn't that unusual?"

"What better time to eradicate the kind of pests they specialize in?" said Mallory.

"I'm no pest," said McGuire. "I'm a thoughtful, considerate, politically moderate bloodsucker who has fears, longings, and sexual needs just like anyone else."

"Stay out here anyway," said Mallory. "Felina, come on."

"It smells bad," she said.

"You know," said Mallory after a moment's consideration, "it might not be a bad idea for you to stay out here too. I can't imagine that you won't put something in your mouth, and probably everything they have is poison."

She sniffed the air. "They have mice."

"They're probably test animals in cages," said Mallory. "Stay outside."

"And birds!" she said, her pupils narrowing to mere slits.

"Stay outside anyway."

"You're mean to me," said Felina. "You hate me. I'll bet the Grundy would be nice to me."

"After he finished torturing you, you mean?"

"But it would be gentle, friendly, considerate torture," she said.

"Boy, I just can't outsmart any of you tonight, can I?" said Mallory sardonically. "I have no more time to waste. Stay with Bats and Nathan."

"Scaly Jim!"

"I stand corrected. Stay with Bats and Jim."

Mallory turned the knob on the door and entered Odd Peter's establishment.

"Anybody here?" he said as the door closed behind him.

"In a minute!" called a voice from a room at the back of the shop.

Mallory looked around. There were rows of tin cans, small jars, and the occasional vial topped by a small cork. Each was meticulously labeled in a calligraphic script.

Finally an old man, bent with age, emerged from the back room. He had the normal number of eyes and ears, but both eyes were to the left of his nose, and both ears were on the right side of his head, one above the other. He had a normal nose, but it was attached horizontally rather than vertically.

"Odd Peter at your service," said the man.

Mallory made no reply.

"You're staring," said Odd Peter.

"I apologize."

"It's all right, I'm used to it. What can I do for you?"

Mallory showed the man his ID. "I'm a detective," he said. "And I'm on the track of a vampire."

"I wish I could help you, but I live upstairs," said Odd Peter. "I haven't been out of the building in years. I've no idea where your vampire might be."

"I just need some information," said Mallory. "This particular vampire seems to have run into some of your product, and bought the makings for an antidote."

"Ah!" said Odd Peter, smiling and revealing two rows of bright blue teeth. "What materials did he assemble?"

"Eye of newt, powdered gorgon nails, baking soda, two harpy feathers, baby aspirin, bay leaves, peach nectar, and peanut butter."

Odd Peter nodded his head knowingly. "Yes, that's mine. The peach nectar is my trademark."

"How many places could he have run into your . . . your whatever-it-was?"

"Vampire repellent," said Odd Peter. "Not fatal. The owner of the premises clearly didn't want a vendetta with any of the vampire's friends and relations. He just wanted to make sure his place wasn't infested by the creatures."

"How many places spread your formula around tonight?"

"It's expensive stuff," answered Odd Peter. "And it loses its potency within a few hours. Only two places have ordered it today—Tassel-Twirling Tessie Twinkle's Five-Star Burlesque Emporium and the Our Lady of Perpetual Frustration Dialysis Center."

"Have you got addresses for them?"

"I believe so. Let me check."

Odd Peter walked to a desk, found a card file, thumbed through it, then wrote two addresses down on a piece of paper, which he handed to Mallory.

"Thanks," said the detective, looking briefly at the paper. "If you don't mind a personal question, how did you get into this business in the first place?"

"My mother was frightened by a Picasso painting," answered Odd Peter. "I decided that my mission in life was to do my best to stop anyone else's mothers from being frightened by anything unnatural."

"I'm surprised you didn't just go around destroying Picasso paintings," said Mallory.

"Do you know how *many* the man painted?" said Odd Peter. "He was inexhaustible. It's much easier to do away with all the nightmare creatures that inhabit Manhattan."

"Well, at least it's a noble undertaking," offered Mallory.

"Noble, schmoble," said Odd Peter. "I just don't want any other kids to grow up looking like *this*." He indicated his own face. "Do you know how long it took me to find a girl I could kiss while looking deep into her eyes?"

"Quite a while, I'd guess."

"Forty-six years!" said Odd Peter. "Of course I married her. I mean, how the hell many other women have their eyes and ears where I do?"

"At least you found a soulmate."

"She's a *yenta* of the first magnitude," growled Odd Peter. "But what was I going to do? Wait another forty-six years to find *another* woman like me?"

"Why don't you just turn out the lights?" said Mallory. "Then it wouldn't matter what your partner looks like."

"Damn!" said Odd Peter. "*Now* you mention it!"

"Thanks for the information," said Mallory. "I hate to grab it and run, but my prey *is* a vampire. I've only got maybe four hours until sunrise."

"You're looking at it all wrong, young man," said Odd Peter. "The very best time to face a vampire is when he's sound asleep. They're a lot less dangerous when they're lying comatose in their coffins."

"I don't know where his coffin *is*," said Mallory. "That's why I'm in a hurry to catch up with him."

"You want a little protection?" said Odd Peter.

"What have you got?"

"I've got a spray that'll eat away at his skin and burn out his eyes, I've some powder that'll make his teeth, his nails, and his genitals fall off, I've got no end of things that'll make him wish he'd never been born." He paused. "The only problem is that you've got to be so close to him that he'll probably just take them away and turn them on you. The average vampire is fourteen times stronger than a man, or is it seventeen? Still, I suppose if you knew exactly where he was going, you could lean out a third-floor window and drop some of this stuff on him, and if the wind didn't blow it onto a bunch of innocent pedestrians, it might very well solve your problem."

"Sounds awfully complicated," said Mallory.

"Well, you *are* going up against one of the Creatures of the Night," replied Odd Peter. "Anything he can reach he can kill."

"Is there any other creature that a vampire is afraid of?" asked Mallory.

Odd Peter shook his head. "I've seen them whip their weight in gorgons, gryphons, ogres, and sea serpents. They're tough dudes, vampires. At least you're not up against one of the Transylvanian ones; they're the worst of all. Well, good luck, young man. Bring back both ears and the tail, or whatever fearless vampire killers bring back these days."

Mallory thanked him and went back out into the street. McGuire and Nathan began walking toward him. He couldn't spot Felina, but a moment later she leaped into the air from atop the awning in front of the shop, did a triple somersault, and landed right next to him.

"Not bad," said Mallory. "I'll give you a nine-point-seven for that."

"Is a nine-point-seven good to eat?" she asked.

"Not without mustard and relish."

"What did you learn?" asked Nathan as he and McGuire reached the detective.

"I learned where Vlad was half an hour ago," said Mallory. "Odd Peter tells me he only delivered two batches of the repellent today."

"Where?"

"One of them was to Tassel-Twirling Tessie Twinkle's burlesque palace," said Mallory.

"Sounds good to me," said McGuire enthusiastically.

"We can eliminate it," said Mallory. "That leaves the Our Lady of Perpetual Frustration Dialysis Center."

"Why not Tessie Twinkle's?" asked McGuire in crestfallen tones. "It's my favorite place in all the world."

"And you know how to get there, don't you?" said Mallory.

"Sure. It's just a block from Times Square."

"Right," said the detective. "In midtown. But we know that Vlad bought his antidote in Greenwich Village, and Our Lady of Perpetual Frustration is right in the heart of the Village, at the corner of Folly and Illusion."

"Makes sense," said Nathan. "I mean, I'm sure he'd love to bite a bunch of gorgeous naked women in the neck, but Tassel-Twirling Tessie Twinkle's always draws a crowd. That means a lot of witnesses. It makes more sense to go to a dialysis unit that deals in blood and probably is all but deserted at three in the morning, even on All Hallows' Eve."

"Why would he *care* if there were witnesses?" asked McGuire. "He's Vlad Dracule. Biting people in the neck is what he does. Who would stop him from biting all those round, ripe, pulsating, undulating . . ."

As he was searching for more adjectives, Mallory spoke up. "Forget it, Bats. Witnesses have nothing to do with it. We know he hit the Dialysis Center because he bought the makings for the antidote in the Village, and if he'd run across Odd Peter's stuff in midtown, he'd never have come all the way to the Village just to find a supermarket."

"So the Dialysis Center is our next destination?" said Nathan.

"Right," said Mallory. "I have a feeling that we're getting closer to him."

It was after 3:30 in the morning, but they were still celebrating All Hallows' Eve all over the Village. Men and women dressed as ghosts, ghouls, and other creatures of the night, and real ghosts, ghouls, and creatures of the night dressed as themselves mingled on the streets, in the alleys, in Washington Square, and on assorted rooftops. Rock bands, jazz bands, and dance bands all played their own riffs on funeral dirges. Puppeteers presented bloody pageants of death and destruction to the delight of human and other children who had been allowed to stay up on this special night.

"I don't suppose it'd do any good to question any of the revelers," remarked Nathan. "So far I've seen at least twenty Draculas."

"He hasn't been here," said Mallory.

"How do you know?"

"No dead bodies."

The detective checked the street signs and building numbers again. "It looks like Folly Place dead ends at that cross street. It's got to be Illusion Circle."

"I can see the sign now," said McGuire. "Our Lady of Perpetual Frustration."

"Yeah, there's the Dialysis Center, right next to the church," said Mallory.

"It looks dark," noted Nathan.

"It *is* dark," said McGuire.

They reached the front door of the center.

"Felina, do you smell anything?"

"Something very strange was here," said the cat-girl, sniffing the air. "But it's gone."

"Is there anyone inside?" asked Mallory.

"Not really."

"What the hell does that mean?"

She just smiled at him, and he gave up trying to get a cogent answer from her. Instead he reached out for the door and was mildly surprised to find that it wasn't locked. He pushed against it, and it swung inward.

"Nathan, stay right here by the door. No one enters, no one leaves."

"Right," said the dragon, holding his spear at the ready.

Mallory walked into the center's outer office. He felt around on the wall until he found a light switch and turned it on.

"*Jesus!*" he said softly as he surveyed the scene. A heavy wooden desk had been thrown against a wall, leaving a huge hole in the wood paneling. A file cabinet had been lifted up and hurled through a window.

Mallory walked over to the desk that lay on its side and tried to lift it. It didn't budge.

"Bats," he said, "grab the other end of this and see if we can move it."

McGuire walked to the far end of the desk, planted his feet, and lifted when Mallory lifted his own end. They raised the desk about an inch and a half but couldn't hold it aloft more than a few seconds.

"What the hell kind of creature could lift this damned thing and throw it halfway across the room into that wall?" mused Mallory.

"The kind we're after," said McGuire grimly.

"Come on," said Mallory, walking to a door that led to the interior of the building. "Let's see what other damage he did."

It didn't take long. Complex dialysis machines were flung against walls. Hospital beds were overturned. Another file cabinet was upended.

"What went on here?" asked McGuire as Felina, more subdued than usual, began sniffing at all the damage, trying to sort out the scents.

"You want a hypothesis?" said Mallory. "Vlad came here looking for blood, but this isn't a blood bank, it's a dialysis facility. They don't store blood here. They cleanse the patient's blood and put it back in his veins. So he made two mistakes: first, he thought this place would provide him with a supply of blood, and it didn't; and second, he never guessed they'd have covered the joint with Odd Peter's formula, and he began itching or burning or whatever the hell it does to him. So he went into a rage and tore the place apart before he went off to buy all the parts of the antidote."

"You're wrong, John Justin," said Felina.

"Oh?"

"You said he didn't get a supply of blood here."

"He didn't."

She smiled and pointed behind an overturned bed.

Mallory walked over and saw that there was a body on the floor. He knelt down next to it. It was a middle-aged woman. Part of her throat had been torn out, and all the blood had been drained from her body.

"That's not a medical uniform," noted Mallory, studying the body. "I'd say she works for a cleaning service, and it makes sense that she'd be here at night, when the place was closed for business." He shook his head. "Just bad timing. He didn't come here looking for her. If she'd shown up fifteen minutes sooner or fifteen minutes later, she'd probably still be alive."

Mallory stood up, walked through the center to make sure there were no other bodies, no one hiding and in need of help, and then, followed by Felina and McGuire, he walked out into the street.

"I take it he wasn't there?" said Nathan.

"Not now. But he was here earlier. He killed a cleaning woman. The cops will learn about it in the morning."

"You look upset," noted the dragon.

"I am."

"Dead bodies never bother the shamus in my books," said Nathan. "I would have thought you'd seen your share of stiffs."

"There's nothing attractive about a dead body, but that's not what's bothering me," said Mallory.

"Then what is?"

"I've been stalking Vlad Dracule all night without really having any idea of what I was up against. Well, I just saw an example of what he can do."

"You're not going to cut and run, are you?" asked Nathan.

"Of course he's not!" said McGuire heatedly. "This is the man who stood up to the Grundy, the most powerful demon on the East Coast."

"Mallory?" said Nathan. "What are you going to do?"

"I can't go up against this Dracule empty-handed," said Mallory. "I've got to arm myself."

"You're not empty-handed," said Nathan. "You showed me your gun, remember?"

"I don't know enough about him or what he can do," said Mallory. "Guns won't stop him. Hell, bullets probably just annoy him. I've got to arm myself with a little knowledge."

"Where do you go for that?" asked Nathan.

"When I needed to learn about unicorns, I went to the Museum of Natural History," said Mallory.

"They won't have anything about Vlad there," said McGuire.

"I know," said Mallory. He looked up. "There's a gas station across the street. You guys wait here. I'm going to borrow their phone book for a minute."

"What for?"

"If there's a Museum of Natural History, there's *got* to be a Museum of Unnatural History," said Mallory, walking toward the gas station. "That's where I'll find my answers."

CHAPTER 25

3:55 AM–4:26 AM

"I never heard of the place," remarked Nathan as they walked up Lexington Avenue, halfway between the Village and midtown.

"Neither did I," answered Mallory. "But I knew *this* Manhattan had to have it, or something like it."

"I don't know what they can tell you about vampires that *I* can't tell you," said McGuire. "After all, I have insider knowledge, so to speak."

"Can you tell me the limits of Vlad's strength?" said Mallory.

"Well, he's stronger than a desk or a file cabinet."

"Or a scared kid or a middle-aged cleaning lady," said the detective. "Yeah, I know. How do I subdue him, or at least protect myself from him?"

"Well . . . ah . . . that is . . ."

"That's why I'm going to the museum," said Mallory. He looked around the deserted street. "It must be later than I thought. We've gone four blocks and haven't run into a single goblin trying to sell us anything."

"You rang?" said a voice from the shadows off to his left.

"I knew it was too good to last," said Mallory.

"I am not here to sell you any products," said the goblin, stepping out under a streetlight. "No authentic oil paintings by the masters, no night-crawlers in case you have an urge to go fishing on your way home, not even any underage oversexed goblin girls."

"That's a pleasant change," said Mallory. "Now leave us alone."

"You *are* John Justin Mallory, are you not?"

"What of it?"

"And you're after the creature that calls itself Vlad Drachma?"

"So?"

"I have been empowered by the Church of the Unfailingly Contrite Sinners to sell you an indulgence for only seventeen dollars and thirty-one cents, which you'll agree is an exceptionally reasonable price to pay for an afterlife in one of the nicer suburbs of heaven, complete with guaranteed tee times at the local golf course."

"Forget it."

"Consider it forgotten," said the goblin. "Since you are clearly determined to face Vlad Drachma without having guaranteed your ascension to heaven, I also have for sale, at a very reasonable price, some of the finest salves and painkillers on the market, just the thing after a hard day in the fiery pits."

"Scaly Jim, stab him with your spear if he says another word," said Mallory.

"With pleasure," said the dragon.

The goblin immediately began acting out the various products and indulgences he was selling, holding up the appropriate number of fingers to indicate how many syllables in each word. The charades continued for another block, after which the goblin lost interest and went off to try to sell cemetery plots to a bearded, robed holy man who was carrying a sign informing one and all that the world would end at 8:43 (Eastern Standard Time) in the morning.

"Why are we slowing down?" asked McGuire.

"We're almost there," said Mallory.

"Nonsense," said McGuire. "We're between Twenty-seventh and Twenty-eighth."

"I'm just following the instructions I got over the phone," said Mallory. They came to an opening between two buildings. He looked up and saw a street sign telling him that he was now at the corner of Lexington and Forgotten Alley. "We turn left here."

"I never heard of it," said McGuire.

"Probably you've never wanted to find it before," replied Mallory. Suddenly he smiled.

"What is it?" asked McGuire.

"I sound like a native," he said. "That's the kind of answer everyone's always giving *me*."

The alley widened and became better lit. Mallory saw a couple of Gnomes of the Subway emerging from an underground station. They immediately began rummaging through a trash container. Finally they pulled out a crumpled newspaper that seemed no different from any of the others and walked off contentedly.

"So where is it?" asked McGuire.

"Somewhere along this alley," answered Mallory. "It's only a block or two long. We'll find it."

They passed a bar filled with goblins, another with elves, and a third with gremlins. A fourth structure was a club with placards announcing that it catered to gentlemen of the reptilian persuasion and featured Slinky Slithering Sally, who shed her clothes and her skin three times nightly and four times on Saturday.

Finally they came to a small stone building with a granite carving of a lamia standing atop a square world, with little ships sailing off the edge.

"This has to be the place," remarked Mallory.

"Yeah, that's about as unnatural as it gets," agreed McGuire. "Imagine anyone still thinking the Earth is square." He chuckled in amusement. "Everyone knows it's a trapezoid."

Mallory climbed the three stone steps to the front door. "Felina, I don't want you to touch anything."

"I won't," she said. "Probably. Unless it's tasty. Or small and defenseless. Or—"

"That's it. You stay outside and wait for me here."

"Maybe I will and maybe I won't."

"That seems fair enough," said Mallory. "Maybe I'll feed you again sometime before you die, and maybe I won't."

"I'll stay right here," she said promptly.

Mallory reached the entrance. "Bats, Nathan, are you coming?"

"Not me," said McGuire. "I don't want to see vampires depicted as unnatural."

"Right," said Mallory. "What's unnatural about being one of the undead and existing on a liquid diet, so to speak?"

"I'm glad you understand," said McGuire. "I'll keep an eye on the cat thing."

"Well, I'm coming," said Nathan. "I go wherever my literary source goes." He paused, lost in thought for a moment. "Have you been to the bathroom since this whole thing started?" he asked Mallory.

"I don't think so. Why?"

"That was very thoughtless of you," said Nathan.

"If you want to go, go," said Mallory. "I'm sure they've got one here. You don't need my permission or my company."

"*I* don't have to go."

"Then what's the problem?"

"I need to see how *you* go, what little idiosyncrasies you may exhibit. It's all for the book. I need to get every detail right."

"I do it like everybody else," said Mallory.

"But if I spend a lot of time watching everybody else, I'll get arrested," complained Nathan.

"That's always a possibility," agreed Mallory pleasantly.

"Maybe I'll just tag along and not worry about every last little detail."

"Sounds good to me," said Mallory.

The detective and the dragon entered the museum. They found themselves in a small lobby that led off in several directions. While they were trying to decide which way to go, a silver-haired man in a lab coat approached them.

"Welcome to the Museum of Unnatural History," he said. "Greetings and felicitations. Happy All Hallows' Eve. Huzzah!" He paused. "Is that enough, do you think?"

"Enough what?" asked Nathan.

"My board told me to join in the celebration if any patrons were around. Allow me to introduce myself. I am Professor Seldon Hari, the chief curator. My specialty is devolution, but I can show you anything you wish to see."

"Devolution?" said Mallory. "What is that?"

"Why, the antithesis of evolution, of course," replied Professor Hari. "Take our children, for example. Seventy-five years ago they listened to the sophisticated jazz stylings of Benny Goodman, and when they spoke of a band they meant Tommy or Jimmy Dorsey's. Fifty years ago their notion of music was Little Richard and Screamin' Jay Hawkins. Another devolution and they worshipped at the altar of Kiss. And today all trace of music is gone, replaced by something call rap." He shook his head. "From Beethoven to this in less than two centuries. If that isn't devolution, I don't know what is."

"You're just choosing one area: music," said Nathan. "Isn't that a little too limiting for you to draw such a conclusion?"

"Take any popular entertainment," answered Professor Hari. "Our taste in humor has devolved from Mort Sahl and the Marx Brothers to Adam Sandler and Borat. Our heroes have devolved from John Wayne to Sean Penn. As our actresses' brains have gotten smaller, their bosoms have gotten bigger. Devolution. Then there's literature. In 1875, the two best-selling books in American history were *Common Sense* and *Huckleberry Finn*. Move the calendar ahead to 1975, and they had been supplanted by *Valley of the Dolls* and *Peyton Place*. Need I say more? Shall we discuss television?"

"I'm afraid I don't have time right now," said Mallory. "I'm after something that hasn't devolved, because it's a few centuries old."

"Ah!" said Professor Hari. "Something mystical and possibly supernatural." He frowned. "Unless it's Miss Morgan, my high school English teacher. She been terrorizing students since the Stone Age."

"It's not your teacher," said Mallory.

"Good! She's the only thing that ever terrified me. Well, except for the seventeenth hole at Pebble Beach, and of course that's an inanimate thing, though sometimes I wonder, given the way the sand traps seem to reach out and grab my golf balls."

"I'm after a vampire from Transylvania," said Mallory. "He's used many names, including Vlad Dracule. I figure if I'm going to learn anything about him, this is the place to do it."

"Ah, vampires!" said Professor Hari, clapping his hands together enthusiastically. "Truly representative of the world's unnatural history. Fascinating creatures!"

"Can you tell me anything about them?"

"I can tell you almost everything about them, young man. For example, did you know they were widely known as *wampyres* until the middle of the twentieth century?"

"No, I didn't."

"Or that they were also known as Nosferatus?"

"I'm sure the origins of their names is endlessly fascinating, but I've got to catch this vampire before sunrise, and I need to know how to protect myself."

"Certainly, certainly," replied Professor Hari. "Once upon a time it was thought that you would be perfectly safe on a small island, or even in a rowboat, that vampires couldn't cross water, but of course they can."

"I know."

"It has also been suggested that a vampire cannot cross your threshold unless you invite him, and it seemed that the ideal way to keep a vampire away was simply not to speak to him." The professor sighed. "Didn't work, of course."

"What *does* work?"

"A silver bullet will kill a werewolf, but it has absolutely no effect on a vampire," continued Professor Hari. He seemed puzzled. "Isn't that odd?"

"How about a stake?" asked Mallory.

"No, thank you," said Professor Hari. "They give me heartburn."

"I mean, how about driving a stake through a vampire's heart?"

"Well, yes, of course, everyone knows that will kill him. The problem, of course, is that you have to get within arm's reach to drive the stake in, and his arm is . . . let me do the math . . . 16.93 times stronger than yours."

"How about crosses or holy water?" asked Mallory.

"I certainly wouldn't want to depend on a cross against a Jewish, Muslim, or Hindu vampire," answered the professor. "There is a strong body of opinion that garlic will keep a vampire at bay."

"Will it?"

Professor Hari shrugged. "I suppose it depends on the vampire. I can state with absolute certainty that when I had it on my breath it held Emmylou Goldberg at bay for an entire evening, but that was, oh, forty-seven years ago, and she may well have overcome her aversion to it by now."

Mallory checked his watch. "Can you tell me *anything* useful about vampires?"

"I thought that was just what I've been doing."

"If you can't tell me how to kill one or hold him at arm's length, can you tell me anything about their habits? Do they all sleep by day? Does sunlight turn them to dust?"

"They have sensitive skins, and they burn easily, but sunlight won't destroy them unless they lie out on the beach in a state of undress for perhaps a week. They prefer to sleep by day, but when the situation demands, they can remain awake in the daytime and sleep at night. The only thing they *must* do is sleep in their native soil."

"Are there any exceptions to that?"

"Well, I suppose there are a few vampires who absolutely cannot remain awake once the sun comes up."

"No, I mean about sleeping in their native soil?"

"No, there are no exceptions," answered Professor Hari. "Disgusting habit. You'd think they would spend half their time showering, but they don't. You know," he continued thoughtfully, "one of the eternal mysteries is why vampires don't have more dirt under their fingernails."

"Thank you, Professor," said Mallory. "You've been very generous with your time, but time is the one commodity that I'm running short of. I've really got to go."

"Are you quite sure?" replied Professor Hari. "We have a wonderful new Yeti display on the second floor, right next to all the exhibits on global warming."

"Perhaps some other time," said Mallory. "Come on, Jim."

Nathan turned and began following him to an exit.

"My goodness, have you been standing there listening all this time?" said Professor Hari. "I thought you were one of the exhibits."

"You're thinking of my aunt Maude," said Nathan. "She's in one of the back rooms."

"Do you really have an aunt Maude on display here?" asked Mallory as they left the building.

"Hell, no. I didn't even know this place existed until twenty minutes ago."

"Then why did you say it?"

"My aunt Maude never gave me a birthday or Christmas present. She ran off with a traveling salesman thirty-two years ago. I'd like to think she wound up here, stuffed and mounted."

McGuire and Felina were waiting where Mallory had left them.

"Did you learn anything?" asked the little vampire.

"Lots," said Mallory. "Most of it useless."

"So what's our next move?"

Mallory checked his watch again. "It's almost 4:30. The sun will be up in another two and a half hours. He's not leaving enough clues for me to track him down before then, so I think we're going to see if we can force him into making a mistake."

"How?" asked Nathan.

"I'm going to call Albert Feinstein and tell him to put a freeze on Vlad's TransEx card. Next time he tries to use it, he'll know someone's on to him. That means he'll have to use cash for all his transactions. We have to figure he hasn't got any, or he wouldn't keep using a traceable card. So he's going to need some quick cash."

"So?"

"He's been trying to keep a low profile. If he robs a store or a citizen, the cops will be after him—and for all he knows, the mark or the store might be under the Grundy's protection. I don't think he'll risk that. The easiest way to get cash at this time of night is to pawn something, and if he does, I know just the guy who can tell me the address on the pawn ticket," said Mallory.

CHAPTER 26

4:26 AM–5:07 AM

Mallory stopped when he came to an all-night coffee shop and entered it.

"I thought time was of the essence," said McGuire, as he, Nathan, and Felina followed the detective inside.

"I phoned Feinstein less than a minute ago. He's probably just freezing the card right now. We're going to have to give Vlad a little time to try to use it and find out it's no good." A young medusa with dark glasses approached them for their orders.

"Three coffees," said Mallory.

"And an elephant," said Felina.

"And a glass of milk," said Mallory.

"What if Vlad doesn't try to use his card before sunrise?" asked Nathan.

"Then we keep trying to hunt down his coffin during the day, and if we don't find it, we hope he tries to use his card tomorrow night."

"And that's *it*?"

"It's like a minimal-information problem," explained Mallory. "Our actions are constricted by what we know, and we don't know very much."

"In situations like this, Wings O'Bannon would renew his finely honed detective instincts," said Nathan.

"With a blonde or a brunette?" asked Mallory.

"First one, then a session at the target range, then the other," answered the dragon.

"I don't know where Wings O'Bannon finds the energy to get through the day," said Mallory.

"Hey, he's a detective," said Nathan, as if that answered everything.

"Let me tell you something, Scaly Jim," said Mallory. "Being a detective is a lot like being a big-game hunter. There are long days of following a trail as it goes this way and that, punctuated by a few seconds of excitement, during which time you wish you were back following the trail."

"That's antithetical to everything in a Wings O'Bannon novel!" protested Nathan.

"Which you write after drawing on your vast experience in the field of detection."

"There's no reason to get personal," said Nathan in hurt tones.

"You want to write about my bathroom habits, and you say there's no reason to get personal?"

"That was business!"

"*This* is business," replied Mallory. "We're on the trail of a cold-blooded killer, and we're beating time, waiting for him to make a mistake."

"You're destroying all my preconceptions," complained Nathan. "The next time Wings O'Bannon takes on a dozen hoods using only his wits and his dukes, I don't know if I can make it believable."

"He must have a brigade of bedmates, if not a whole division," said Mallory. "Have them help."

"Let's not be ridiculous," said Nathan with dignity.

"Right. No sense messing with the sense of realism that permeates the books."

"I'm glad you understand."

The medusa returned with their order. Felina grabbed her milk right off the tray, while the medusa handed each of the others their coffee.

Mallory took a sip, made a face, and poured in some cream. He tried again, didn't like it any better, and added sweetener. It didn't help.

"Try the ketchup next," suggested McGuire.

"I'll pass," said Mallory. He watched as the little vampire took the top off the bottle. "You're not really going to pour ketchup into your coffee, are you?"

"It's red," replied McGuire.

"So what?" asked Nathan.

"I have an urge to drink red things."

"You're never going to convince your body that it's blood," said the dragon.

"Speak for yourself," said McGuire. "My body is incredibly naïve and trusting." He paused. "Tomato soup would have been even better, now that I think of it."

"Why don't you just drink some blood and be done with it?" asked Nathan.

"Disgusting stuff," said McGuire.

"That's a hell of thing for a vampire to say," replied Nathan.

"Do I tell you to go out and kill knights in armor?" shot back McGuire. "Don't tell me how to be a vampire."

"Knock it off, both of you," said Mallory at last. "Try to remember who the real enemy is."

They spent another twenty minutes trying not to think about how their coffee tasted. Finally Mallory left some money on the table and stood up. "I think we've killed enough time. Let's go see if Vlad's noticed that his TransEx card's no good."

They went out onto the street. It began drizzling as Mallory turned left. They walked a few blocks and then came to a darkened building that covered an entire city block.

"Why are we stopping?" asked McGuire.

"We're here," said Mallory.

"But it's just an old warehouse."

"Right," said Mallory. "In point of fact, it's the Old Abandoned Warehouse."

"I heard about this place," said Nathan, frowning. "Isn't it owned by a duke or an earl or something?"

"The Prince of Whales, the biggest fence in the city," replied Mallory. "He's an old friend."

"It looks like he doesn't want any company," noted McGuire, indicating a quartet of leprechauns who were standing guard at the front door.

"Halt!" cried a leprechaun. "Who goes there?"

Mallory stepped forward. "You know who I am. Step aside and let me through."

"Nobody enters this building!" said the leprechaun.

"I haven't got time for the usual fun and games," said Mallory. "Just tell your boss that John Justin Mallory is here."

"You *look* like John Justin Mallory," said another leprechaun. "You *sound* like John Justin Mallory. You're as rude and aggressive and ill-mannered as John Justin Mallory. But how can we be sure?"

"Cut the crap. I've got to see the Prince."

"The only way to prove you're Mallory is to give us the passwords."

"Felina," said Mallory, "kill any leprechaun who tries to stop me."

"The very words!" said the leprechaun hastily. "'Felina, kill any leprechaun who tries to stop me.' You can enter."

The leprechauns fell all over themselves stepping aside to let Mallory and his party enter the building. The detective led the way through the rows of goods to a well-appointed office.

"Your security force is about as useful as ever," said Mallory.

A huge blue-skinned man in a purple sharkskin suit, light blue shirt, violet tie, and navy blue shoes and socks stood up from his desk. He was just under seven feet tall and weighed in the vicinity of five hundred pounds.

"Mallory!" he said in a deep voice. "Good to see you again!" He glanced at the detective's companions. "I see you still haven't managed to get rid of the cat creature. And who are these other two?"

"Bats McGuire and Scaly Jim Chandler," replied Mallory. "They're working with me on a case."

"Scaly Jim Chandler?" repeated the Prince of Whales. "I must have three hundred copies of your latest book here."

"You do?" said Nathan, surprised.

"Yeah. Some idiot thought you were the other Chandler and stole them. Tell you what—as long as you're a friend of Mallory's, come by anytime and you can cart them away."

"Really?" said Nathan happily. "That's very generous of you."

"Any friend of Mallory's is a friend of mine," said the Prince. "Besides, they're a drag on the market. I can't give the damned things away. They need more sex and violence." He turned to Mallory. "So what brings you here?"

"I need a favor."

"Anything for the man who put my evil twin Skippy behind bars. Just name it."

"I'm after a vampire who called himself Vlad Drachma. I had his credit card frozen, and I think if he needs money he'll either pawn something of his own or swipe something and pawn it."

"Drachma, Drachma," repeated the Prince of Whales. "No, he hasn't been here."

"You remember every fence and pawnbroker in the city," said Mallory. "Can you find out if he's pawned anything in the last half hour?"

"I can try."

"We'll wait."

"And that's all you want to know?" continued the Prince. "Just if he pawned anything?"

"And the address he gave on the pawn ticket."

"Ah!" said the Prince. "Let me get to work on it."

He had the answer four minutes later.

"He pawned a velvet cape at Stella Houston's," announced the Prince.

"Stella Houston's?"

"She used to be Stella Dallas before that incident with the entire Texas Oilwells football team," replied the Prince. "The one that made all the tabloids. Anyway, the address your vampire gave was the Kringleman Arms Hotel. Ever hear of it?"

"Yeah," said Mallory. "It's a boardinghouse for Santas, all those old guys you see on street corners in red suits and beards at Christmastime, ringing bells for charity." He frowned. "This doesn't make any sense. He'd stand out like a sore thumb there."

"Could there be two Kringleman Arms?" asked Nathan.

"Not a chance," said Mallory. "There's just the one. I was there on a case. It's owned by Nick the Saint, a high roller from up North."

"I remember him," said the Prince. "Got a blue-nosed reindeer, drives a hard bargain."

"That's the one," said Mallory. "I have a feeling this is a dead end, but we'd better check it out anyway. Thanks for your help."

"Any time," said the Prince, escorting them to the door.

"We'll take the subway," Mallory told his companions. "It's got to be fifty blocks from here. No sense walking it."

There was a station at the corner. They descended on an escalator, then waited about a minute for a subway train to pull up.

"What'll it be?" asked McGuire. "The observation car or the dining car?"

"This is an express," said Mallory. "We're getting off at the next stop. Just find a seat."

"You know," said Nathan, "I've never tried the sauna car. I understand it's unisex. I should scout it out, just to see if I want to put Wings O'Bannon there in my next book."

"If there are naked women, what's to scout out?" asked Mallory. "Of course you'll put him there."

"True, true," agreed Nathan. "It'll help him relieve all the tension from the chase that leads him to the train in the first place."

"I prefer the observation car," said McGuire. "Why work up a sweat when you're getting off in less than two minutes?"

"Bats, this is the subway," said Mallory. "There's nothing to observe."

"True," agreed McGuire. "But you can observe it from much closer range in the observation car."

"You observe what you want, and Wings will observe what *he* wants," said Nathan.

The train began screeching to a halt.

"We're here," said Mallory, looking at the station platform. "Let's go."

"Just over a minute and a half," noted Nathan as he followed Mallory out onto the platform. "Wings O'Bannon would have had time for seconds."

"He can't have satisfied his partners at that speed," noted Mallory.

"He's *Wings O'Bannon*," said Nathan. "Being with him is all the satisfaction they need."

"I apologize," said Mallory. "I wasn't thinking clearly."

The four of them took the escalator to the street level and stepped out into the cold drizzle.

"There it is, right across the street," said Mallory.

"It looks homey," observed McGuire.

"It looks full," said Nathan.

"Santas need a place to stay even when it's not Christmas," said Mallory. "Come on, let's go see if he's there."

They crossed the street and entered the hotel's lobby. Mallory walked up to the desk, where a bored young man greeted him.

"Good evening, and welcome to the Kringleman Arms, ho ho ho," he said. "How may I help you?"

"I'm looking for one of your borders," said Mallory. "Name of Vlad Drachma."

"No such person registered here, ho ho ho," said the clerk.

"How about Vlad Dracule?"

"Nope."

"Count Dracula?"

The clerk stared at him for a long moment. "Okay, where is it?"

"Where is *what*?"

"Come on," he said. "This is *Candid Camera*, right? I mean, who the hell else would ask for Count Dracula?" He looked around the lobby. "Where's the camera?"

"You're too smart for me, fella," said Mallory. "It's in the door handle."

He and his companions left the hotel as the clerk combed his hair, straightened his tie, and grinned stupidly at the handle on the front door.

"Was he telling the truth, do you think?" asked Nathan.

"Yeah," said Mallory. "He's too stupid to lie."

"Then we're out of leads. What do we do now?"

"Wait for a break in the case," answered Mallory. "Could take an hour, could take a day, could take a month."

He was wrong. It took ninety-three seconds.

"What if there *isn't* a break?" asked Nathan.

"Then he wins and we lose," said Mallory. "Your books to the contrary, the good guys don't always come out on top."

"That's unacceptable," said the dragon. "How am I going to sell *Stalking the Vampire* if we don't catch him?"

"Have him steal some of Wings O'Bannon's women," replied Mallory. "Love stories about vampires outsell hard-boiled detective novels twenty-to-one."

"I won't do it," said Nathan. "I have my pride." He paused thoughtfully. "Of course, I could always turn him into a detective, kind of like McGuire here, but good-looking and sexually irresistible."

Suddenly there was a thunderclap and a puff of smoke, and the Grundy was standing in front of them. Nathan jumped back, startled. McGuire fainted dead away. Felina paid him no attention whatsoever.

"If you've come to gloat because we've lost him, it's five in the morning and I'm not in the mood for it," said Mallory irritably.

"I have come to render you a favor," replied the demon.

"Concerning Vlad?"

"Yes."

"I thought your nature wouldn't let you interfere," said Mallory suspiciously.

"Eventually Albert Feinstein would locate you and transmit the same message. I am merely hastening the process, not precipitating or changing it."

"Why don't you save me a phone call and just tell me what he wants me to know?"

"I can't."

"Yeah, I know," said Mallory. "All those restrictions that you don't think are there. Still, you've done your good deed for tonight. I owe you one."

223

"I am incapable of committing a good deed," said the Grundy with a touch of repugnance at the concept. "I have merely performed a minor service for a worthy competitor."

"Competitor?" repeated Mallory, frowning.

"Rival, if you prefer."

"Fine. Where's the nearest phone?"

"You don't really expect me to tell you, do you?" said the Grundy.

"No, I suppose not. Thanks for the service. I'll take it from here. And by the way, you were right."

"Doubtless," replied the Grundy. "But what is this in reference to?"

"This case is a lot more complicated than just finding Aristotle Draconis."

"That is why it has sought you out."

"I beg your pardon?"

"For every prey animal, there is a predator uniquely suited to find and kill it. For every yang there is a yin. And for every crime, there is one and only one detective perfectly equipped to solve it."

"It may seem predestined to you that I'm going to nail him," said Mallory, "but he's killed at least two people tonight, I've only got about two hours of darkness left to find him, and every lead has turned out to be a dead end."

But the detective found that he was speaking to empty air.

"Where did he go?" he asked Felina.

"Away," she said.

"He's not still hanging around where I can't see him?"

She shook her head.

"Okay. Then I'd better get in touch with Feinstein." He looked around. "There must be some all-night diner or bar with a pay phone around here."

"Why don't you just use your cell phone?" asked Nathan.

"I don't have one," answered Mallory. "There has to be *some* time when no one can bother you."

"Just turn it off," said Nathan. "You don't have to leave it on, you know."

"If I'm going to leave it turned off, then why have it in the first place?"

"You know, I just hate questions like that," said Nathan, his brow furrowed in thought.

"Since you're so keen on cell phones, loan me yours," said Mallory.

"I can't."

"Why not?"

"I left it at home," said the dragon uncomfortably. "It just doesn't fit the image—a fierce, spear-carrying dragon with a cell phone."

"Then with your permission, I'm going to find a pay phone, like I was before we started this idiot conversation."

Mallory began walking down the block. When he'd made it halfway to the next corner, he came to a still-open bar.

"The Kretchma," he said, reading the sign on the window. "This place looks as likely as any." He turned to his companions. "You guys wait out here."

He entered the bar. There was a fiddler playing morbid Russian songs, a bartender who kept crying at each new one, and a waiter who finally came by with a menu tucked under his arm.

"May I get you a *wodka*, Comrade?" he asked.

"No, I just need to use a phone," answered Mallory. "Where can I find one?"

"In telephone stores, most kitchens, some bedrooms, the occasional hunting lodge, the ladies' lounge, the Hellhound Bus Station . . . There's no end of places where you can find a telephone, Comrade."

"How about right here?"

"Right where you're sitting?" said the waiter. "No, I don't see one there."

"Right here in the Kretchma," Mallory amended.

"There's one behind the bar and another just outside the men's room," said the waiter, holding out his hand for a tip.

"Thanks," said Mallory, taking his hand and shaking it. "Always nice to speak to someone who remembers his manners."

He walked to the phone by the men's room, where he would be less likely to be overheard, just in case he said something that was worth overhearing, then put a coin in the machine and tapped out Feinstein's number. A moment later the hacker picked up the receiver.

"Hi, Albert, this is Mallory," said the detective. "A mutual friend suggested that you wanted to speak to me."

"If he's the same one who's responsible for every disaster and death that takes place within the city limits, I prefer to think of him as a mutual acquaintance."

"Enough with the semantics," said Mallory. "What have you got for me?"

"Vlad contacted TransEx about ten minutes ago to report that his card was lost or stolen," said Feinstein. "They've issued him a new one. He hasn't got it yet, of course, but he's got the number, so he can use it to charge just about anything he wants by phone."

"He knows we're on to him," said Mallory. "That means he wouldn't have ordered a replacement card if he didn't need it. Keep an eye on him. I can almost guarantee he's going to use it, and soon."

"Will do."

"I'll check in with you every few minutes."

"Just give me your cell phone number," said Feinstein. "I'll call you the second he charges anything."

"I'll call you," repeated Mallory.

"I hadn't realized you had that many enemies," said Feinstein. "Yes, use untraceable public phones, by all means."

"Keep this line open," said Mallory.

"No problem," said Feinstein. "You're the only one who ever calls me. Everyone else contacts me via e-mail."

"Catch you soon," said Mallory, hanging up.

The waiter approached him the moment he was through with the phone. "Your *wodka*, Comrade."

"I didn't order any."

"It's goes with the phone."

"How much?"

"The *wodka* is free. The phone is six dollars."

"For a local call?"

"For a local call and a glass of Glorious Revolution."

Mallory left a five and a one on the waiter's tray and took a sip of the drink.

"What do you think?" asked the waiter, watching him intently.

"That's powerful stuff," rasped Mallory, certain that his throat was on fire.

"It's the same brand Stalin gave to Roosevelt right before they reached the Yalta Agreement."

"Figures," said Mallory. "I used to blame Roosevelt for giving away

Eastern Europe and setting up the conditions for the Cold War. Now I can see he'd have signed anything if it let him get away so he could get to a source of water and rinse his mouth out. Damned clever, these KGB."

"NKVD," the waiter corrected him. "Fiends of an earlier era."

The phone rang behind the bar. The bartender picked it up, listened for a moment, frowned, and held the receiver up. "Anyone here named Mallory?"

"Yeah, I am," said Mallory.

The bartender handed him the phone. "It's for you."

Mallory took the phone from him, staring at it curiously. Finally he placed it to his ear. "Hello?"

"Hi, Mallory," said the familiar voice at the other end. "This is Feinstein. I had my computer trace the call you just put through to me."

"What's up?"

"He just paid for a room at the Waldorf."

"Thanks, Albert. I'm on my way."

Mallory gave the phone back to the bartender.

"Not bad news I hope, Comrade?" said the waiter.

"Good news, actually," replied Mallory. "Nice meeting you."

"You have to leave right now?"

"Yeah."

"What a pity. You'll miss Natasha."

"Natasha?"

"Our singer," said the waiter. "Each song more heartbreaking than the last."

"Some other time," said the detective.

He had almost reached the door when the phone rang again.

"Mallory, it's for you," said the bartender in bored tones.

Mallory took the phone from him and held it to his ear. "Yeah?"

"Feinstein again," said the hacker. "He just checked into the Plaza."

"He didn't like the Waldorf?"

"He hasn't checked *out* of the Waldorf," said Feinstein. "Hold on a minute. Now he's got a room at the Leamington."

"He's playing games," said Mallory. "He's trying to send me on a wild goose chase all the hell over town, from one hotel to another. It's an old trick."

"Yeah," said Feinstein. "He just got a room at the Pierre. And here comes one at the Hyatt."

"You don't have to keep count," said Mallory. "He's not at any of them."

"He's probably at some little run-down hotel, laughing his head off at the thought of you checking out every hotel where he reserved a room."

"He's not at any hotel, luxurious or run-down," said Mallory.

"How do you know?" said Feinstein. "We're not that far from dawn. He needs a place to lie up."

"He's not in a hotel, because no hotel will let him bring his coffin up to his room."

"If he tips them enough, they *all* will."

"He knows that if *he* can tip them enough to break the rules, then whoever's chasing him can tip them enough to find out what hotel room's holding a Transylvanian casket."

"Then why is he going to all this trouble?"

"To keep us busy until dawn, while he goes to where he's always planned to go."

"And where is that?" asked Feinstein.

"His coffin," said Mallory.

"Well, of course his coffin," said Feinstein. "But where is it?"

"You're going to tell me, Albert."

"Me?"

"Yeah," said Mallory. "A while back you told me you traced my first call to this number."

"That's right," said Feinstein. "Piece of cake."

"Can you find out where Vlad was when he requested his new TransEx card?"

"I can do better than that!" said Einstein, suddenly enthused. "I can pinpoint where he's reserving all those hotel rooms from."

"Good," said Mallory. "Once you do, have your computer locate the nearest mortuary."

"Don't leave the Kretchma," said Feinstein. "This won't take more than a few minutes."

Mallory hung up the phone. "I guess I'll listen to Natasha after all," he told the waiter.

He sat down on a stool at the bar and turned to face the small stage, where the singer had just appeared. She had a fine figure, with the usual low-cut gown, but her songs were so morbid, her face so streaked with tears, that Mallory never looked below her neck. The first two songs ended in her suicide, the third in the murder of her lover, his parents, and her kid sister. The fourth song was cheerful by comparison; only the mailman died, ripped to shreds by the singer's guard dog, who mistook him for the stepfather who had sexually abused her in her youth.

Natasha had just taken her bows and exited when the bartender announced that there was another phone call for Mallory.

"Thanks," said the detective, taking the received from him.

"You ever think of getting a cell phone, Mac?"

"This should be the last call," Mallory assured him. He put the receiver to his year. "Albert?"

"Right here," Feinstein assured him.

"Did it work?"

"You'll have to go there, and then you can tell me," said Feinstein. "You ever hear of the Hills of Home Mortuary, Cemetery, and Delicatessen?"

"A place with a name like that actually exists?"

"You'd better hope so," said Feinstein. "Because it's two blocks from where he made the calls, and there's not another within a mile of him."

"We're on our way," said Mallory.

"Anything else I can do for you?"

"See if you can contact my partner, Winnifred Carruthers, and tell her to meet me back at the office."

"Roger, over and out," said the hacker.

Mallory retuurned the phone to the bartender, then walked out into the street, where he found his crew waiting for him.

"Did you learn anything useful?" asked Nathan.

"That's what we're going to find out," said Mallory.

CHAPTER 28

5:33 AM–6:01 AM

"Are we getting close, do you think?" asked McGuire as they walked through the lightly falling rain.

"Another two blocks," said Mallory.

"I mean to Vlad, not to the cemetery."

Mallory shrugged. "I don't know. I hope not."

"*What?*"

"You know the damage he can do. Are *you* ready to come face to face with him?"

"Then why are we trying to hunt him down?" demanded Nathan.

"It's like sports, or to use an example you'd understand better, it's like sex," answered Mallory. "Everything depends on timing."

"I *don't* understand," protested the dragon. "Are you trying to find him or not?"

"Yes, of course I am."

"Then what are you talking about?"

"If he's waiting for us at the entrance to the cemetery, he's meeting us on his terms," said Mallory. "I prefer to meet him on mine."

"*Have* you any terms?" persisted the dragon.

"I'm working on it."

"I know you must be good at your job," said McGuire, "or the Grundy would have killed you a long time ago. But I sure as hell don't see how you can meet Vlad on any terms other than his own."

"That's why I'm the detective and you're the sidekick," answered Mallory.

"Is that the only answer I'm going to get?" demanded the little vampire.

"For the time being."

"Oh, this is *good!*" said Nathan enthusiastically.

"What is?" asked Mallory.

"My book!" answered the dragon. "Well, *our* book. The hero has figured out the mystery, and now the readers have to see if they're as smart as he is." Nathan took out his notebook and began scribbling furiously.

"There's no mystery," said Mallory. "We know that Vlad killed Rupert Newton. And I'll give plenty of eight-to-one that we've already solved the location of his coffin."

"Say, that's right," said Nathan. "Good. Now we're done with the hard part. This is the point where Wings O'Bannon refreshes his spirit one last time—"

"By which you mean he beds one last 42-23-35 nymphomaniac," interjected Mallory.

"—and goes in with guns blazing to take care of the bad guy."

"You think blazing guns will take care of Vlad Dracule, do you?" said Mallory.

"Well, blazing wits," amended Nathan.

"Can you accept a gentle criticism, Scaly Jim?" said the detective.

"What is it?"

"Don't give up your day job."

"Well, if you're not going to shoot him, and you can't outfight him, and you're not going to confront him, what *are* you going to do?"

"Improvise."

"You're a very frustrating person to talk to," complained Nathan. "How can I do my research if you won't share with me?"

The Hills of Home Mortuary, Cemetery, and Delicatessen loomed just ahead of them. There was a large building right at the street, with the cemetery spread out behind it.

"I suggest that you start researching where his casket is," said the detective.

"There are dead people here," said Felina, sniffing the air.

"There usually are at a cemetery," replied Mallory.

"Not all of them are in the ground," she added.

"Let's go in and find out where the rest of them are," suggested Mallory, walking up to the building that held the mortuary and the deli.

"Maybe I should stand guard out here," said McGuire nervously.

"Suit yourself," said Mallory.

"Of course," continued the little vampire, "if something attacks, I'd be facing it alone, wouldn't I?"

"Why would anything attack you? You belong here, in a manner of speaking."

"I most certainly do not," said McGuire, his gaze darting from one shadow to another. "I belong in my room, under my covers, reading a good book."

"I'll be happy to give you one if we survive the next two hours," offered Nathan. "Real cerebral stuff, with an exquisite felicity of expression, a certain *je ne c'est quois*, and a lot of guns and broads."

"*Lots* of dead things," said Felina, staring into the darkness at something only she could see.

"Maybe I'll come inside with you," said McGuire. "After all, I did volunteer to protect you."

"Whatever makes you happy," said Mallory, opening the door.

"Welcome to the Hills of Home," said a cheerful white-haired man. "Are you the bereaved or the newly deceased?" He stared at McGuire. "Or a little of both?"

"I'm just here to ask a few questions," said Mallory.

"Wonderful!" said the man. "I love quizzes! While we're taking it, I can offer you a beautiful velvet-lined coffin, or perhaps a knish and some chopped liver, depending on your needs?" He studied Felina. "Or maybe some lox?"

"Let's start with the questions," said Mallory.

"Ready," said the man. "Gypsy Rose Lee, an hour and thirteen minutes, and Butte, Montana, in September of 1926."

"What are you talking about?" asked Mallory, confused.

"My first three answers, of course," said the man. "Now let's see if the quality of your questions is up to the quality of my answers."

"Why don't you let me ask my questions first, and then try to answer them?" suggested Mallory.

"But that's so commonplace," protested the man. "By the way, we haven't been introduced." He extended his hand. "My name is Hermes."

"Mallory."

"No, Hermes."

"I meant that *I'm* Mallory."

"Pleased to meet you," said Hermes. "You sure I can't interest you in some cheese blintzes, covered with sour cream and topped off with cinnamon sugar? Or maybe a funeral in any of the seventy-four most popular religions, with two hundred guaranteed mourners, at least three of which will have hysterics and have to be sedated?"

"Blintzes!" said Felina.

"You don't even know what a blintz is," said Mallory.

"If it's smaller than me, who cares?" said Felina. She smiled. "It doesn't even have to be dead. Yet."

"Later," said Mallory, as the cat-girl turned her back on him and began assiduously licking a forearm.

"So, Mr. Mallory," said Hermes, "can I get you something from the deli, or are we going to play more guessing games?"

"Let's try a question," said Mallory. "How many vampires leave their coffins here?"

"None," replied Hermes. "Sooner or later they all take them away."

"Let me rephrase that: How many vampires currently have their coffins here?"

The old man scratched his head. "Maybe thirty, maybe thirty-five. Can't be more than forty, and that's a fact."

"Why not?"

"Only got forty private mausoleums. Wouldn't do for a vampire to bury his coffin in the ground. He'd have to dig it up every time he wanted to catch forty winks."

"What's a wink?" asked Felina, turning to face him. "Are they good to eat?"

"Next question," said Mallory.

"You didn't answer your ladyfriend's question," noted Hermes.

"She's not my ladyfriend, and I'm asking the questions, not answering them," said Mallory. "Next question: Do any of the mausoleums have a coffin from Transylvania?"

"Is that anywhere near Pennsylvania?" asked the old man.

"Let's try another," said Mallory. "The particular vampire I'm after has been in Manhattan for less than a week. How many coffins have you taken in during the past six or seven days?"

"Maybe fifteen or so," said Hermes. "They travel a lot, vampires. Always seeking fresh blood, so to speak."

"Have you got a list of those fifteen most recent arrivals?" asked Mallory.

"Sure have."

"Can I see it?"

"No reason why not," said Hermes. "I'm always open to negotiation."

"How much?"

"I can't take a bribe to reveal confidential information," said the old man. "That's against the law."

Mallory frowned. "What do you want, then?"

"Your cat-girl sounded pretty hungry. How'd you like to buy her two pounds of gefilte fish?"

"Deal," said Mallory. "We'll pick it up on our way out of here."

"Give me a minute to make up the list," said Hermes, pulling out a thick ledger, a sheet of paper, and a quill pen.

"I want my gifted fish now," said Felina.

"They're your payment for helping me," said Mallory. "First you work, then you eat."

"How soon?" she demanded.

"Very soon."

"Good. I've never had a gifted fish before. Maybe we can have a nice educational chat before I kill it."

"Here you are," said Hermes, handing a sheet of paper to Mallory.

"I don't understand," said Mallory, reading the paper. "These aren't numbers."

"The mausoleums aren't numbered. Each one has a classical or mythical name. These are the names of the ones that have the recent arrivals."

"And where are they?"

"Out back," said Hermes, pointing. "You can't miss them. Or maybe you can." He handed Mallory a flashlight. "Here. You'd better take this."

"Thanks."

Mallory led his companions out to the rows of stone mausoleums. As he came to one that's name matched a name on the paper, he opened the door and called Felina over.

"We're looking for the same person who was at the dialysis center in the Village," he told her. "Take a whiff and tell me if this is where he lives."

"He doesn't *live* at all," said Felina.

"Where he stays," amended the detective.

They went through the first dozen mausoleums with no luck. Then they came to the one marked *Styx*. As soon as Mallory cracked the door open Felina's entire posture changed.

"This is it, isn't it?" asked Mallory.

She nodded.

"Is he here now?"

"No."

"Let's hope you're right," said Mallory, entering the small structure, followed by Felina, Nathan, and McGuire.

There was a hardwood coffin lying on the floor. It had numerous words carved on it, in a language Mallory couldn't read.

"Let's open it up," he said.

"What if Vlad's in it and we wake him up?" asked McGuire nervously.

"He's not," answered Mallory. "Felina would know if he was here."

"What if she's wrong?"

"I don't know about you," said Mallory, unlatching the top of the coffin, "but I'll be very unhappy about it. Come on, Nathan—give me a hand."

The detective and the dragon opened the coffin and looked in. The bottom was covered by perhaps an inch of dirt. Mallory reached down and picked up a handful.

"Pure Transylvanian soil," he said, letting it slide out through his fingers.

"Okay, we found his coffin," said Nathan. "He's due back sometime in the next hour and a half, so now what do we do?"

"Now we get to work," said Mallory. "Nathan, there's got to be a caretaker's cabin around here, and there has to be some grave-digging equipment. See if you can scare up a shovel or two. If not, I suppose even a dustpan will do."

"Right," said the dragon.

"Bats," continued Mallory, "stay here and if Vlad shows up, give a holler."

"I'll give a scream you wouldn't believe," answered McGuire. "Right before I take off like a Bats out of hell."

"Felina," said Mallory as he left the mausoleum and headed back to the main building, "you come with me."

When Mallory arrived, Hermes was waiting for him.

"Got my flashlight?" asked the old man.

"I'll need it a little longer," replied Mallory. He pulled some cash out of his pocket and handed it to Hermes. "For the gefilte fish. She earned it. And toss in some lox, too."

"It's a pleasure doing . . . whatever it is we're doing, with you, young man," said Hermes.

"I need two more favors," said Mallory. "First, have you got a couple of buckets, or if not, some sturdy garbage bags?"

"Got both," said the old man. "Take your choice."

"Thanks. And can I borrow a phone for a couple of local calls?"

"Sure."

He led the detective to a telephone. Mallory dialed his office. Winnifred wasn't there yet, but he left her a message telling her what he wanted her to do. He made one more call, and then, while Felina happily stuffed her face with gefilte fish, he found two empty buckets in the deli's kitchen and went back to the mausoleum.

"Is Nathan back yet?" he asked McGuire, who was guarding the door.

"Yes," said the little vampire. "He's inside."

"Good. Come in with me and make yourself useful."

They entered the mausoleum.

"What did you find, Nathan?" asked Mallory.

"A shovel and a dustpan," answered the dragon. "I hope you're not going to suggest that we dig a grave and bury the coffin."

"Nothing that complicated," said Mallory. He placed the buckets on the floor next to the coffin. "I want the two of you to scoop all the dirt out of the coffin and put it in here."

"Then what?"

"Then I'll tell you what to do next."

"I hope you know what you're doing," said McGuire, grabbing the dustpan and beginning to scoop the soil out of the coffin.

"That makes two of us," said Mallory.

It took the dragon and the vampire about five minutes to complete the job.

"Now what?"

Mallory pulled two business cards out of his wallet. On the back of the first he scribbled an address.

"Now you take the buckets *here*," he said, handing the card to Nathan. "Someone will be waiting for you and will tell you what to do with them."

"What about Felina?"

"If she hasn't made herself sick already, she can come back to the office with me. Otherwise she can spend the night here."

"You're going back to your office?" said Nathan.

"Yeah," said Mallory. "Your story needs an ending, doesn't it? And I might as well play out the final chapter where the whole thing began."

"All alone?" said the dragon with a puzzled frown.

"I won't be alone," said Mallory, and with that, he leaned over and laid the other business card face up on the floor of the coffin.

It took Mallory fifteen minutes to get back to his office. Felina had gorged herself on the fish, and he left her at the Hills of Home.

The first thing he did was check the answering machine. His message to Winnifred had been erased, so at least he knew she received it. He looked around for some sign that she'd done what he asked, and finally he found it: a small "Paid" receipt placed carefully beneath his *Racing Form*.

"Hey, Periwinkle," he said, "are you awake?"

"I am *now*," grumbled his magic mirror.

"I've been up all night. Show me something that'll keep me alert."

"With or without pasties and g-strings?" asked Periwinkle.

"Spare me your sarcasm," said Mallory. "I need something fast-paced and exciting."

"To which I repeat: With or without pasties and g-strings?"

"I have a feeling that Wings O'Bannon has spoiled that particular form of entertainment for me, at least for a few days. How about a nice cheerful musical?"

"Perhaps *Pygmalion?*" suggested Periwinkle.

"You mean *My Fair Lady*."

"I mean *Pygmalion*, the musical that Rodgers and Hammerstein were commissioned to write. Lerner and Loewe wrote *My Fair Lady* only after Rodgers and Hammerstein abandoned the project."

"Yeah, I suppose that could be interesting."

"You don't seem wildly enthused," noted the mirror.

"I'm just killing time."

"Until what?"

"You'll see soon enough," said Mallory.

"If you need to get your adrenaline flowing, I could show you a partic-

239

ular 1949 Roller Derby in which Tuffy Bresheen put three girls from the opposing team into the hospital."

"That's before I was born," complained Mallory. "Why do you always insist on showing me Tuffy Bresheen?"

"She was my ideal," answered Periwinkle. "One hundred sixty pounds of muscle and savagery. Give me fifty like her and I could conquer the world."

"I got a feeling I could use all fifty of them before sunrise," said Mallory. He lit a cigarette.

"I thought you were trying to give those up," said the mirror.

"Tomorrow. Right after I start my diet."

"Yes, of course. And now, since you seem unable to decide upon an entertainment, I'm going back to sleep."

"Yeah, go ahead," said Mallory. "I'm sorry I disturbed you."

Periwinkle made no reply, and Mallory assumed the mirror was already asleep. He checked his watch. It was 6:27.

He walked over to Winnifred's desk, picked up a book, and thumbed through the pages. It concerned the coming of age of a young woman in nineteenth-century London. Mallory was sure it was a fine book, filled with historical accuracy and brilliant insights, but somehow he had a feeling he'd be more comfortable with a Wings O'Bannon adventure.

He went back to his desk and checked the time again: 6:41. He looked out the window. The sun would be up in less than an hour.

He picked up a magazine, thumbed through it, studied the center spread with a practiced eye, admitted to himself that he didn't really buy it for the articles, and replaced it in a desk drawer.

Suddenly he heard wings flapping in the next room. He didn't have to look to know what it was. He had left the window open about a foot, big enough for a large bat to get through. Then he heard something that was far too large and too heavy to fit through the window land on the floor.

Mallory swiveled his chair so that he was facing the room in question. A moment later a man of moderate build, clad all in black, entered the room.

There was something strange, something *dead*, about his eyes. His skin was gray and wizened, his hair black with gray streaks on the side, his nose thin and aquiline, his lips also thin, his mouth broad, his teeth—even his large canines—yellow with age and lack of care. He stood and walked as if each movement caused him discomfort if not pain, yet he exuded an air of power.

"I have come for that which is mine," he said in a voice that seemed too strong for his body.

"You have come because I sent for you," replied Mallory.

"And why *have* you sent for me? I have never seen you before. Your name was unknown to me prior to this morning."

"Yeah, well, your name is not unknown to me. One of them, anyway. Welcome to my humble office, Vlad Dracule."

"So you know," remarked the vampire. Then he shrugged. "It makes no difference. It is a piece of knowledge that will die with you."

Mallory looked out a window. "The sun's coming up in about forty-five minutes. I know where *I'm* sleeping." He turned back to the vampire. "Do you know where *you're* taking your next nap?"

"So *that* is what this is about," said Vlad. "What do you want for the return of my soil?"

"It's not for sale."

Vlad Dracule frowned. "Explain yourself."

Mallory stood stock-still for a moment. Then he heard the sound he had been waiting for from the next room, and he turned his attention back to the vampire.

"I don't want your money," said Mallory. "You are an evil, unclean *thing* who killed the wrong person—the young man you first bit on the *Moribund Manatee*."

"I think we must come to an understanding, John Justin Mallory," said the vampire. "I am very old, older than I think you can imagine. I was here before Prague and Budapest, before Rome, even before Troy. Look at me, Mr. Mallory. My skin is like parchment, my bones frail. I am tired of living, yet the life force remains strong within me. For many decades now I have wished I could die, just lay down the burden of my years and my millennia and cease to exist, but that was not to be. I am what I am, and I am here for the remainder of Time, for better or for worse."

Even as he spoke the years seemed to melt off Vlad Dracule's body, and when he was finished, he faced Mallory, awesome and frightening in his new-found vitality and strength.

"Do you do card tricks too?" asked Mallory, trying to sound much less impressed and frightened than he felt. .

The vampire half hissed, half roared his rage. "You know what I've come for! I cannot be killed. Now give me that which you have stolen or suffer the consequences!"

"Keep your threats to yourself," said Mallory with more confidence than he felt. "That is, if you want to know where your soil is." Mallory studied him. "And you *do* want to know, don't you? I don't know why a night's sleep is so valuable to you—I haven't had one, and I'm still going strong—but it's obvious that you need it."

Vlad made an almost physical effort to control his rising anger.

"You are meddling in things that you know nothing about, areas that can be of no concern to you," he said. "Give me the soil this minute and I may let you live."

"You're in no bargaining position," Mallory pointed out. "I have something you want. You have nothing that is of any interest to me."

"Then what *do* you want?"

"I want you to return to Transylvania and never come back here."

Vlad Dracule drew himself up to his full height, which seemed considerably taller than only a moment earlier. "I come and go where I please."

"Save it for people who don't have any bargaining chips," said Mallory. "I've got your soil, and if you didn't need it back, you wouldn't be here. Let me know when you're through making empty threats and are willing to talk business."

"You have already stated your demand," said Vlad. "It is unacceptable. Give me what I came for or prepare to suffer the consequences."

"I can't give it to you," answered Mallory.

"Why not?" thundered the vampire.

"Because it is currently in a coffin aboard a ship bound for Eastern Europe."

Vlad Dracule emitted a roar of fury. His eyes narrowed, his face became elongated, and suddenly he was exposing truly phenomenal canines.

"Prepare to die!" he thundered.

"If I die, I won't die alone," said Mallory. "Now shut up and listen."

The vampire glared at the detective, but remained where he was.

"Let me tell you what your options are," said Mallory. "First, you can kill me, but if you do you're never going to learn the name and location of the ship that's about to leave with your coffin."

"I will find it," growled Vlad Dracule.

Mallory shook his head. "You can't even leave this office without my help. Do you remember what you felt like when you ripped the dialysis center apart earlier tonight? While I was at the cemetery, my partner treated all the doors and windows with a much stronger solution, courtesy of a gentleman named Odd Peter. If I don't open the door for you, you're stuck here."

"Fool!" rasped the vampire. "How do you think I entered?"

"You entered through the one untreated window, which I left open for you. But my partner was standing outside the building, and the moment she saw you fly in, she closed the window and treated it. But don't take *my* word for it; go see if it's still open."

Vlad raced to the window in the next room. His roar of anger when he saw it was closed was almost deafening.

"Your second option," said Mallory when the vampire returned to the office, "is to agree to my terms. Swear to me that you will never return to this country, and I'll let you out." He looked out a window. "I think you'll have time to make it to the ship just ahead of the sun."

Vlad Dracule stared at him with more hate than Mallory had ever seen on a face, human or otherwise.

"While you're considering which option to choose, it's only fair that I tell you that I have two friends aboard the ship who have been instructed to seal your coffin the moment you're in it, and the ship's personnel have orders not to unseal it until it has been returned to Transylvania." Mallory met the vampire's gaze. "Now it's up to you. Are you really as tired of living as you say, or would you like to take your chances in the old country?"

"How little you know of things!" hissed Vlad Dracule. "You cannot kill me."

"Maybe so, maybe not," replied Mallory, "but I can keep you in this office until they tear the building down. And while I don't know quite what your need for that soil is, I know that if we talk for another couple of minutes, it's gone and you're stranded here without it."

The vampire stared at him curiously. "You have absolutely no fear of me, have you?"

"Wings O'Bannon has no fear of you," said Mallory. "And he'd have been dead five minutes into this case. Me, I'm scared to death of you. That's why I took all the precautions I took." He glanced out the window again. "The sun's up in another few minutes. What's your decision?"

For just a moment Mallory thought Vlad was going to pounce on him and tear him apart. Then all the vampire's energy seemed to vanish, and he was once again the old and wizened man that had first entered the office.

"We have an agreement," he said. "Now let me out. I *must* reach that ship before sunrise."

Mallory walked him to the office door and opened it.

"Go to the same set of docks where you arrived last week," said Mallory as they walked out onto the street. "At Pier 66 you'll find a ship called the *Cryptic Corpse*. Go to the cargo hold—there will be a window opened to accommodate you—and you'll find your coffin."

"I will not thank you," said Vlad Dracule. "But I will give you a piece of advice."

"Yes?"

"If you should go abroad in the future, stay out of Transylvania."

"Words to live by," said Mallory sardonically.

"Precisely," said Vlad—and suddenly there was a pile of black clothes at Mallory's feet, and a huge bat was flying south and east across the night sky.

As he returned to his office, Mallory heard a familiar voice say: "Not bad, John Justin Mallory. Not bad at all. Next week we shall be at hazard again, but in honor of your accomplishment I hereby declare a one-week truce."

"So I got rid of the vampire *and* impressed the Grundy," said Mallory as he sat down at his desk. "Let's see Wings O'Bannon pull *that* off."

CHAPTER 30

Sunrise

"How are we going to clean Odd Peter's formula off the doors and windows?" asked Winnifred as she and Mallory sat in their office.

"Why bother?" replied Mallory. "It only affects vampires. Maybe Vlad had friends."

She looked surprised. "Do you really think so?"

"Him? Friends?" Mallory shook his head. "Not a chance."

"I still feel badly that we let him go," said Winnifred. "We should have done something more."

"Like what?" said Mallory. "Instead of feeling badly, you ought to try feeling lucky that you and your trolls didn't run into him during the night. I think bullets would just have annoyed him—even from a .550 Nitro Express."

"Not *these* bullets," said Winnifred. She reached into her purse, pulled one out, and tossed it to the detective.

"Well, I'll be damned!" said Mallory. "I've heard of hard-nosed bullets and soft-nosed bullets, but this is the first time I've ever seen a wood-nosed bullet. Still, I don't know if it would have done the trick. When all is said and done, it's not a stake."

"It's wood and it would have pierced his heart."

"I think maybe the reason for a stake is to keep the wound distended. These would have passed right through him, always assuming they could even pierce his skin." He grimaced. "Besides, all this talk about killing him is academic."

"I don't follow you, John Justin."

"He was already dead."

She sighed. "I keep forgetting that."

The phone rang, and Mallory picked it up. "Yeah?"

"Just reporting in," said Nathan.

"He showed up?"

"He beat the sun by less than a minute," said the dragon.

"And you sealed him in?"

"Yes. What do we do now?"

"Why don't you come by the office, and we'll all go out for some break-fast?" said Mallory.

"I've never been there."

"Bats knows the way."

"Okay, we'll leave just as soon as he finishes sloshing on his sunscreen and remembering where he stashed his shades."

Mallory hung up the phone. "He's in his coffin."

"Who was that?"

"Scaly Jim Chandler."

"The dragon," she said, nodding. "And what happened to the little vampire?"

"Bats McGuire," said Mallory. "He's with Nathan. They're on their way here now. They stuck by me all night. I figure the least we can do is buy them breakfast."

"Certainly," she agreed. She looked around the office. "I don't see Felina. She isn't . . . ?"

"No," replied the detective. "She just lost a battle with some gefilte fish."

There was a scratching at the office door. Winnifred got up and opened it, and Felina, her belly a bit distended, staggered in.

"I'm dying!" moaned the cat-girl.

"Come on now," said Mallory. "You ought to be over it by now."

"After you left we had tuna, and then sardines, and smoked fish, and more lox, and more gifted fish, and I'm dying."

She lay down on the floor, curled up in a fetal ball.

"What's this all about, John Justin?" asked Winnifred.

"It's about a cat whose eyes were bigger than her stomach."

Felina rolled onto her back and pointed to her belly. "*Nothing's* bigger than my stomach!"

"Win a few, lose a few," commented Mallory. "Or maybe I should say, eat a lot, lose a lot."

"Don't make jokes," moaned the cat-girl. "If I die, whose back will you skritch?"

"I haven't really thought that far ahead," said Mallory.

"She really seems to be in some distress," observed Winnifred.

"So would you be if you'd eaten half the population of the Atlantic Ocean," answered Mallory. "Let her lie where she is. She'll be fine in another month or two."

Felina hissed at him and began crawling across the floor. "I'm going into the next room to die. Then you'll be sorry."

"I'm already sorry," said Mallory.

"You are?" she asked, her face brightening a bit.

"Yeah. I hate to think of the bill the guy at the deli is going to send us."

"You're cruel and heartless," whispered Felina as she reached the next room, waited until she was sure they were both watching her, and collapsed.

"I thought I just saved us all from someone who was cruel and heartless."

"I hate you."

"Remember that the next time you want your back scratched."

"*Skritched!*" she moaned.

"Should we do anything for her?" asked Winnifred in worried tones.

"Maybe just buy her a blackboard and make her write 'I will not eat seventy-three pounds of fish at one sitting' a few hundred times." The rays of the sun began pouring in through the window. "By the way, have you made funeral arrangements for Rupert?"

"Yes, I took care of it when I claimed his body at the morgue." She paused. "Tell me about this Odd Peter. I never heard of his establishment before."

Mallory spent the next twenty minutes describing his evening, from the Vampire State Building to the morgue to the Zombies' Ball to the Gryphon's Roost to the Battery to the dialysis center to Odd Peter's to the waterfront to the Hills of Home. He had just finished when Nathan and McGuire showed up.

"What the hell have you got on your door?" asked McGuire as Nathan opened it and the little vampire stepped into the office.

"A little something Odd Peter mixed up for us," replied the detective. "Don't touch the windows, and let someone else open the door for you, and you'll be okay."

"Hello again, ma'am," said Nathan. He looked around the office. "Where is she?"

"Where is *who*?" asked Mallory.

"You really and truly don't have a gorgeous oversexed secretary named Velma?"

Winnifred and Mallory exchanged looks.

"She's on vacation," said Winnifred.

"Hah!" said Nathan. "I *knew* he was putting me on."

"Okay," said Mallory, "are we all ready for breakfast?"

He could have guessed what was coming next, as ninety-plus pounds of cat-girl landed on his back. "*I'm* ready, John Justin!" said Felina, stifling a little ladylike belch.

The five of them walked out into the early morning sunlight.

"We missed All Hallows' Eve," said Winnifred, her face reflecting her disappointment. "The parties, the pageants, the celebrations, all the ghosts and spirits are gone for another year." She sighed. "Everything's back to normal."

"Out of the way, Mac!" yelled a goblin with a satchel slung over its shoulder, sitting atop a yellow elephant that missed trampling the detective by inches. "The US Mail stops for no man!"

"Yeah," grated Mallory. "Everything's back to normal."

Stalking the Vampire

by Col. Winnifred Carruthers

(speech delivered before the Blood Sports Enthusiasts
of Lower South Manhattan)

I have been asked many times: What is the best weapon to use against a vampire?

Are you better off with a wooden stake, or perhaps a wood-shafted arrow shot from a crossbow that has been blessed by a priest? I have even heard of one gentleman who created wooden bullets, which doubtless seemed like a brilliant idea until the first one lost its structural integrity upon firing and caused the pistol to explode in his hand.

The answer, of course, is the very best weapon to use is your brain. Wooden stakes and arrows and other traditional anti-vampiric weapons are all very well and good, but we're not speaking of a dumb herbivore like a gazelle or a unicorn here, an animal that seeks only to escape. No, my friends, the vampire is endowed with a brain every bit as good as your own and is as anxious to kill you as you are to kill him. Never forget that: he is *not* trying to escape, and while you may trick him from time to time, you are no more likely to outsmart him than he is to outsmart you—perhaps less so, since in all likelihood he has been around longer and has certainly been hunting men longer than you have been hunting vampires.

I suggest that you study the beasts of the field. The predator never seeks out the strongest member of the herd; he goes after the young, the ancient, and the infirm. It is not a bad principle to apply when hunting the vampire.

No, you won't find any young ones, and the ancient ones are as strong as any of the others. But the principle holds true: you attack the weakest, and since there is no way to differentiate, you attack when your prey is *at* his weakest—in broad daylight, when he's asleep in his coffin.

So just as the predator knows that sooner or later his prey must come to the water hole to slake its thirst, the vampire hunter knows that every day at sunrise the vampire must seek out his coffin, lie down in his native soil, and remain there until sunset.

Which means that just as our hypothetical predator must know the terrain, must know every water hole, every place of concealment, so must the vampire hunter learn *his* terrain, which is to say, he must become intimately acquainted with cemeteries, mausoleums, mortuaries, and any other place where a vampire is likely to store his coffin.

The predator stakes out his territory, usually by leaving signatures of urine or dung on the grass and shrubbery, signals that his rivals can read. It is essential that the vampire hunter stake out *his* territory as well, though by more socially acceptable means, because the mature vampire has heightened senses of perception and will be as likely to spot three or four of his predators as just one.

Just as the rhino has his tick birds to warn him of approaching danger, just as the gorgon has his smerps, so the vampire has *his* helpers. Usually they are called renfields, though the names vary with the territory. They are the once-bitten and twice-bitten who are in thrall to the vampire and serve as his lookouts, his informers, and his late-night snacks, or frequently all three. So if you see a renfield walking through the mortuary, keep perfectly still until he has given the all-clear sign to his dark master, and even then you would be wise to wait until the vampire is safely ensconced inside his coffin before showing yourself. Most renfields are cowards at heart, and even those who aren't can usually be bought off with a handful of insects and spiders, which form the staple of their daily diet.

Then it is simply a matter of waiting until the renfield is gone, opening the coffin, and driving home that wooden stake. I prefer hickory, but oak, maple, and even redwood have been used with some success. I would beware of the wood of the African accacia tree, as you never know if a witch doctor has cursed it.

I see some unhappy faces out there. I know, I know—this runs contrary to your sporting instincts, as it doesn't give the vampire a sporting chance to escape. The thing I have to keep emphasizing is that he doesn't *want* to escape. Nor will he meet you on equal footing: when he is awake and on the stalk, even a bullet from a .550 Nitro Express won't slow him down. If you can get close enough to drive in that wooden stake, you'll kill him, of course, but he is as aware of that as you are and will be on his guard.

How would you approach a vampire?

Again, your greatest weapon is your brain. Let me give you a few examples.

Vampires, as you know, leave no reflection in the mirror. You might stare at him, frown, and offer him a comb. It's a reasonable thing to do, since he has no idea how his hair looks, and as he reaches out to accept the comb, you move in quickly with the stake.

If you are a woman, and this works not only for vampires but for any other human-appearing creatures you cannot kill from afar, just stare at his crotch and pretend you are trying very hard to repress a giggle. He will wonder what is wrong, perhaps even ask you. Just blush and say that of course nothing is wrong, then put your hand over your mouth to stifle a laugh. Sooner or later he'll look down to see if his fly is unzipped, and that is the instant you'll move in for the kill.

Or here's one that almost never fails to work. You plan to attend a crowded party, and you know that the vampire has spotted you following him and will try to neutralize you there. You go to the local pet store and buy a small mouse; even a lab rat will do. Then you give it to a confederate who will also be attending the party. When the confederate sees that the vampire has separated you out from the pack, so to speak, and has you cornered, he releases the mouse. Invariably the first woman to see it will scream (and if not, the confederate can always goose her to elicit a shriek). You will look in her direction with great concern and say words to the effect that a vampire has just attacked a beautiful young woman in front of everyone. The real vampire, whose instinct is to defend his territory, will of course turn to look—and that's when you'll strike.

There are numerous other tried-and-true methods, but every last one of them requires brainpower, since in all other areas—except the way your pupils adjust to bright sunlight—he is your superior.

There is one method I have to address, simply because it runs against all the finer instincts of blood sports enthusiasts. A number of you have not been members of the Lower South Manhattan Blood Sports Enthusiasts Club as long as I have, so you may not know why Dr. Theodore Van Rhysling was expelled. Dr. Van Rhysling, for those of you who are not aware of the case, specialized in rare blood diseases, and when he found one that was both virulent and incurable, he sent his patient out every night until the vampire that had been terrorizing Dr. Van Rhysling's neighborhood encountered him, took a bite, and died a slow and horrible death. If any of you have had the same idea, be warned that your membership, like Dr. Van Rhysling's, will be revoked. *The true sportsman never uses poisoned bait.*

Let us say that something goes wrong, that the inevitable happens when your prey realizes that he is as close to you as you are to him, and you receive that dreaded first bite. Most people rush to the hospital for an emergency transfusion of blood or plasma, which does absolutely no good, since the bloodstream is already infected and this does nothing to eradicate it. My own suggestion is that you immediately apply leeches to the wound; even ten minutes after being bitten is too late, so carry some leeches with you on the hunt. If sunrise arrives and you still haven't come face to face with a vampire, well, the leeches make a hearty breakfast, especially when fried, breaded, and served alongside some scrambled gorgon eggs.

A final warning: Numbers mean nothing, so leave your faithful trolls behind. Strength means nothing, so don't take along your pet leopard or lamia. Your only advantage is your brain, and I wouldn't become overconfident, as the last two vampires I killed were a professor of ethics at Harvard and a successful Hollywood agent, truly awesome bloodsuckers both.

So study your prey, learn the territory, sharpen those stakes, gather those leeches, and good hunting to you!

— end of speech —

Debunking the Vampire

monograph by Professor Seldon Hari,
Chief Curator of the Museum of Unnatural History

A lot of myths have grown up about the vampire, most of them almost entirely mythical. It is time for the Museum of Unnatural History to debunk them, or, failing that, to show them to be totally false, except for the ones that aren't.

Vampires are a misunderstood lot. Most people think they take enormous joy in ripping out the throats of their victims and drinking their blood. Wrong. They are psychologically compelled to do so, just as the lion would prefer to lie down with the lamb but for his conditioning.

The average vampire spends ten hours a day sleeping in his native soil. Not a bed, mind you, or even a recliner chair in front of the television set. No, he sleeps in dirt, which lends to his feelings of isolation and inferiority.

His skin is extremely sensitive to the sun. He burns easily. He must beware of skin cancers. So of course he prefers to go out at night, a lifestyle choice which is invariably misunderstood, even though its advantages are obvious to anyone who takes the trouble to consider them. I mean, seriously now, how many nightclubs are open at noontime? If the lonely, downtrodden vampire seeks a companion, have you ever heard the expression "Ladies of the Afternoon"? He hides his insecurity by wearing formal clothes and even a cape, which appear ludicrous when observed at 11:03 AM or even 2:45 PM.

And since society disapproves of his meager attempts at self-respect, he in turn develops what can only be termed antisocial aspects to his behavior. Yet even here vampires are both maligned and misunderstood.

For example, precious few men and women know that the average vampire is incredibly farsighted. He can spot a gorgeous young woman standing in the moonlight at six hundred yards, but he cannot make out her features at three feet. He does not seek to bite the necks of the women he loves (or, let us be honest, merely lusts for). When embracing he closes his eyes, which cannot focus at such short distances, and invariably his lips come into contact with his partner's neck rather than her own lips. This so humiliates and embarrasses him that he pulls his lips back, forgetting that one of the features of vampirism is long and razor-sharp canines.

It has been suggested that garlic will keep a vampire at bay, and indeed it will—but not by hanging it. If you have an unnatural prejudice against vampires, simply chew some garlic right before you come into contact with them. If garlic is unavailable, onions will do. Or simply don't brush your teeth for twenty-four hours in advance. Vampires, as I've pointed out, are very sensitive souls.

It has been suggested that no vampire can enter your domicile unless you invite him in. This of course is ridiculous. The truth of the matter is that vampires have impeccable manners and hence no vampire *will* enter your premises unless you invite him in.

Can vampires cross water? Clearly this is a corruption of a long-lost observation, doubtless made by a religious fanatic. Priests cross themselves, and Jesus walks on water, and I am at a loss to understand what either of them has to do with vampires. True, I have never known a vampire to take a boat across water, but that is because vampires are exceptionally thrifty—there are very few night-shift jobs available, compared to the number of vampires applying for them—and since they are already dead and have no need to breathe, they tend to walk from one shore to the other *under* water, saving them the cost of passage aboard a commercial vessel. (It is true that cargo ships charge their few passengers far less, but vampires are a social lot, and the lack of passengers acts as a deterrent.)

There's another myth to the effect that vampires leave no reflection in mirrors. Absolutely false. Doubtless it stems from the fact that vampires cannot see themselves in mirrors, but this comes from their extreme farsightedness. In point of fact, any vampire can see his image in a mirror, provided that you hold the mirror up at a distance of four hundred paces or more. (This also explains why male vampires have such a frightening appearance. Without access to mirrors, their hair must be slicked down with oil since they cannot see it to comb it; they are unable to perceive the shadows under their eyes and hence do nothing to cover them up; and aware that they cannot go out in the sun without risking severe sunburn or worse, they rouge their faces and apply bright red lipstick to their lips, which gives them the appearance—of which they are totally unaware—of having just drunk tomato juice, a ham sandwich with too much ketchup, or a voluptuous young maiden's lifeblood.)

The most egregious myth of all is that vampires can be killed with a steak to the heart. I am here to tell you from long and painful personal experience that they cannot be killed with a steak, or with veal, chicken, guinea fowl, or roast turkey. If anything can kill them, I suspect it's my wife's jambalaya, especially after she's seasoned it with all that green pepper.

I trust this dispels the more notorious myths and lies about vampires.

What do they really want?

The same as you and me: a full stomach, a safe place to sleep, and a loving partner of the opposite sex who is always there when the need arises.

Next week: Our Friend the Gorgon.

Stalking the Vampire
by Scaly Jim Chandler

(excerpt)

She was prime stuff. She had long blonde hair, cool blue eyes, curves in places where most broads didn't even have places, and only the floor stopped her legs from going on forever. I looked at that full heaving neckline and figured if she heaved it just a little harder I could catch it without getting up from my chair.

"You were recommended to me, Mr. O'Bannon," she said.

"Was it Fifi?" I asked. "Fatima? Bubbles? Mitzie?"

"Malcolm Burke," she said.

"Oh," I replied. "So it's business."

"I'm in desperate trouble, Mr. O'Bannon!"

"Call me Wings," I replied.

"I'm being blackmailed, Mr. O'Bannon!"

"Wings," I said.

"All right—Wings," she said. "You've got to help me."

"What seems to be the problem?" I asked.

"It's so humiliating."

"Yeah, it usually is," I said. "You want a hit from the office bottle?"

She shook her head. "I am Mrs. Wilbur Carlisle . . ." she began.

"Are we talking about *the* Wilbur Carlisle?" I asked. "The eccentric reclusive millionaire?"

"Yes." Then: "Well, no, actually. He's a billionaire."

I frowned. "Isn't he something like seventy-five years old?"

"Ninety-eight," she corrected me.

"If we add your 38-22-36 all together, he's still got you beat by a couple of years."

"Wilbur and I are very much in love," she assured me.

"He's probably mistaking you for your great-grandmother," I suggested.

"Are you going to help me or insult me?" she demanded.

"I thought I was insulting your husband," I said. "But let's get down to business. I get seventy-five a day plus expenses."

"Agreed."

"Velma—that's my secretary—is on her lunch break," I told her. "I'll have her draw up a contract when she gets back."

She pulled a handful of C-notes from her purse and held them out to me. "Will this be enough, Mr. O'Bannon?"

"Wings," I said, taking the cash and sticking it in a vest pocket. "Yeah, it'll do fine. Now suppose you tell me about your problem."

"We were at a high-society party," she said. "Do you know the Cuthbertson-Smythes?"

"How many of them are there?" I asked.

"Just two."

"All right," I said, "fill me in. All my experience has been in low society."

"We were all drinking and laughing and having a fine time," she said. "And then . . . well, I guess I must have drunk more than I thought, because I can't remember another thing."

"Sounds like someone slipped you a Mickey Finn," I said.

"Is that his name?"

"Whose name?" I asked.

"I guess I'd better explain. You see, I woke up in a strange hotel room— and there was a dead man on the floor. His throat had been slit from ear to ear. Is *he* Mickey Finn?"

"Probably not," I said. "And someone's blackmailing you, threatening to expose you as a murderess?"

She shook her head. "He was a nobody. Wilbur could have bought the police off in a minute, if anyone even cared who killed him."

"I can believe it, Mrs. Carlyle."

"My name is Moira," she said.

"If you don't mind sharing a hotel room with a stiff, I fail to see what your problem is, Moira."

"That was yesterday." She reached into her purse. "Today I received *this* in the mail." She pulled out a plain manila envelope but didn't offer it to me.

"I get plain manila envelopes in the mail all the time," I said. "Usually girlie magazines, sometimes bills."

"This contains some very humiliating photographs of me with a man I've never seen before," she said. "If Wilbur saw them . . ."

"He'd throw you out?" I suggested.

She shook her head. "He'd get so excited he might keel over with a heart attack."

"Let's have 'em," I said, reaching my hand out.

"I'm too embarrassed to show them to you."

"I've got to know what they are before I can do anything about it."

She walked around the desk. "I'm ashamed to show you the pictures. I'd rather just show you what I did."

"That's less embarrassing than the photos?" I asked.

"My hair was a mess," she explained, slipping out of her clothes.

She was a Moira, all right, with an emphasis on the "Moi." I slid my hand down her back, over the lush smooth curve of her hips, and

{censored}

"Oh!" she moaned. "Don't stop!"

{censored}

"Oh God God God!" she breathed.

{censored, next three pages of manuscript burned, octogenarian proofreader hospitalized}

"Okay, Moira," I said, fixing my tie. "I'll be in touch."

"Again?" she said hopefully.

"By phone," I said.

She looked like someone had run over her pet chimera with a car—probably a Mercedes convertible with gull-wing doors, or maybe a Lambroghini, given the circles she traveled in—and undulated out of the office.

"Can I come in now?" Velma's sultry voice came through the side door.

"Why not?" I said. "Have you been there long?"

"Long enough to be jealous," she said, slinking into the room.

"You could have joined us," I said.

"You have a filthy mind, Wings," she chided me.

"Yeah, but I clean under my fingernails," I shot back.

"So is she your new client?" she asked.

"Yeah, looks like it."

"What's her problem?"

"I'll show you," I said, reaching out for her. Her blouse came away in my hand.

"Velcro," she said. "It was getting expensive, replacing all the clothes you're always ripping off me."

"And some people still think I didn't hire you for your brains," I said as I grabbed her and pulled her to me.

An hour later we began getting dressed again.

"Wow!" said Velma, her face still flushed. "That's some problem!"

"That's why she came to me," I said. "She's being blackmailed."

"Blackmail is an ugly word," said Velma with a shudder that would have had most men baying the moon.

"So is *myxophyceae*," I said. "But *myxophyceae's* not against the law except in Albania."

The phone rang and I picked it up. For a moment all I could hear was the sound of heavy breathing.

"It's for you," I said, offering the receiver to Velma.

"No, it's for you, Shamus!" said a voice at the other end of the phone. "It took me a minute to catch my breath. I had to beat an old lady to the phone booth."

"Why don't you get a cell phone?" I said.

"You gonna listen or you gonna criticize?"

"Who am I talking to?" I asked.

"Don't worry about that now," said the voice. "I got an important message for you."

"If it's that important, use Western Union and stop keeping little old ladies from calling their grandkids."

"Listen to me and listen good, Shamus!" said the voice. "We're gonna be watching your every move. Don't take the Carlisle case or you're a dead man."

"Carlisle who?" I asked innocently.

"You know," said the voice. "She's the dame who . . ." It took him half an hour to finish describing what was going on in the photos, by which time

I was breathing as hard as he was, and he was drooling so much that he finally shorted out his phone.

"Who was it, Wings?" asked Velma, who was sitting at her desk reading a gossip magazine.

"Just another death threat," I said with a shrug.

"That's your ninth this week," she noted.

"Yeah," I said. "Business has been slow." Then I did some serious thinking. "Listen, Angel," I told her, "I've got to start working on the Carlisle case before she asks for her retainer back, and I don't need any interference from a bunch of hired gunsels, so I think we're going to outsmart them."

"How?" she asked, wide-eyed with wonder.

"I've got an extra suit in the closet," I said. "I want you to get into it, wear my hat, and go for a nice long walk in the park. They'll think it's me, they won't shoot as long as you're not following leads for Mrs. Carlisle, and that'll leave me free to operate."

"It'll never work, Wings," said Velma.

"Why not?"

"Because I'm a 44-D," she said, taking a deep breath and thrusting back her shoulders.

"No problem," I said. "My chest is 44 normal and 46 expanded."

"Gee!" she said with a smile. "Maybe it'll work after all."

"Right," I said. "Anyone approaches you, just grunt, lower your voice, and talk about baseball. They'll never spot the difference."

"You're a genius, Wings," she said admiringly.

"Hey, thinking is my business," I said. "Getting shot at all the time is just for exercise."

It took her about five minutes to change into my suit, and then she left by the front door. I waited another ten minutes, then cut out the back way.

I knew that my first order of business was to find out who had taken the photos. There weren't more than six, maybe seven thousand professional pornographers in town, plus another twelve thousand talented amateurs, which meant I had my work cut out for me, hitting porn studio after porn studio, beating time with all the naked oversexed girls until the photographers had time to speak to me. Still, it *might* prove distracting; there were probably as many as twenty girls I'd never met before.

Then I started doing the math and realized I'd never hit all the pornographers before I ran through my retainer, so even though it wasn't going to be as much fun, I decided that the easiest way to get the job done was to go have a chat with Blind Benny, who works the ritziest part of town, tin cup in hand.

It took me about twenty minutes to get there, and it wasn't long before I heard Blind Benny begging for alms while adding that he'd also settle for any bill that had Ben Franklin's or Andy Jackson's likeness on it.

"Hi, Benny," I said, walking up to him and giving Buster, his guide dog, a friendly pat on the head.

"Hiya, Wings," he said, studying me through his dark glasses. "You're looking well."

"Yeah," I replied. "I haven't had a shoot-out in a week. How are things with you?"

"Just trying to get used to this new dog," said Blind Benny.

"Isn't that Buster?"

"Nah. I sold Buster to some guy who needed him for an art film."

"I thought you loved that dog," I said.

"Loving dogs is another union," said Blind Benny. "I *liked* him. Still, this guy paid through the nose for him. I guess he planned to make a killing off that rich Carlisle broad, and—"

"*Moira* Carlisle?" I interrupted.

"Unless there are two knockouts married to billionaires named Carlisle," said Blind Benny.

"Where can I find him?"

"Carlisle? Penthouse of the Diamond Tower."

"No, the guy who bought your dog."

"It's kind of complicated," said Blind Benny, pulling a pen and a sheet of paper out of his pocket. "I'd better draw you a map."

"He won't be using it," said a voice from behind me.

I spun around and found myself facing two tough-looking gunsels.

"I never saw a tail," I said, surprised.

"We didn't follow you," said the taller of the two.

"Then what are you doing here?"

"We took a cab," he said. "Everyone knows that whenever you need information you come to Blind Benny."

"Right," said the shorter one. "You think we don't read your books?"

"You do?" I said, surprised.

"Everyone does," said the shorter one. He pulled out a copy of *The Bloody Corpse Cries Foul* and walked up to me. "Would you autograph it?"

"Sure," I said, reaching for a pen.

"Could you say 'To Vinnie, the one man I was always afeared of'?"

"You got to excuse my partner," said the taller gunsel. "He ain't never got past third grade. It's 'the one man I was always ascared of.'"

"I *liked* third grade," said Vinnie defensively.

I scribbled an inscription and handed it back to him.

"I can't read your signature," said Vinnie, peering at it.

"That's okay," I told him. "I didn't write it anyway. I thought everyone knew that Scaly Jim Chandler writes them."

"*That's* why it's so good!" exclaimed the taller gunsel.

"I really appreciate this, Wings," said Vinnie. "It almost makes me sorry about what I got to do next."

He slugged me in the belly, and as I doubled over he cracked me over the head with a club I hadn't even seen in his hand.

I spat blood. It tasted salty. The salt invigorated me, and I caught Vinnie with a roundhouse left, but before I could follow up his partner had sapped me from behind with a blackjack. I started seeing images of Velma with her clothes on, so I knew they'd done me some serious damage. I came up swinging, catching Vinnie with a right to the jaw and Blind Benny with a left to the solar plexus.

"What the hell are you hitting *me* for?" he demanded.

"When I have time for aimed shots, you'll be the first to know," I grated through torn lips.

The blackjack caught me on the side of the head again, and as I fell to the ground Vinnie and his partner began covering my unprotected body with kicks that would have done a soccer player proud. Time after time one foot or another would crunch into my face. I felt the cartilage in my nose give way, and I heard the sharp *crack!* as my jaw broke.

Finally Vinnie pulled out a pistol and aimed it at me.

"You can't say you wasn't warned, Shamus," he said, pulling the trigger. Five shots buried themselves deep in my liver and spleen.

That did it. Before I'd merely been annoyed. Now I was *mad*.

— end of excerpt —

About the Author

Locus, *the trade journal of science fiction, keeps a list of the winners of major science fiction awards on its Web page. Mike Resnick is currently fourth in the all-time standings, ahead of Isaac Asimov, Sir Arthur C. Clarke, Ray Bradbury, and Robert A. Heinlein. He is the leading award-winner among all authors, living and dead, for short science fiction.*

* * * * * *

Mike was born on March 5, 1942. He sold his first article in 1957, his first short story in 1959, and his first book in 1962.

He attended the University of Chicago from 1959 through 1961, won three letters on the fencing team, and met and married Carol. Their daughter, Laura, was born in 1962, and has since become a writer herself, winning three awards for her romance novels and the 1993 Campbell Award for Best New Science Fiction Writer.

Mike and Carol discovered science fiction fandom in 1962, attended their first Worldcon in 1963, and more than fifty science fiction books into his career, Mike still considers himself a fan and frequently contributes articles to fanzines. He and Carol appeared in five Worldcon masquerades in the 1970s in costumes that she created, and they won four of them.

Mike labored anonymously but profitably from 1964 through 1976, selling more than two hundred novels, three hundred short stories, and two thousand articles, almost all of them under pseudonyms, most of them in the "adult" field. He edited seven different tabloid newspapers, and a trio of men's magazines as well.

In 1968 Mike and Carol became serious breeders and exhibitors of

collies, a pursuit they continued through 1981. During that time they
bred and/or exhibited twenty-seven champion collies, and they were
the country's leading breeders and exhibitors during various years
along the way.

This led them to purchase the Briarwood Pet Motel in Cincinnati
in 1976. It was the country's second-largest luxury boarding and
grooming establishment, and they worked full-time at it for the next
few years. By 1980 the kennel was being run by a staff of twenty-one,
and Mike was free to return to his first love, science fiction, albeit at
a far slower pace than his previous writing. They sold the kennel in
1993.

Mike's first novel in this "second career" was *The Soul Eater*, which
was followed shortly by *Birthright: The Book of Man*, *Walpurgis III*, the
four-book Tales of the Galactic Midway series, *The Branch*, the four-
book Tales of the Velvet Comet series, and *Adventures*, all from Signet.
His breakthrough novel was the international best seller *Santiago*,
published by Tor in 1986. Tor has since published *Stalking the Unicorn*,
The Dark Lady, *Ivory*, *Second Contact*, *Paradise*, *Purgatory*, *Inferno*, the
Double *Bwana/Bully!*, and the collection *Will the Last Person to Leave
the Planet Please Shut Off the Sun?* His most recent Tor releases were *A
Miracle of Rare Design*, *A Hunger in the Soul*, *The Outpost*, and *The Return
of Santiago*.

Even at his reduced rate, Mike is too prolific for one publisher, and
in the 1990s Ace published *Soothsayer*, *Oracle*, and *Prophet*; Questar
published *Lucifer Jones*; Bantam brought out the *Locus* best-selling
trilogy of *The Widowmaker*, *The Widowmaker Reborn*, and *The Widowmaker Unleashed*; and Del Rey published *Kirinyaga: A Fable of Utopia*
and *Lara Croft, Tomb Raider: The Amulet of Power*. His current releases
include *A Gathering of Widowmakers* for Meisha Merlin, *Dragon America*
for Phobos, and *Lady with an Alien*, *A Club in Montmarte*, *The World
behind the Door* for Watson-Guptill, and *The Alternate Teddy Roosevelts*
for Subterranean Press.

Beginning with *Shaggy B.E.M. Stories* in 1988, Mike has also become an anthology editor (and was nominated for a Best Editor Hugo in 1994 and 1995). His list of anthologies in print and in press totals forty-eight, and includes *Alternate Presidents*, *Alternate Kennedys*, *Sherlock Holmes in Orbit*, *By Any Other Fame*, *Dinosaur Fantastic*, and *Christmas Ghosts*, plus the recent *Stars*, coedited with superstar singer Janis Ian, and *The Dragon Done It*, coedited with best seller Eric Flint.

Mike has always supported the "specialty press," and he has numerous books and collections out in limited editions from such diverse publishers as Phantasia Press, Axolotl Press, Misfit Press, Pulphouse Publishing, Wildside Press, Dark Regions Press, NESFA Press, WSFA Press, Obscura Press, Farthest Star, and others. He recently served a stint as the science fiction editor for BenBella Books, and in 2006 he became the executive editor of *Jim Baen's Universe*.

Mike was never interested in writing short stories early in his career, producing only seven between 1976 and 1986. Then something clicked, and he has written and sold more than 200 stories since 1986, and now spends more time on short fiction than on novels. The writing that has brought him the most acclaim thus far in his career is the Kirinyaga series, which, with sixty-seven major and minor awards and nominations to date, is the most honored series of stories in the history of science fiction.

He also began writing short nonfiction as well. He sold a four-part series, "Forgotten Treasures," to the *Magazine of Fantasy and Science Fiction*, was a regular columnist for *Speculations* ("Ask Bwana") for twelve years, currently appears in every issue of the *SFWA Bulletin* ("The Resnick/Malzberg Dialogues"), and wrote a biweekly column for the late, lamented GalaxyOnline.com.

Carol has always been Mike's uncredited collaborator on his science fiction, but in the past few years they have sold two movie scripts— *Santiago* and *The Widowmaker*, both based on Mike's books—and Carol *is* listed as his collaborator on those.

Readers of Mike's works are aware of his fascination with Africa, and the many uses to which he has put it in his science fiction. Mike and Carol have taken numerous safaris, visiting Kenya (four times), Tanzania, Malawi, Zimbabwe, Egypt, Botswana, and Uganda. Mike edited the Library of African Adventure series for St. Martin's Press and is currently editing *The Resnick Library of African Adventure* and, with Carol as coeditor, *The Resnick Library of Worldwide Adventure* for Alexander Books.

Since 1989, Mike has won five Hugo Awards (for "Kirinyaga," "The Manamouki," "Seven Views of Olduvai Gorge," "The 43 Antarean Dynasties," and "Travels with My Cats") and a Nebula Award (for "Seven Views of Olduvai Gorge"), and has been nominated for thirty-one Hugos, eleven Nebulas, a Clarke (British), and six Seiun-sho (Japanese). He has also won a Seiun-sho, a Prix Tour Eiffel (French), two Prix Ozones (French), ten HOMer Awards, an Alexander Award, a Golden Pagoda Award, a Hayakawa SF Award (Japanese), a Locus Award, three Ignotus Awards (Spanish), a Xatafi-Cyberdark Award (Spanish), a Futura Award (Croatian), an El Melocoton Mechanico (Spanish), two Sfinks Awards (Polish), and a Fantastyka Award (Polish), and has topped the Science Fiction Chronicle Poll six times, the Scifi Weekly Hugo Straw Poll three times, and the Asimov's Readers Poll five times. In 1993 he was awarded the Skylark Award for Lifetime Achievement in Science Fiction, and both in 2001 and in 2004 he was named Fictionwise.com's Author of the Year.

His work has been translated into French, Italian, German, Spanish, Japanese, Korean, Bulgarian, Hungarian, Hebrew, Russian, Latvian, Lithuanian, Polish, Czech, Dutch, Swedish, Romanian, Finnish, Danish, Chinese, and Croatian.

He was recently the subject of Fiona Kelleghan's massive *Mike Resnick: An Annotated Bibliography and Guide to His Work*. Adrienne Gormley is currently preparing a second edition.